KNIFE SKILLS for Beginners

www.penguin.co.uk

Also by Orlando Murrin

Cookbooks

The Clever Cookbook

Can't Go Wrong Cookbook

No Cook Cookbook

A Table in the Tarn

Two's Company

Two's Company Simple

KNIFE SKILLS *for Beginners*

ORLANDO MURRIN

bantam

TRANSWORLD PUBLISHERS
Penguin Random House, One Embassy Gardens,
8 Viaduct Gardens, London SW11 7BW
www.penguin.co.uk

Transworld is part of the Penguin Random House group of companies
whose addresses can be found at global.penguinrandomhouse.com

First published in Great Britain in 2024 by Bantam
an imprint of Transworld Publishers

A CIP catalogue record for this book is available from the British Library.

ISBNs 9781787636811 (cased)
9781787636828 (tpb)

Text design by Couper Street Type Co.

Typeset in 13/16pt Dante MT Pro by Jouve (UK), Milton Keynes.
Printed and bound in Great Britain by Clays Ltd, Elcograf S.p.A.

The authorized representative in the EEA is Penguin Random House Ireland,
Morrison Chambers, 32 Nassau Street, Dublin D02 YH68.

'They were all victims. Whatever happened inside that house none of them deserves to be punished for it. None of them.'

The Family Remains, Lisa Jewell

AMUSE-GUEULE

Sunday 29/6/2003

Chef made me promise to keep a recipe diary. Essential for anyone with ambitions to open his own place or write a cookbook. As if.

He's had me working on a cheese biscuit to serve as an 'amuse', so here we go. There's this new guy at work called Paul (posh boy, far too full of himself) who had the idea of rolling the dough into a tube and coating it in seeds. Then you slice and bake so the biscuits are decorated round the edge. It took a lot of work but in the end I cracked it. Brilliant, though I say so myself.

So here it is: Christian's Cookbook, recipe #1.

PARMESAN BITES

Process together into a dough 170g plain flour, 150g each of grated parmesan and chilled, cubed butter, 1 teaspoon black pepper (freshly ground, as ALWAYS), ½ teaspoon flaky salt and a big pinch of cayenne.

Roll into two neat cylinders about an inch in diameter and chill until firm. Brush with beaten egg and roll in a mixture of sesame, nigella and poppy seeds (about 2 tablespoons of each) and chill again. Slice into thick coins and bake off at 160°C fan for 16–18 minutes until darkly golden.

Makes 50–60. They keep well in a plastic box and go great with sherry. The key is not to add water to the dough. We left one batch in too long and discovered they taste better if you overbake them. Happy accident.

PROLOGUE

Sunday

I'm looking at my watch for the tenth time, when in he strides.

'Ouch,' I say, 'you look terrible. What on earth happened?'

'Looks worse than it is,' he replies, upbeat as ever. 'Disagreement with an escalator.'

We're in one of those high-pitched bar-restaurants on Sloane Square with too many mirrors, too many people checking their hair in them and Taittinger by the glass. Christian's right arm is in a plaster cast with just the fingers sticking out, the left one bandaged at the wrist. Not ideal for a chef.

He orders a vodka Negroni, asking for it to be served in a highball glass so it's easier for him to hold, and shoots a look at a pair of young women perched near by, which despite the bruises on his face has its usual effect. Warm eyes, winning smile – he's never had to try very hard.

It being a Sunday, I go for a Bloody Mary.

'Been too long, mate,' he says, and holds out his glass for me to clink. 'I'm sorry about Marcus – how are you doing?'

'Sorry I didn't return your calls. It's been a difficult time. But I'm getting there, slowly.'

'How long is it now?'

'Almost ten months.' Three hundred and one days, to be precise.

'Oh,' he says, then in an attempt to brighten the mood: 'Still living in the lap of luxury, though?' It comes out a bit tactlessly, and he knows it. 'That little gem of a house round the corner you two used to share,' he quickly adds.

'Jubilee Cottage,' I reply. 'One or two problems, but I'm hanging on in there.' Maybe it's all the months of moping around, but I seem to have lost the art of small talk.

'I was thinking back to that gig we did in Cannes a few years back,' he continues. 'Wild times! Remember the langoustine that came to life in the *fruits de mer* and bit Kate Beckinsale? I'll never cook on a yacht again as long as I live.'

I smile and stir my drink with its oversize stick of celery. A dish of grilled Padrón peppers arrives, and I sprinkle them with salt flakes. Spain is a land of bright colours – go bold with the seasoning.

'Anyway . . . Hoping you may be able to save the day, help out an old friend. Does Chester Square Cookery School mean anything to you?'

I must have walked past the place a thousand times on my way to Victoria – typical Belgravia mansion with decorative white stucco, like icing on a wedding cake. Somewhat grander than your average cookery school, and news to me that Christian works there.

'It was after my business went into liquidation – the owner's an old friend of mine. She took pity on me, I guess. The job comes with a nice little flat at the back, and I don't mind having to charm the punters while I cook. Which brings me to my point.'

It seems Christian has a problem. During September, the school runs short residential courses for amateur cooks wishing to take their culinary skills 'to the next level'. There's one starting tomorrow, but he can hardly teach it one-handed.

'I thought – if I do the meet-and-greets, who better than my old friend Paul to cover me in the classroom? I meant to bring the schedule along, but it's basic stuff really – knife skills, roasting, chocolate. Mainly ladies who lunch, enjoying a break from their husbands. The sort of stuff an expert like you can teach with one arm tied behind your back.' He wiggles his fingers and laughs.

Poor old Christian; he sure has come down in the world since the glory days of *Pass the Gravy!* and two Michelin stars. His latest failure – he seems to be the master of bad timing – was a chain of brasseries, which I gather cost a lot of people a lot of money.

I weigh up his offer. Chester Square is less than a ten-minute walk from home, so I can hardly complain about the commute. On the other hand, am I ready to throw myself into a classroom, in front of new faces, strangers? I'm out of practice – I'd rather stay at home.

'Embarrassing question,' I say. 'How much will they pay?'

He sits up a little straighter, tension visibly easing.

'We'll sort that out, no worries there. But great that you'll do it – weight off my mind.'

'I'm not saying yes for definite – I need to check my diary,' I protest. What am I letting myself in for? 'Look, I'll phone you.'

This he chooses to ignore. 'So see you tomorrow – I'll introduce you to the team, give you the tour, before the students arrive.'

He lays his left hand lightly on my arm, the bandage somewhat grubby. 'I'm sorry about Marcus, and I mean that.'

Then he stands up, teases the girls with another of his steel-grey glances, and bounds out of the bar. Leaving me to pay the bill.

* * *

I hate to go on about money, but since Marcus died I've discovered how totally clueless I am. He knew how to manage finances, handle any sort of tricky situation, whereas I always seem to be out of my depth and chasing my tail. I can't believe how much it costs to run a house – even one as tiny as mine. Thank God for my freelance work for *Escape*, which covers the basics; an eight-pager every month – recipes *and* food styling. And thank God for Julie, who happens to be the magazine's food editor and commissions me.

Back at Jubilee Cottage, I phone her to tell her about Christian. Early evening on a Sunday, she may even pick up. Party Girl is out carousing with some noisy media friends in a bar in Covent Garden – a Montmartre vibe, apparently. 'I'll call you back on FaceTime,' she screams. She thinks modern technology is marvellous, whereas I can take it or leave it.

A few seconds later my phone vibrates and her smiling face appears. Tonight she's gone for a Latin look, with hair swept up and dramatic eyeliner. 'That's better,' she says, to the background bleat and swell of accordions. 'It's crazy here – you should come and join us!' My barfly days with Julie are over but it's kind of her to ask.

'Funnily enough, I've been out to drinks myself,' I say, with a hint of pride. For weeks she's been trying to persuade me to stir my stumps and go out. 'But you'll never guess who with.'

'Lady Gaga? Elton John? Dolly Parton?'

'Better than that – *Christian*!'

She's amazed – hasn't seen him since the brasserie launch. 'That's great! But I thought he'd crashed and burned. Is he still as gorgeous as ever?'

'Some wear and tear,' I say, ungenerously.

'Remember that time he got mixed up with the oligarch's daughter and we were convinced he'd been sent to Siberia?'

Or the time he was fan-mobbed in Tokyo, or cooked at

the White House: no shortage of material for a future biographer.

I tell her about Christian's accident, and that he wants me to step in and save the day. As expected, Julie turns protective. 'Are they paying you properly?' I confess this hasn't been finalized. 'Pin them down, Paul, and insist on half upfront. Otherwise – if you want my opinion – it's a brilliant idea.'

'The only thing is, I was promising myself a few days off after last week,' I say lamely.

'But you're a fantastic teacher – it'll be fun. Get you out of the house, and you can treat yourself to a holiday on the proceeds. A proper holiday, like you deserve.'

It's true: I could do with a week on a beach. Early September means Christmas to magazine people, and we've just completed a nerve-shredding two-day photoshoot for *Escape*'s festive number. The theme was *The Nutcracker*. As well as the inevitable groaning turkey and trimmings, our editor insisted on a twelve-foot Christmas tree (fully festooned in blue and silver), three small kids (ditto) and a French bulldog (blue and white bandana). Everywhere you looked, bewhiskered toy soldiers, plus – I can feel sweat breaking out at the memory – a crackling log fire, on the hottest day of the year.

'I just hope she's OK with the pictures,' I say. 'She' is our editor, Dena, a tyrant who stubs out careers as casually as the Dunhills she still smokes in the office because no one has the nerve to object.

'I'll text you tomorrow morning the moment she's seen them. And *please* say yes to Christian.' As we talk I catch sight of myself in the mirror. It's hard to look at your own reflection objectively, but the last couple of years haven't been kind: Marcus's dreadful illness, followed by the inevitable. For forty-two, I guess I'm in reasonable shape – not that I take any exercise apart from racing around for work. But there's sadness in my eyes, a sort of wariness that wasn't there before. Hair's getting greyer, too – which on Marcus was distinguished, but makes me look somehow faded. Worn down by grief, if you want to know the truth. I try smiling, and it's a big improvement.

Maybe Julie's right, and this Chester Square gig will take me out of myself, stop me rattling around in an empty house missing Marcus. Maybe I'll get a glimpse of the Christian I used to know and love before the ex-girlfriends and Inland Revenue knocked the stuffing out of him.

'OK, I'll think about it,' I say. 'Speak tomorrow.'

CHAPTER I

Monday

The front door of number forty-one is not in Chester Square at all but to one side of the property, in Eccleston Street. This particular house has always intrigued me because at some point the owners built a square extension at the back, with clerestory windows running around the top – a gallery, or perhaps a library?

By Belgravia standards, the place looks shabby. The Grosvenor Estate, which owns everything around here, has draconian rules on exterior maintenance, so it's not a case of peeling paint or cracked windows, but there's something unloved about it. Cinerarias in the window boxes look as if they'd benefit from a feed and water, and the steps could do with a sweep.

Beside the door – regulation black gloss, somewhat scuffed – is a touchpad with numbers, and a round button marked VISITORS. I press this and there's a jangling of bells, followed by the clash of electric locks leaping back. The door half opens, and a pale, slender young woman in a high-necked white chef's tunic looks me up and down. It's as if she's gone out of her way to be unmemorable: no make-up or jewellery, wishy-washy hair.

'I'm Suzie,' she says. 'Suzie Wheeler.'

Not the enthusiastic welcome one might have hoped for . . . *Thank you for coming to the rescue at short notice, Paul!* Or: *You must be Paul Delamare – our knight in shining armour!*

'I'll show you up. Christian isn't here yet.' She's a rhotic speaker – burrs her *r*s as they do in the West Country; my mother was too. As the door closes behind us I notice she bites her nails.

'Is there a code so I can get in and out by myself?' I ask.

'1904,' she replies.

I've set the questions for a few food quizzes in my time, so I parry this with, 'Invention of the tea bag.'

'Also the boss's birthday.' She smiles, cautiously. 'Not the year, obviously – the nineteenth of April.'

My first impression on stepping inside is the smell. I have an especially keen sense of smell – it's something chefs develop. This is that instantly recognizable 'institutional' pall, of dinners and disinfectant. Otherwise no surprises: a thick but well-worn carpet in burnt gold, console tables with magazines and tired vases of chrysanthemums, dingy Victorian landscapes hanging from picture rails.

I follow Suzie up a broad flight of stairs – 'The Grand Staircase,' she says with a sniff – and along a landing. If downstairs is like a waiting room, this has more of an auction house vibe, crowded with lumber and glass display cases. I'll take a proper look later, but we seem to have a collector in our midst – of antique cooking equipment.

We pick our way to a door bearing a hand-painted plaque: SHELLEY ROOM. Suzie taps on it, calls out, 'Your visitor, Mrs Hoyt,' then melts away. I step into the oak-panelled lair of the cookery school's proprietor-cum-principal.

She's standing at tall French windows, facing away from me. Her silhouette is trim – braid-edged tweed suit, ash-blonde hair swept back under a wide headband – against the green backdrop of the planes in the square's central garden.

In the middle of the room stands a large antique desk of the bank manager sort, topped with green leather, framed photographs and a laptop. A few tidy piles of paper are kept in check by antique brass weights, the bell-shaped type with a handle at the top. Running along the walls are further display cabinets and an ornate cast-iron strongbox, with a coat of arms traced in gilt. Hanging on the panelling: prints of herbs, fruits and spices; framed advertisements for Victorian bakeware and gadgetry; one of those School of Arcimboldo oil paintings in which the subject's face is modelled from vegetables.

I'm busy taking all this in when the woman wheels round. She's not that much older than I am – late forties, perhaps – elegantly made-up and presented, but holds her face to one side, as if hiding something.

'Rose Hoyt,' she says, extending a hand for me to shake. With the other, she dabs her eye with a handkerchief. 'You must excuse my appearance. I presume from your surprised expression that Christian didn't mention it.'

I fumble an apology and turn away. Her face appears to have fallen at one side, perhaps because of a stroke or palsy. Something similar happened to a matron at school during the school holidays – we were terrified it might be catching.

'Anyway,' says Rose, fidgeting with her hands, 'I did ask him to try and be punctual.' As well as engagement and wedding rings I see a big fat cushion-cut emerald in a diamond surround, probably Art Deco, worth more than I earn in a year.

'While we're waiting, let me tell you a little about the school and what we do here. This house has been in my family – the Strangs – since 1900, and I have lived here all my life. As you can see, it's on the large side. After my husband died – Hoyt is my married name – our daughter took a course at Leith's. It struck me we might be able to set up something along similar lines here.

'We teach what I call "classic cookery". A lot of the cookery schools seem only interested in jumping on the latest bandwagon – "Macaroon Masterclass", "Vegan in a Hurry", you know the sort of thing. But if you study here, you learn real cooking – how to make a proper béchamel, French-trim lamb cutlets or poach a salmon. Proper culinary practice, in other words.

'You will be teaching a class of eight. It's a residential arrangement. I think part of our appeal is that students get to stay in Belgravia, which would normally cost them a king's ransom. From our point of view, if we have all these spare bedrooms, we may as well fill them.'

She checks her watch again. According to mine, it's four minutes fast, but maybe she likes it that way. 'Did Christian take you through the syllabus?'

'No,' I reply, and she hands me a printed sheet. I'm about to raise the question of my fee, but she's already stood up and crossed to the fireplace, beside which an ornate gilt handle is set in a decorative plaster border. She gives it a crank, and noticing my look of interest, comments, 'You'll find that in many ways we're rather old-tech here. This is one of the original servants' bells from the nineteenth century, although of course Papa had them electrified.'

I look down the list of lessons. *Yikes!* This is also like stepping back in time – to a 1970s catering college. *Mastering the Art of Pastry. Well-tempered Chocolate. Syrups, Spun Sugar and Sugarcraft.* What has Christian landed me with?

'Erm, is there any flexibility with this?' I ask.

'I think you'll find it well structured – it covers the basic techniques and gives a satisfactory balance across the days. I know some schools design their courses so the students effectively cook their own meals, but I find that a little, well, cheap. Besides, that's what Suzie is here for,' she adds, as the young woman enters.

'You rang, Mrs Hoyt.' Very *Downton Abbey*.

'No sign of him, I suppose?' asks Rose.

'I think he was late back last night,' replies Suzie.

Rose fiddles with an earring. 'In that case, please show Mr Delamare around and make sure he knows where everything is.'

I follow Suzie out and, as soon as the door is shut, say to her, '"Mr Delamare" makes me feel about a hundred. Please call me Paul.'

She nods and we file back past the museum exhibits.

'I do feel a bit let down by Christian,' I continue, hoping she'll tell me what's happening. 'He promised to be here.' She shrugs – barely perceptibly – then leads me downstairs to a stately door with an enormous brass gong to one side. The nameplate is inscribed PINK ROOM.

'This is where we eat,' she says, swinging it open. There's something about pink dining rooms that makes me feel bilious, though I have to admit the space itself is gracious enough, facing out over Chester Square and gleaming with mahogany. On one wall, discreetly let into the beeswaxed panelling, I notice a dumb waiter, and ask Suzie if it's still in operation.

I'm a sucker for old-fashioned mod-cons. When I was a child, my mother used to take me to a china shop in South Audley Street that had a magic doormat: when you stepped on it, your weight triggered a mechanism that set the doors juddering open. My first suit came from a men's outfitters that used pneumatic tubes to whizz cash and change between the shop floor and the accounts department upstairs.

'Right to the top,' she replies. Useful no doubt in olden days, for servants ferrying breakfast in bed to their indolent masters and mistresses. 'But Mrs Hoyt doesn't like the disturbance while people are eating, so I still do a lot of traipsing up and down.' Suzie indicates a door covered in green baize – the real thing, which you rarely see nowadays except on gaming and billiard tables.

Leaving the Pink Room behind us, she leads me back into the hall, past the funeral flowers to the rear of the building. I knew these properties were big, but this one seems to go on for ever. We step out into a dark little courtyard, towered over by brickwork, with a huge black steel door at the back which Suzie says opens into Eaton Mews. A narrow cast-iron stairway – like an old-fashioned fire escape – leads up to a glazed door. Christian told me he had a flat above the old coach house, and this is it.

Suzie climbs up the stairway and taps at the door, waits for a minute then descends.

'Any idea where he might have got to?' I ask.

She raises an eyebrow, to indicate that it's no concern of hers, and I follow her back into the house. A fleeting idea passes through my head – why not slip out of the front door and go home, pretend none of this ever happened? Then I think of Julie, and how I'd be letting her down.

I trail Suzie along a broad passageway lit by skylights and down a short ramp. She taps a green button and doors whoosh open. 'The Old Ballroom,' she announces.

Not a gallery, nor a library – but a ballroom. Of course! And now the HQ of the Chester Square Cookery School. At one end, a demonstration bench, with mirrors above to give students an aerial view. Two rows of workstations, each with its own hob and sink. Ovens down one wall, fridges another. Marble, stainless steel, Gaggenau, Liebherr – I'm impressed.

There's a clanging of the doorbell – the students have started to arrive – but before disappearing to answer it, Suzie indicates a piece of paper on the bench.

NAME	**NOTES**	**PAYMENT STATUS**
Lady Brash (Serena)	Travelling from Bath.	✓
The Hon. Harriet Brash (daughter)	"	✓
S. Cartwright	London SE25	Concession (under 26)
De'Lyse	Press/Media	Complimentary
Gregory Greenleaf	Arr. Gatwick, 9.10 a.m.	✓
Victoria Mortimore	From Kings Lynn. No avocadoes.	✓
Lilith Mostyn	North Wales. Gluten-free.	✓
Melanie Hardy-Powell	*Friend of R.H.*	*(Pay on arrival)*

The woman scribbled in at the bottom must have booked at the last minute – always beware friends of the boss. The name Gregory Greenleaf rings a bell, but I can't think why.

CHAPTER 2

There's something about the light in the Old Ballroom – which comes in from above – that reminds me of our old gymnasium at school. On a sunny day it must be lovely, but today it feels cold and grey – like a prison. After turning lights on and off, which doesn't help, I log into the Chester Square Wi-Fi – password *LobsterThermidor* – and check for messages. Julie knows what I think about emojis, which only seems to encourage her.

> 🤨 🧙‍♀️'s 🚪 closed all morning! 🦃 pics 😻 but something's⚠️. 🌕 in ⚱️= 😈🕰️🕰️➡️. Trust you made it to Chester 🔲?

Quite understandably, my friend is worried I bailed out on the cookery school; part of me wishes I had. The bit before that means 'Full moon in Aquarius – strange times ahead.' She believes in astrology, or pretends to, so I get a daily customized horoscope.

The first part of the message, however, is a bit more worrying. Roughly translated: 'Not sure what's going on, but Dena –' that's the witch symbol – 'has been shut up in her office all morning. Photographs from turkey shoot look lovely, but something's up.'

Hmm . . . as every journalist knows, editors only close their doors when trouble is brewing. I call Julie, even though she won't pick up, and leave a message asking her to keep me updated. That photoshoot nearly killed me, and I won't rest easy till Dena's signed it off.

Back in the real world, I do a quick survey of fridges, drawers and cupboards, wondering all the time where Christian's got to. With any luck he's joined the students in the Pink Room, for Rose's welcome chat about fire exits and defibrillators.

I use the interlude to lay out my knives. Like every professional chef, I travel with my own, though you have to be careful nowadays carrying them about in a place like London. (Mine are transported in a rather dashing leather affair with straps and buckles, tucked in my backpack, and no dilly-dallying on the way.)

First out is my trusty steel – of no great financial value, but one of my most treasured possessions. It was given to me on my eighteenth birthday by our local butcher, after Mum told him I was interested in cooking. She encouraged me to believe I could succeed as a chef (Dad wanted me to do something more 'worthwhile') and whenever I use this steel I like to think of her looking over my shoulder.

Next to it on the bench I place my small and medium chef's knives; German, engraved with my initials and polished with an occasional drop of camellia oil, as used by the Japanese; applying it makes me think of waxy blossoms and *Madame Butterfly*; or should that be *La Traviata*?

My next choice is a modest *couteau à pamplemousse* bought in a Toulouse department store fifteen years ago. Small, serrated and shaped like a scimitar, it's the best three euros I ever spent – swift, deadly, and the only thing for slicing tomatoes and segmenting citrus. Apart from that, my armoury includes a pair of ceramic knives and my much-prized carbon-steel filleting knife. The latter's long, narrow, slightly flexible blade sweeps through smoked salmon and cold meats, and laughs in the face of jamón ibérico.

It's not going to be much of a lesson if we don't have anything to cut, so I sort out a selection of vegetables and check out the fridge, where two shelves are devoted to meat and poultry. Interesting selection; I'm setting aside one package in particular, hoping my students aren't the squeamish type, when the double doors swing open and down the ramp they charge.

CHAPTER 3

The women lead the march, including one extremely eye-catching one. Bringing up the rear are a very young man and – wheezing along behind – what could be his grandfather.

At the sight of me, they all stop dead. Grandpa realizes too late and steps on the heels of the woman in front, who squeals. They peer round the room, squinting into corners and up to the ceiling, then the leader of the pack, a purposeful, upright woman in a trouser suit, steps forward and barks: 'Where is he, then?'

'I'm sorry,' I say, smiling her in the eye. 'I'm Paul Delamare. I'm leading this week's course.' The general out-breath of disappointment sounds like a balloon deflating.

'But we're here because of Christian,' she protests, looking round for support and tapping her foot. They shrug and shoot me accusing looks, as if I've locked him in a cupboard so I can teach his class.

'I'm sorry,' I say, in as cordial a tone as I can muster. 'I thought Christian might have joined you for coffee. Didn't Mrs Hoyt explain?'

I see that the ringleader has brought along a less purposeful and upright version of herself – a sort of Mini-Me. According to my crib, this must be the mother–daughter duo, Lady Brash and the Hon. Harriet.

'Explain what?' declares her ladyship, jabbing her daughter with an elbow for no reason in particular.

'About the accident?'

More muttering and head shaking. I'm seething: how dare Rose leave me to break the news about Christian! And where the hell is he? Nevertheless, I take a deep breath and say, in my most soothing tones, 'Christian will be along shortly – I'll explain everything after you've settled in. Choose yourself a workbench and get comfortable.'

There's a clamour for the spaces at the back – wouldn't have happened if the main attraction had shown up – but the older man isn't quick enough, and is forced to shuffle to the front. Name badges might have helped, though something tells me this is Gregory Greenleaf – he looks like a Gregory.

I know that teachers, when faced with a classroom full of new faces, employ mnemonics to remember names, so I rack my brain to think of something for Gregory. Gregorian chant? No, nothing monkish here. With his horn-rimmed glasses, baggy eyes and beaky nose, he looks more like a bird – a bird of prey. Gregory *Peck*; that'll have to do.

Once they're all settled, I hand out our official Chester Square Cookery School aprons – austere in white, with a black line drawing of the facade. It never ceases to amaze me how even millionaires love a freebie, and it seems to lift their spirits.

I kick off by explaining about Christian's accident, although the escalator story comes out sounding a little thin, and I see Lady Brash purse her lips.

Then I say a few words about myself. I've done just about everything you can think of in the food world, but what people *really* want to know is what's it like being on TV? (Answer – frightening, blinding lights, swarms of production people buzzing round you like flying ants.) And have I met such-and-such TV chef? (Answer – we all know each other and, except for one I'm not naming, get on just fine.) A couple of students say they recognize me, or maybe they're just being polite. Then I ask everyone to introduce themselves and tell us what they hope to get out of the course.

A young black woman goes first. This is De'Lyse, who according to Rose is a successful blogger ('Callaloo and Bammy') with about a trillion followers on social media. She waves around her iPhone – latest model, waterproof, telephoto lens – and announces she'll be Instagramming and posting videos throughout the course. 'If anyone doesn't want to be in the videos, just keep out of shot.' I notice Lady B curl her lip.

I'm no expert, but you wouldn't want to be queuing for the bathroom when De'Lyse applies her *maquillage* in the morning. Carefully applied contouring, iridescent eye shadow, glossy smile. More catwalk than kitchen, but we shall see.

Next, her ladyship broadcasts, without pausing to draw breath: 'Lady Brash but please call me Serena and this is my daughter Harriet who's getting married in spring so we thought: time to brush up on one's cookery skills!' De'Lyse rolls her eyes. '*So* disappointing about Christian, we met him on quite a few occasions at his restaurant in Bath.'

She picks what appears to be a long silky hair from her sleeve; a Collie hair, if I'm not mistaken. Collies need to be walked for at least two hours a day; explains why she's so trim. Next, I smile encouragingly at the honourable daughter.

'As Mummy said, I'm Harriet.' She adds, 'Sorry! Slightly carsick after the taxi from Paddington. I'll brighten up in a bit.'

After that, I catch Gregory's eye. Now that he's under the lights I can see that his residual tufts of hair are tinted a sandy colour; they tone with his mustard corduroys. I've observed that corduroys are often the choice of the older gentleman, but there's something about the fabric that accentuates a paunch.

'Basically, from Warwickshire but I live much of the year

in Biarritz.' Murmurs of approval or envy. 'Small apartment – view of the sea – flew in this morning. My real interest is fine wine – specifically claret – but read about the course in the *FT* and thought it time to, er, broaden my culinary repertoire.' I notice he has a habit of shutting his eyes when he's talking; often signals a lack of confidence.

Next, a vivacious woman in her late forties puts up her hand and flutters it like an eager schoolgirl. She has wide green eyes, freckles and a tumble of red hair; a feline version of Fergie, Duchess of York. She's called Melanie – my mother's name, so that's easy to remember. Melanie Hardy-Powell lives in Tite Street, Chelsea (a very good address, as Marcus would say), and is an old friend of Rose's, though they don't meet up often because they're both so busy.

I ask if she's going home each evening. (About five minutes by taxi.) No, the course is all-in, so she thought, why not take a break from domestic responsibilities – enjoy some fine dining in pleasant company? With this she shoots me a flirtatious smile – including a flash of teeth.

Now it's the turn of the student who caught my eye earlier. She's gone for broke with one of those novelty hair colours that seem to be all the rage: the first word that springs to mind is mauve. Lilith comes from a tongue-twisting town in North Wales and was given the course as a birthday present by her other half. She has one of those gentle Welsh accents that makes you think of valleys and waterfalls. Generously built, rainbow-coloured and named after a Biblical bad girl, I know I'm going to remember her with no problem.

At the bench next to her – something tells me these two will be either friends or foes – sits 'Call me Vicky', a pharmacist from Norfolk. I can just see her poring over prescriptions through her goggle glasses and telling customers to come back tomorrow. She and hubby take separate holidays (said with a wink) and she's joined the course because she'd like to make more use of her freezer; not very inspiring, but I promise to bear it in mind. As she's sporting a snakeskin-print outfit, this one's easy: Viper Vicky. It's not as if she'll ever know.

That leaves a timid young fellow who looks as if he's wandered in by mistake, having meant to book a class in watercolours or playing the flute. Stephen Cartwright has Harry Potter glasses, the shortest possible buzz cut and smooth, pale skin. He looks too young to grow a beard, and I would put him at early twenties.

He's been sent on the course by his employer because he's considering retraining as a chef. Who's his employer? The Royal Parks. I know how it feels when everyone around you is older than you – and larger than life – so decide to keep a friendly eye out for him.

At this point I hear a squeal from the back row. The Hon. Harriet has found a spider in her knife block and Mama is hunting it down with a wooden spoon.

'No need to kill him,' says the Hon. 'He's only tiny.'

'Get a grip, Harriet,' returns the mother. 'You've been feeble all morning – serves you right for skipping breakfast.'

Harriet watches tight-jawed as her mother pursues the hapless arachnid down the side of the workbench, at which point it disappears between two floorboards. 'Blast,' she says, screwing her foot on the spot. 'Got away.'

I'm about to begin the lesson when a pale-faced Harriet stands up, excuses herself and – accompanied by glares from her mother – makes a swift exit.

CHAPTER 4

'Anyone here like quizzes?' I ask, once order is restored and the Hon. Harriet – still looking pale and unsteady – reinstalled at her workbench. 'What's the most important thing in your kitchen?'

'The Aga,' declares Lady B. Julie and I have a private joke that if someone has an Aga, they tell you about it in the first five minutes. Her ladyship, Gregory and Melanie of York all have Agas, and I notice them casting pitying looks towards Lilith, who tries to join in, but only has a Rayburn.

'Nope,' I reply. 'Knife sharpener. And I'm not talking about gimmicky little ones with spinning wheels, or the electric type that shave away the edge till you've no blade left. If this is all you learn during the week, you'll have got your money's worth.

'What you need is a *sharpening steel*. If you haven't got one, fifteen quid on Amazon. Grab it by the handle and hold it upright on the worktop. Take your knife in your other hand and sweep it down, pulling towards you so the whole length of the edge makes contact with the steel. Listen – you should hear it sing.'

Every bench has its own set of knives, so we pass the steel around and they try it for themselves. Despite everything, I find I'm slightly enjoying myself; it's interesting seeing novices at work. De'Lyse goes in with an impatient slashing action, and takes a lump out of her chopping board. Vicky and Lilith squabble about who's going first and decide to toss for it, by which time it's been passed to bird man Gregory, who taps and scrapes like a woodpecker on a tree trunk. The Hon. Harriet gets her mother to do hers because the sound sets her teeth on edge, after which Melanie talks her into swapping knives because she prefers the colour of Harriet's handle. Stephen seems to be moving everything in the wrong direction, and it turns out he's left-handed.

Blades honed and gleaming, it's showtime. Some people are natural dancers, others marvellous in bed, but – not wishing to boast – I'm good with a knife. Most chefs are: next time you see one at work, note their elegant turn of wrist, the grace, fluidity, finesse.

Give me a blade and I'll take your breath away. Nothing gives me greater pleasure than transforming a knobbly pineapple into a pile of golden chunks with a few deft twists and turns, or peeling a Granny Smith so the skin twirls off in one shiny green ribbon.

Knife techniques aren't difficult to learn, I explain, but you have to start by holding the implement correctly. To find the comfortable, natural position, 'shake hands' with it; your spare hand, meanwhile, forming a 'claw', to keep fingers out of danger.

The 'bounce' is where you keep your wrist free and ricochet the blade rapidly up and down in a tapping movement. I once timed myself at 190 slices a minute, and duly demonstrate on a row of mushrooms, which disappear in a blur. The 'seesaw' is where you rock the blade from handle to point, zig-zagging across the food as you do so. In seconds I transform a bunch of parsley into verdant dust. The 'mash' is where you use the blade flat against the board, in a squashing motion. Crush, press – crush, press – repeat. Result: liquid garlic.

In the East, knives are handled differently – you slice rather than chop. It's kinder on the knife and your wrist. I get out my trusty Kyocera – white ceramic blade, black pakka-wood handle – and show the students a trick taught me by a Korean friend. Fifty-six inscrutable cuts later – plus a few extra feints and dodges for the benefit of De'Lyse, who is videoing – and an onion is reduced to 1,104 tiny identical cubes.

I'm somewhat flattered when this is met by rapturous applause. It feels strange but oddly energizing to find myself the centre of attention after all those months of hibernation: I take a bow.

Now it's their turn. Melanie first. She fixes her eyes on the onion, like a cat eyeing a mouse, then goes in at speed. I remind everyone – *please!* – to keep their non-chopping fingers curled and out of the way. Kitchens can be death traps.

Lilith drops her onion on the floor and it rolls away under a workbench. I suggest she uses another – retrieves the lost one later – but no, she'll chop that one or none at all. I sense she's going to be disruptive: there's one in every class.

Lady B uses an exaggerated sawing motion, as if she's conducting an orchestra, while her daughter seems abstracted, and gives up halfway through. Vicky announces she buys her onions pre-chopped from the freezer centre.

'Freezer centre?' echoes Lady B scornfully.

'Frozen food has more nutrients,' she declares, and I back her up, because in most cases it's true.

Quiet Stephen is 'in the zone', studiously rocking the knife backwards and forwards between his delicate hands. Of everyone in the room, I feel he may be the one with actual culinary flair, although it's early days.

* * *

I'm relieved, if slightly embarrassed, when the theme from *Strictly* suddenly bursts forth from my phone – the alarm I set for the end of class. Another of Julie's pranks . . . I should never have let her loose on my settings.

'We've almost finished for today,' I announce, 'but before we do, I'd like us to get the meat set up for tomorrow's session, called, erm, *The Noble Art of Meat Cookery*. Just to double-check – no vegetarians in the class?' You'd be surprised how often one slips through the net.

Viper Vicky jumps in. 'I went veggie five years ago, but gave up last Bonfire Night. It was the sausages.'

Not to be outdone, Lilith raises a hand, bedecked with glittery acrylics. 'Gluten-free,' she says proudly.

I nod and continue. 'Now, there's endless debate about whether you should season meat before or during or after cooking, but for larger cuts and whole birds I strongly recommend the day before.'

I lay out a selection of joints and poultry; Chester Square's supplier is the most expensive butcher in London, which means Rose is forking out £70 for a leg of lamb.

I start by butterflying the latter: I remove the aitch bone, then the ball and socket (the tricky bit), and finally the shank. There's a sharp intake of breath from Vicky when I season it. 'Isn't that rather a lot of salt?'

'Most chefs use far more salt than you would at home – also more cream and butter: it's why restaurant food is so tasty and luxurious. The argument is that eating out is, for most people, a special occasion – not about healthy eating. It's up to you, of course, but this is a large piece of meat, and we want it to be tasty right to the centre.' Gregory nods away, like a bird on a telegraph wire, as if to say he knew all this.

After that I spatchcock a chicken and bone out some short ribs, before finishing up with my pièce de résistance. I'm a firm believer that there's no place for timidity in the kitchen, and I go to the fridge to take out the package I set aside earlier: it's pigeon time. Lilith pulls a face.

'Wood pigeons, not the ones flapping about in Trafalgar Square,' I say.

My own cleaver doesn't fit in my knife roll, so I've pulled out the cookery school's, a jaunty affair with a bright red handle. There are audible gasps as one pigeon head lands in the bin, swiftly followed by the other.

'First rule of butchery: off with his head.'

And into this mêlée walks Christian.

CHAPTER 5

Six foot three of pure virility. Magnificent head of greying hair, freshly cut and styled. Perfectly tailored jeans and slim-fit shirt, open at the neck to reveal just enough spray-tanned chest. A waft of Tom Ford for Men.

He's even managed to give his injuries sex appeal. The wrist is wrapped in a crisp new bandage. The sleeve over the other arm is rolled up (how did he even get the shirt on?) to reveal his plaster cast. This is decorated with his initials – C. S. W. – in snazzy graffiti style, plus a red balloon heart in homage to Banksy. An irresistible blend of masculinity and vulnerability – and the perfect reminder of why his public love him. Or did.

'It's Christian!' I announce – unnecessarily, as he's already surrounded by a gaggle of admirers.

I'd be embarrassed to receive this kind of adulation. Everyone wants a selfie with him, and Lady B produces her *Pass the Gravy!* cookbook to be autographed. *To the gorgeous Lady Serena*, he squiggles (funny how his hand suddenly got better).

De'Lyse grabs him for a mini-interview, with the others clustered around. 'Is it true you're going on *I'm A Celebrity*?' she demands. He makes a zipping motion across his mouth and they squeal with laughter.

'Are you doing a Christmas special?'

'Wait and see!' he teases back. I doubt it – he's past his sell-by date – but his admirers whoop and giggle.

It dawns on me that his fan club is entirely women. Gregory has slipped out for a loo break, but where's Stephen? I look around and see to my horror that he's slid off his stool and is lying prone on the floor, ignored in the hysteria all around. This is terrible!

I dash across to kneel beside him and check his pulse, which is what you're supposed to do. My braggadocio with the cleaver must have been too much for him; I've always believed that handling meat is an important part of learning to cook, but times are changing, and I should remove that trick from my repertoire.

Next, I hear a woman shouting, 'Coming through, coming through!' (I think – strictly speaking – that's for emergencies involving crowds) and Lilith plonks herself down beside me. 'St John's Ambulance,' she cries, and yanks at the young man's collar to pull open his shirt. He looks very pale, and I notice he has a tattoo on his neck: a little cherub plucking a harp. I don't care for tattoos but at least this one is subtle. And then Suzie materializes next to us and pounces on him.

'I've got this,' she says, pushing a surprised Lilith out of the way. We watch as she rearranges his clothes and puts back his glasses. 'I'm Health and Safety Officer here. He's fainted, that's all. Leave it to me.' A minute later Stephen is sitting on a chair and Lilith is sent off to make a cup of tea. 'He takes one sugar,' calls Suzie.

Stephen realizes everyone is looking at him. 'Sorry,' he mumbles. 'Suddenly felt peculiar.'

'I don't normally have that effect on people,' says Christian, and everyone laughs. 'Anyway, I must love you and leave you – doctor's orders!' There's more cooing and preening as he makes his exit; I try to catch his eye but it's clear I'm being given the brush-off.

Amid the chit-chat, I notice a whispered confab happening

at the doorway. Christian has been intercepted on his way out by Harriet and an extraordinary sequence of reactions is passing across his handsome face. Surprise – dread – and . . . I can't quite work out what else.

* * *

By the time they've all left the Old Ballroom, I've an hour and a half till dinner. I'm furious with Christian – dashing in for a cameo appearance without so much as acknowledging my existence – and what was that odd exchange in the doorway all about? I'm mulling it over when it occurs to me I still haven't heard from Julie. Did Dena give the pictures the thumbs up, or will we be thrown to the lions?

This gives me an idea. Chester Square is on Julie's way home; she lives in a bright, spacious flat near Putney Bridge, half-buried in books and music scores and mid-century furniture. Instead of going back to Jubilee Cottage to change and freshen up, I could stay put and ask her to stop off for a catch-up and guided tour.

Thinking it would be polite to check first with Rose, I make my way up to the Shelley Room, remembering on the way that I *still* haven't dared ask how much I'm going to be paid, and I know Julie will ask.

The door is open and as I approach I can see the principal is upset, Suzie comforting her, with one hand resting on her arm. 'Such a betrayal,' Rose is saying, picking up pieces of paper distractedly and putting them down again. 'And just when we are on a knife edge . . .'

At my entrance, she dabs the tears from her face. 'Suzie is being very kind,' she says. She pronounces it *Soo-Zee*, as if it's an exotic fruit. 'What with students fainting, and Christian playing fancy-free, I can't seem to concentrate. Soo-Zee assures me that all is well, and of course Christian is such a marvellous tutor.' Her hand grips the edge of the desk and I take the empty seat opposite her.

She wipes her eyes and breathes deeply. 'It's been a very hard couple of years for the school. The cost of maintaining a large historic property . . . Prices spiralling . . . Frankly we live from one course to the next.' More distracted paper shuffling.

It plainly isn't the time for me to talk about my fee, but I ask if she minds Julie calling round.

'Of course, invite your friend,' Rose says through her handkerchief, bravely attempting a smile. 'Tell her the code for the front door so the bell doesn't give everyone a fright.'

I leave the two of them together, feeling I've misjudged Suzie. She may come across as cool and detached, but this incident has shown a more caring side to her: she's mature for her age.

I send Julie a text inviting her over and give her the door code as instructed. Seconds later, I get a reply.

Soz, stuck in office. 🆘 meeting tomoz am, all dept 👥. 🙀. Rumours ✈️. ⚫ in 🐏 = 😲 🛣️

The last bit seems to be an updated horoscope – 'Mars in Aries – surprise on the way'. Had enough of those lately.

Neither is the rest of the message great news. 'Emergency meeting tomorrow morning, all department heads. Worried. Rumours flying.'

I decide to have a walk and clear my head. It's a warm, humid evening, and the lawnmowers have been at work in the square's communal garden. The idea of emergency meetings at the magazine gives me the jitters, but the sweet grassy smell is pleasant and calming. I peer enviously through the hedge, where locals – or more likely, their maids or paid dog-walkers – are giving their cockapoos and chihuahuas an evening stroll among the spotty laurels and rhododendrons.

I pass one of the gates into the garden, sternly emblazoned Keyholders Only, and glance in. There, sitting on a bench and intently studying a sheaf of documents in the golden light, is none other than De'Lyse. Alongside her is a younger woman, dressed in a business suit, with striking ash-blonde hair.

Sensing perhaps that someone's peeking at them through the greenery, De'Lyse whispers something to her companion and they disappear with their paperwork behind a clump of hydrangeas.

CHAPTER 6

There seems to be more going on at Chester Square than I anticipated – or perhaps I'm out of practice with normal life. And now a new ordeal: dinner.

We're summoned to the Pink Room by a clash of gong so tremendous that I count the reverberations for a full five seconds. On arrival I find Suzie gliding about in her chef's whites, arranging plates and serving apparatus on the sideboard and lighting candles. Tonight is a help-yourself affair, with students and staff sitting wherever they choose around the long dining table. It's laid out attractively, with Strang family silver and posies of flowers, but the atmosphere – like everything else around here – creaks.

Wine is available at a side table, with an honesty book alongside; I don't know how long the Grenache has been hanging around – not a wine that keeps well once open – so I break into a Merlot.

Feeling somewhat on duty, I circulate to make sure everyone feels included. I ask Lady B if she is happy with her accommodation, and she replies tersely, 'Spacious'; Rose is three feet away so perhaps that's not the full story. The Hon. Harriet is hovering about in the shadow of her mama as usual. I continue to puzzle over her odd behaviour, and wonder if it can be put down to wedding jitters.

Melanie of York and Gregory Peck are comparing notes on the Île-de-Ré, where Melanie's stepdaughter worked as an au pair last summer. (Disaster, came home in a sulk after three days when asked to clean out the family fridge.) I ask Melanie if she was named after Olivia de Havilland's character in *Gone with the Wind*, as was my mother.

She laughs – a wide laugh with teeth on display. A fine set of whiskers would not look amiss, and a saucer of milk. 'Absolutely not – Melanie the singer.'

Gregory starts crooning – not very melodiously – '*Look what they've done to my song, Ma . . .*'

Melanie gives him a polite nod and cuts in, 'That's the one. My parents were hippies – they went to Woodstock,' Melanie says.

'Mel is a Flower Child,' announces Gregory. The others eye her with new curiosity, as if expecting her to plonk herself down on the floor and spark up a spliff.

'I wasn't conceived in a field, if that's what you mean,' she replies, with a shake of her mane. 'Also, no one calls me Mel.'

I knew a young chef who was brought up in a commune near Lampeter and rebelled against his hippy parents by marrying an estate agent and settling down in Croydon. Judging by her cashmere polo and tailored skirt, I would say Melanie has gone the same way: more Brora than Bohemia.

I notice Rose standing alone, away from the light, and move towards her.

'I think we'd better start without him,' she says, glancing at her watch. This is overheard by the students, and sets them off again. Considering my valiant efforts to make today's sessions interesting and amusing, this constant twittering about *Christian Christian Christian* is driving me nuts. Rose tinkles a little handbell – the brass type they hang round the necks of Swiss cows – and we take our places around the table; at which point Suzie brings the food to the sideboard, and the elbows come out.

As an appetiser, we are offered a choice of three savoury

tarts in foil containers. From Marks and Spencer at Victoria station, if I'm not mistaken; at least she's bothered to warm them up. Lilith asks pointedly where she'll find the gluten-free option and Suzie points to a fluorescent prawn cocktail in a plastic pot. Main course is a slimy fish pie – fresh from the freezer – served with baked potatoes (why?), plus a 'vegetable medley' of carrots, peas and sweetcorn.

If this is the typical Chester Square student dining experience, Rose should be ashamed of herself; being within spitting distance of some of London's finest food shops, she could do so much better. Think good bread and olive oil to dip it in, a few exciting salads, Italian cured meats and a cheeseboard . . . nothing that need break the bank. Before the week is out, maybe I can make some discreet suggestions to Suzie, or even take her on a shopping expedition.

Conversation fluctuates, and at one point, when people seem to be talking in pairs rather than generally, I turn to De'Lyse, sitting to one side of me. I casually mention that I saw her earlier in the communal garden.

'It looks so peaceful in there, away from the cars and buses. I think you were with a friend?'

'Oh, yes,' she says. Does she seem a little flustered? 'That was a fan. I get recognized all the time.'

Next, I tune into a conversation further down the table, which isn't difficult because they're shouting. Lady B has discovered Gregory knows her ex, who has moved to Cheltenham. Indeed, Gregory has been to dinner with Lord Brash.

'How *very* interesting,' drawls her ladyship, licking her lips. 'I hear they've decorated the house in *screaming* bad taste – murals, fake pillars, silk flowers everywhere. She's half-Lebanese, you know.'

Viper Vicky appears to be in what psychologist Mihaly Csikszentmihalyi described as a 'state of flow': laboriously separating the tiny cubes of her medley into individual piles. They look like tesserae waiting to be glued into a mosaic.

'What are you doing that for?' asks Lilith; rather forward but it's what we're all wondering.

'I like to be organized, that's all,' says Vicky, looking up. 'Stay on top of things.'

'You missed a bit of sweetcorn,' says Lilith, pointing with her knife.

Vicky ignores this and resumes her triage.

'Doesn't your dinner get cold?' says Lilith.

'Only if people keep interrupting.'

* * *

I am at the sideboard, trying to find a potato that isn't raw in the middle, when the door swings open and in comes you-know-who. As ever, the effect is electrifying.

'Hi, everyone!' he says, showing off his perfect smile. (New, incidentally.) 'Hope no one minds if I join you for ten minutes. What I really fancied was baked beans but I couldn't open the tin.' General laughter. Christian is the archetypal ladies' man – women fall at his feet while men see through him like glass. 'Suzie, be a doll and serve me a little of everything? Cut it up for the wounded soldier?'

I notice Gregory's eyes fixed unblinkingly on Christian. It's a few seconds before Christian notices him, but when he does his smile drops. The exchange is over so quickly that I wonder if I imagined it.

Suzie goes silently to the sideboard – I don't think young women appreciate being addressed as 'doll' nowadays – and there's a scramble at the table to make space for Christian. For a second it looks as if Melanie will win, but Lady B succeeds in barging her aside and laying a place between herself and the Hon., who looks uncomfortable about the arrangement and buries herself in her handbag. As Christian sits down, he clocks young Stephen at the other end of the table, trying to make himself invisible.

'Hey!' Christian calls over, waving his plaster cast and brandishing a fork. 'Any more fainting fits? You youngsters, you're oversensitive . . . need to man up a bit!' Stephen blushes while Christian leads the laughter.

Conversation centres on broken limbs; never having suffered one, I don't find it of great interest. Vicky broke her ankle ice-skating, which is quickly capped by Melanie, who snapped a femur on a black run at Megève.

'My problem is, I'm drawn to danger,' Melanie confides, talking across Lady B, to her evident displeasure. 'Put me in a helicopter or a Ferrari and I'm anybody's.'

Christian laps it up. 'Sounds like you ladies are on the wrong course. Ask Paul if he can slip in a session on bungee jumping!' Hardly hilarious, but they titter away like budgerigars.

Christian's oddly elated mood continues until, quite abruptly, he gets up to leave. He and Gregory still have not spoken a word, I notice, and he's scarcely acknowledged me.

'Don't know about anyone else round here, but I've been prescribed bed rest,' he announces, managing to make that prospect sound anything but restful. 'Nighty night!'

Despite his fast getaway, I'm not going to let him out of my clutches this time. Feeling my blood rise, I make a beeline for the door and manage to get there first.

'Christian, you've dropped me in it!' I hiss, trying to keep it sotto voce. 'I feel completely abandoned – where have you been?'

'Sorry, mate, something came up,' he replies, but he's not really listening. It's as if he's away in some dream world.

'So will you be around tomorrow?'

'I can't do this right now – catch up later, OK?'

'You said we were in this together, but it's the same old, same old. Just occasionally, you need to think about someone other than yourself.'

A faint smile seems to flicker across his face as he squeezes past and escapes. I turn around to see ten pairs of eyes trained on me.

'There was no need for that display,' mutters Rose under her breath as I sit back down.

CHAPTER 7

Shortly afterwards, a huge dish of Eton Mess is produced. I'm not the only one made queasy by the sight of the swirled mountain of whipped cream, meringue and strawberries. The Hon. Harriet, who has hardly said a word all evening, heads straight for the door. Stephen makes to leave too but I manage to catch up with him.

'I'm sorry Christian embarrassed you,' I say quietly. 'He doesn't mean any harm, but it's not the sort of thing you say to people nowadays. There's no place for attitudes like that.'

A blush – or is it more like a shadow? – passes over the young man's face before he gives the slightest hint of a nod and scurries away.

To add the final, deathly flourish to this lacklustre soirée, Suzie returns, bearing aloft a black lacquer tray laden with cafetières and some dusty-looking '*gourmandises*'. Lilith adds three lumps of sugar, which seems excessive for such small cups. I see Gregory drop his half-nibbled truffle into a potted aspidistra.

After the guests have trickled away, I help Suzie load up the dumb waiter; she seems surprised. 'Most people scarper when it's time to clear up. I s'pose they think they're on holiday.' Last night I took a look online at the fees Rose charges for these short courses, and I think they might be justified.

'When do you get to eat?' I ask.

'Before or after. There's always loads left over.'

Hardly surprising, if tonight was anything to go by, but she doesn't exactly bounce with health.

'Rose seems to be going through a bad patch,' I continue, passing her cups and cutlery. She shrugs. 'Big responsibility, running a cookery school single-handed,' I add, and notice her bite her lip. 'It can't help that Christian's so unreliable.'

She hesitates for a moment, then leans closer and lowers her voice. 'Everyone loves him, but if you ask me, he's a disaster for the school. Unreliable, rude to the students . . .'

'I had no idea. It must put extra pressure on you – on everybody.'

'It's got to the stage where Mrs Hoyt just wants him out, but he's demanding a huge pay-off. You won't tell her I said that, will you?'

'Of course not,' I say, and she turns back to the dishes. 'She must have known what he was like,' I continue. 'Why did she employ him in the first place?' I watch as she needlessly rearranges the contents of the dumb waiter.

Finally, she says, 'They've been sweet on each other for years – they're an item.'

My goodness . . . Rose and Christian? They come from different worlds. Or perhaps that's the attraction.

Suzie continues: 'Till the bust-up, that is. In January, Mrs Hoyt found out he was up to his old tricks – a barista he picked up in the King's Road – and they had a showdown. She woke up next morning and only one eye would open. Imagine looking in the mirror and seeing that.'

'I can well imagine,' I say.

'By the way – you didn't hear it from me,' she concludes, jabbing the button to send the dumb waiter down. 'Jobs like this aren't two a penny and the old bat is OK once you get used to her.'

The dark wooden doors of the contraption slide shut,

reminding me of something I can't quite place, and she disappears behind the green baize to her basement hideaway.

* * *

Everyone is in bed by the time I leave for home, but I catch the sound of voices. Glancing across the courtyard, I see the coach-house flat ablaze with light. With his back to the window is the unmistakable outline of Christian, pouring wine into someone's glass. Kind of him to invite me to the after-party.

So, home I trudge. There's something a bit rum about the school (to use an expression of my father's), plus it's run by the Addams Family . . . but heck, it's only a few days, so I might as well make the best of it.

I pass the Duke of Wellington (known to us locals as the Duke of Boots), walk up Caroline Terrace and turn right into Bourne Street. People imagine it must be amazing to live where I do – and of course it is. But Jubilee Cottage is neither big nor grand; in fact, Marcus wanted to put up a blue plaque declaring it 'the smallest house in Belgravia'.

It's tucked down an alley off a narrow cul-de-sac called Skinner Place. Strictly speaking, I live in a cul-de-sac within a cul-de-sac. There are many such anomalies in this area. The other houses are built of London stock brick, usually a sort of tawny colour, but mine is the odd one out, in red brick. It's also the smallest: basement, two-up and two-down, with a tiny yard at the back. It originally housed a railway manager and his family, which must have been convenient, because we're virtually above Sloane Square underground station. From my yard I could abseil down onto the platform, and if I open my bedroom window I can listen to the announcements on the District and Circle lines.

As I turn into the alley, I stop in my tracks. Lying on its

side at the front door of Jubilee Cottage is my dustbin, the black one for all the yucky stuff you can't recycle. And some MORON has upended the contents down my basement steps.

I feel bile rise in my throat and my chest tightens. I know exactly who that moron is. I was assured we'd put this behind us, that he'd left the country. But he's back, and he wants me to know it.

CHAPTER 8

Tuesday

My next-door neighbour does Airbnb, and I see a pyjama-clad couple peering down at me from their upstairs window as I stomp about in heavy-duty Marigolds. It takes me a full ten minutes to clean up the sticky, smelly mess, including the multiple cigarette butts which are my unwanted visitor's calling card, a greasy portion of fish and chips from God-knows-where and half a dozen scratch cards; at which point I look up and see the man filming me on his phone. *Look what these funny Londoners get up to at night!* I give him a sardonic wave, bag everything up and hose down the area before going back inside.

There's no point in going to bed until I've calmed down, so I sit up for a bit. My gaze falls inevitably on Marcus's law books – they're piled up all over the place. Beside the fireplace is his favourite chair, one of the very few things he managed to salvage after breaking up with Olinda. On the desk lies his fountain pen, and in the bathroom, on the shelf, you'll find a bottle of his cologne. A hideous Toby jug, inherited from his godfather, takes pride of place on the mantelpiece.

I used to be a marvellous sleeper, but those days are over.

When I finally go to bed, I toss and turn, thinking about Marcus and wondering if I'll ever stop missing him so acutely.

* * *

At six o'clock – long before the alarm sounds – I find myself getting up. I spin breakfast out as best I can, then set off for Chester Square hours before I need to. Catching sight of my black bin, I experience a sinking feeling: I'm going to have to start watching my back. There's a chill in the air so I'm wearing a light jacket for the first time in months. If I get the chance, I'll grab Christian before class for a quick chat and to clear the air.

I let myself in through the front door and step past the coats and umbrellas into the hallway. I turn right underneath the Grand Staircase and along the glazed passageway leading towards the Old Ballroom.

The windows here look onto the rear courtyard, which is dark and shady as usual, but with a glittering, frosty appearance. On closer examination this appears to be caused by a crystalline scattering of broken glass. I take the door leading out, glance up towards Christian's flat and see his glass door is broken.

Did he trip and fall into it? Go on a bender after dinner and smash the place up? Has he been burgled as he slept?

I gingerly climb the cast-iron steps, trying to avoid the worst of the chips and splinters. At the top, I call out for him – not too loud because I don't want to wake the whole of Chester Square.

I push at the door, but it's locked. Nothing odd about that, except I feel a pounding sensation in my chest and my breath quickening. Taking great care to avoid the jagged shards at the edges of the frame, I reach inside and feel for a key, which

I turn successfully. This admits me into a narrow hallway. Apart from more broken glass, all seems to be in order: coat hanging on a peg, shoes and boots lined up neatly to one side. I note all this down in my mind, though I'm not sure why.

On one wall is a cork board stuck with a couple of appointment cards and a *Racing Post* calendar. Opposite, on the windowsill, is a piece of scrunched-up giftwrap and a colourful scarf. This is neatly rolled, as if never tried on, and hand-knitted – you can always tell. Soft music is playing in the background – something old-fashioned, a foxtrot.

Adrenaline kicks in. For a chef, it's a familiar feeling, this hyper-alertness, the sense of danger. I blink, and notice my hands shaking: like dinner service in a packed restaurant when the plates are being called at triple speed.

I try again. 'Christian . . . Christian?' My voice sounds more high-pitched than usual.

I follow the music through a door left slightly ajar, and step into a modest sitting room. The blinds are closed. When I saw him last night, hitting the booze, they were open.

There's a fragrance in the room I half recognize; the kind of heavy, old-fashioned scent that lingers on upholstery and soft furnishings hours after the wearer has departed.

On the coffee table are: a folder marked 'Farson Holdings'; the student list – same as mine, though without the addition of Melanie; two glasses, smeary, containing wine dregs; bottle of wine – Château Palmer 2017, quarter full, no cork or corkscrew. A flash of gold on the carpet catches my eye. It's a lipstick, in a softish hue, labelled at the bottom 'Old Flame'. (Who thinks up the names?)

The song, which is coming from an iPad, draws to a close and a voice starts waffling: I recognize one of the presenters from Sentimental FM. Next up is 'All I Have To Do Is Dream' by the Everly Brothers. A favourite of mine, but I don't hum along.

I go back into the hall and knock loudly at the other door, which is closed. I open it a crack: a tap is dripping and there's an odd smell I can't at first place. Not a good one. The room has no external window, so I flick on the light.

Kitchens have lost their individuality nowadays, and there's nothing remarkable about this one. White cupboard units in an L-shape, stainless-steel appliances, tiled floor . . . probably IKEA top to bottom.

Except for one thing. Lying face down on the sizeable French farmhouse table is the body of a man with his head hacked almost off. A red-handled cleaver has been driven into the tabletop beside it. Thick greying hair is clotted with blood, which has also dripped down onto the tiled floor. I know immediately this is Christian. And that there's no point in checking for his pulse.

I've only ever seen a dead body once before. This one is unearthly, sculptural. I can make out the sinews and muscle groups of his neck and torso, and if it were the carcass of a heifer or pig, I could name them all: chuck, jowel, brisket. So much blood; what a job it'll be to scrub it out of the table.

What was it I said in class yesterday? 'First rule of butchery: off with his head!' Someone's had a damned good try at doing just that.

I feel sweat break out and my head starts to pound. This is *Christian.* Christian – erstwhile celebrity chef, restaurateur, pin-up. Christian – who only hours ago was bursting with charm and vitality, working the room as only he can. Or rather, could. Christian – my old friend.

All those years of working together, laughing together, sharing confidences as we scaled the culinary ladder. And how does our friendship end? With an outburst of bile and bitterness from me, in full view of his fan club. And now this.

A sob rises within me and I take a gasp of air. It is foul – the thick ferrous taint of recently spilled blood, mingled with Tom Ford – and, faint with horror, I feel myself toppling towards the floor.

* * *

I come round – no idea how much later – and become aware of a blurred outline moving about. It gradually solidifies, then leans over me. 'Paul, it's OK, I'm here,' says a soft voice. I see a flash of white, and someone takes my hand. 'Let me help you.' It's Suzie, thank God.

I've managed to escape the pool of blood, but I've landed on something else, which crunches under my weight as I try and sit up. Dried pasta. For no reason at all, or perhaps as a last pathetic reminder of Christian, I grab a handful and stick it in my jacket pocket.

Suzie steadies me as I stagger to my feet. 'Lucky I came over,' she says, her eyes fixed on the spreadeagled body. I take a look at my friend: the swept-back hair, the strong shoulders, the plaster cast on which some admirer has lovingly doodled a little snake shape in felt-tip. 'Mrs Hoyt asked me to make sure Christian made it into class today,' Suzie says, leading me gently away. 'We'd better get out of here and raise the alarm.'

HORS D'OEUVRE

Monday, 26th July '04
Big day tomorrow – audition at Millbank. The TV guys asked me to come up with a 'retro canapé'. Not really my thing (fiddly), but I decided on something dead easy so I can relax and SMILE at the camera.

Paul had one of his daft ideas – serving the eggs on a bed of shredded lettuce. I thought he was taking the piss at first (has been known) but it looks a bit special. Like straw – only you can eat it.

So: coming to your screen shortly (with any luck) The Christian Wagner Show. Or Christian's Cookalong. Or – if they fancy calling it something cheeky – Pass the Gravy!

DEVILLED EGGS

Hardboil 7 eggs and cool. Peel, halve neatly and remove the yolks to a bowl. Discard the two worst-looking whites and feed them to the dog.

Mash the yolks with 3 tablespoons mayo, 1 teaspoon seedy mustard, ½ teaspoon wine or cider vinegar and a splash of Worcestershire Sauce; plus generous seasoning. Pipe into the whites if you want to impress the in-laws, or use a spoon.

Nestle in a layer of shredded lettuce (+ vinaigrette). Makes a nice starter or lunch, in which case serve three halves per person.

They asked me to suggest variations: you can mix into the yolks fried chopped bacon; mashed crabmeat; blue cheese. I said a dab of caviar would go down a treat but the tightwad production people won't cough up for it.

CHAPTER 9

Some people lead rotten lives, but I honestly can't complain. Happy childhood, loving parents (even if they died too young), never any shortage of money then. Ten amazing years with Marcus, the love of my life. Interesting job, heavenly little home, Julie! I am blessed.

How pointless it all seems, however – how vain and petty life's struggles and triumphs – when you find yourself faced with something like this. Not just an untimely, sudden death – but *murder*. And of the most cruel and gruesome kind. A man hacked up like an animal . . . except that if Christian had been an animal, the job would have been done decently, with at least a modicum of dignity.

For the next few minutes, I am numb. I know I am following Suzie down the cast-iron stairs, because I can see my feet hit the steps; and I know I'm drinking tea, because she has put a mug in my hand and I can hear the liquid glug down my throat. But I'm outside my body somehow, as if this is happening to someone else.

Then the numbness fades, and the horror returns. I'm not going to pretend that Christian was like a brother to me, or that he'll leave a huge hole in my life – all the platitudes that get trotted out when an old pop star or veteran football manager 'passes'. He was no saint. But we were friends for twenty years, and for the first few of those, we worked together, shoulder-to-shoulder. Unless you're a chef yourself, you can't imagine the attention to detail, the patience, the level of collaboration it takes to knock out a hundred covers at Michelin-star level. Then afterwards, the high you get when the boss says, 'Thank you, team.' It's more than camaraderie, it's bonding.

And despite the selfishness, the philandering, the business disasters, Christian was good-hearted and loved life. I think that's why he always looked so marvellous – it shone through. Even yesterday, frayed around the edges and knocked about a bit, he lit up the room.

And never let anyone forget: when he wanted to, he could out-cook *anyone*.

I remember eating at the Oxford branch of Christian's Brasserie just after it opened, about three years ago, with our old friend Jerome. This was Christian's great comeback, after being spat out by Channel 4 and bankruptcy, and he was flush with new investment, fired up and ready to succeed. Most important of all, he was in the kitchen, leading his brigade.

As long as he was in there, the food was impeccable, and his team loved him. He didn't scream and shout: he led by example, with total concentration on whatever he was doing, whether that was shaping quenelles of mousse to float in a bisque or whisking a *beurre blanc* into flaxen silk. The problems started when he wasn't there, either because he was opening the next brasserie, or else having one of his periodic lapses of interest, usually after he'd acquired a new woman. This is why roll-outs, or chains, or 'diffusion-line' restaurants – whatever you want to call them – invariably disappoint. If you want to clone restaurants, first learn to clone chefs.

My starter on the Oxford visit was a duck liver parfait, served with bergamot marmalade and brioche soldiers. Christian could have got away with a trad presentation, but instead the butter-smooth pâté had been shaped into a small pear – which is what a bergamot looks like – and the toast arranged in criss-cross formation, military style.

I don't take photographs when I'm in a restaurant unless I have a good reason to do so. It feels like showing off: 'Look at me, everyone, I'm having dinner at Sketch!!!!' (The loos really *are* amazing, by the way.) On this occasion, however, I did. I wanted to show Marcus when I got home how clever Christian could be when he put his mind to it, because he'd heard so much about the fallen *Wunderkind* from me.

For my main, I went for that French bistro classic, steak frites. The steak was from the top of the rump, a forgotten cut he brought back into fashion. I'll never forget the chips – a sort of bird's nest of crisp shoestrings. Christian told me he'd developed a formula for sauce béarnaise that could be kept warm for hours or even reheated. I wonder if he ever wrote it down.

I'm not a dessert man, but Jerome insisted on sharing his – a new take on sticky toffee pudding. Imagine a velvety caramel sponge topped with crunchy nougatine and popping-candy ice cream.

Afterwards I couldn't wait to get back and tell Marcus what he'd missed. It breaks my heart to remember this, but later I discovered that the reason he couldn't join me in Oxford that day was that he was in Wimpole Street, receiving the results of some ominous medical tests he hadn't told me about. Marcus never got to eat that sublime food. And now no one ever will again.

* * *

I find myself sitting in the Shelley Room when the clock on the mantelpiece strikes eight. Rose has been on the phone, answering questions and giving instructions in a quiet voice.

'No, I am not related to Mr Wagner. We have – a business relationship.'

If she still loves him, saying those words must strike a dagger to her heart.

'Please may I request that your officers don't arrive with flashing lights and sirens. It is not necessary and I do not wish to alarm our neighbours in the square.'

Does she really imagine she's going to keep a lid on this?

She crosses to the window and stands there as if frozen, gazing out into the square, as when I first saw her.

I can't stop myself from thinking: could she have done that to Christian? Those years of bottled-up rage – the torment of seeing him flaunt new young paramours in front of her – his threat to ruin the school?

I feel exhausted. I remember that's how I was after Marcus died – that sense of being dragged down by a force stronger than gravity. Except he died a natural, peaceful death, surrounded by people who loved him, tended by caring doctors and nurses. Although it was sudden at the end, he died as he'd lived, with courage, dignity, consideration. Not butchered on a slab.

As I stand up to leave, a text bleeps in from Julie. It feels inconceivable that the world is still turning on its axis, normal life continuing, when all I want to do is curl into a ball and hide. But she's my best friend in the world, and I must attend to it.

📞 u l8r. Meeting postponed to pm. 🧙‍♀️🔥. ⚡💨 = ⏰⏰

CHAPTER 10

I can't tell from Julie's emojis whether Dena's burst into flames or had a ciggy and set off the smoke alarms (again), but either way it's bad news. She's brewing trouble, and her team are going to catch it.

One of her most infuriating habits is the way she rewrites history, so nothing is ever her fault. For a recent 'Inner Radiance' special, she sent the beauty team off to write about the latest celeb craze for detoxifying with leeches, then when the copy came in, complained it was cruel to animals. (According to Julie, all beauty editors are nuts, by the way; it comes from writing nonsense for a living.)

I guess the last bit is my horoscope for the day. Electricity in the air and double alarm clocks: *Emergency!* Say *that* again.

I tell Rose I'm going down to the Old Ballroom – she doesn't register any reaction – and manage to dodge out of sight of Lady B descending from an upper floor. I am in no fit state for *Good morning! Sleep well? What are we learning today?* For some reason her ladyship is in a rage, and I fear for the staircase. *Stomp STOMP stomp STOMP stomp stomp stomp stomp*, like Stravinsky's *The Rite of Spring*. Dragged behind her, like a fish on a hook, is a wan-faced Harriet.

I hurry along the hallway, averting my eyes from the courtyard of horror, and tap the green button to release the doors. They fly open in their usual way – it's like living in an airport. If you ask me, they need adjusting before someone gets hurt.

After the mayhem I've just lived through, the Old Ballroom is an oasis of peace and order. My knife roll is exactly where I left it, my knives all present and correct.

Which brings me to the matter of the cleaver. If the one I saw earlier this morning was the same one I used yesterday to prep the pigeons, how did it find its way up to Christian's flat? It certainly seemed to have the same red handle.

I phone Julie back, but she doesn't pick up. I should have expected as much but can't for the life of me think what voicemail to leave. *Day got off to bad start.* (You can say that again.) *Just found Christian with a cleaver through his head.* (She'll think I'm kidding.) Finally, I say something that hits the right note. 'Erm . . . I'm OK but something terrible's happened at the school. Phone me when you can. And I do mean phone, not a string of silly faces and unicorns.'

I'm finishing the call when the doors whoosh open again. It's Suzie, ushering in a pair of police officers, male and female.

The male, with a crown of curly fair hair, is in a dark suit and tie, and announces himself as a detective sergeant; the woman, in full police clobber, is a sergeant. How hot and tiring it must be to traipse around all day in a stiff stab-proof vest, weighed down with baton, handcuffs, radio, bodycam, CS spray, notebook, pen and Lord-knows-what. The detective asks Suzie to leave the room, then his partner-in-crime-prevention goes into a sort of monotone, as if she's reading the Last Rites.

'Please tell us what happened, Mr Delamare. Take your time.' Hushed, polite, sympathetic, as if Christian were my nearest and dearest, rather than just my happy-go-lucky old friend.

I don't really register what they or I say – all I know is that the sergeant keeps clicking her pen and I wish she'd stop. Finally the pair of them give up.

'We'll chat again when you're feeling – a bit more steady,' she says. They start gabbling into their radios, at which point Suzie returns and escorts them away.

My natural instinct is to trust the police: quite a few of my mother's family were in law enforcement in one way or another, so I was brought up to think of them as the good guys. This isn't to say that I've always stayed on the right side of them . . . but that was only once, and thanks to Marcus, and of course Julie, it will never happen again.

Julie will, needless to say, go into full defence mode when she hears what's happened. She's addicted to true crime programmes on TV (her other favoured genres currently being 'idiots in cars' and 'wedding fails') and knows all about interrogation techniques and body-language analysis. More often than not, she says, the person who reports a crime is the person who committed it. Which puts me in a very bad place.

When Suzie comes back I ask if by any chance there's brandy on the premises because: 'It's not every day you trip over a corpse on your way to work.'

She shows no sign of amusement but goes to a bank of cupboards, takes out her keys and unlocks one.

'Christian's locker,' she explains. He probably keeps a bottle hidden away for the old flambé trick, and as I knock back a swig, the Courvoisier honestly seems to help.

'I can't thank you enough for earlier – helping me,' I say. 'But are you OK?'

She shakes her head sorrowfully. 'Not really. Just keeping my head down, doing what I can for Mrs Hoyt.'

'So has she told the students?' I ask.

'All they know is, there's been an accident.'

I feel anger flare up. 'You're joking! You mean she didn't tell them? Surely they'll seal the place off – send us all home?'

'Not yet,' Suzie says. 'The police say everyone needs to

hang around until we're given permission to leave. And a message from Mrs Hoyt – we're to expect the counterterrorism people along shortly.'

'What on earth for?' I snap.

'The way it was done,' she replies, adding under her voice, 'You know . . . jihadists, beheading. You can't rule anything out. Anyway, I've worked out a route through the house so the students don't get tangled up with the police.'

'You can't be serious! Rose hasn't thought this through. It's disrespectful.'

Suzie seems to agree, adding apologetically: 'She says she can't afford to refund everyone.'

The doors open, and in the students troop, perky and enthusiastic. Someone's going to have to tell them at some point, but I don't see why it should be me.

'Hi, everyone. Not great news about – the accident,' I say. Chatter and giggles. Next thing they're all tying on their aprons.

'If anyone doesn't feel up to it, I'll quite understand,' I add. My eye is drawn to the Hon. Harriet, who is ghostly pale and has her hand to her mouth. She abruptly leaves the room, tracked by the gorgon glare of her mother.

'I was wondering if we should give this morning's class a rain check,' I continue tentatively.

There's a rustling sound, which I locate to Lilith. She's chinwagging with Vicky, mop of mauve hair swishing up and down like a horse's tail swatting flies.

'Some of us have come a long way to be here,' says Lilith slowly, with a hint of menace.

Vicky nods and fixes me with her eyes through the goggle lenses. 'It's only an accident, after all.' She holds up her copy of the curriculum, encased in a see-through plastic wallet and emblazoned with stickers. '*Stock, Sauces and Jus* – I was looking forward to that one.'

'Bad luck to have two accidents in such quick succession,' mutters Melanie.

De'Lyse is looking nervous. 'There were police cars outside. Maybe it's worse than we think.'

'Rose assured us there's nothing anyone can do at this point,' says Gregory.

I feel like screaming and slamming my head against the workbench.

Instead I take a deep breath and handle the crisis in the only way I know: throw myself into some cooking. It's healing balm for the chef, and exactly what Christian would do.

CHAPTER 11

Stock is one of those kitchen processes that the experienced cook learns to do automatically, while thinking of other things. Sometimes, after a particularly stressful time – and there have been a few of those in the last couple of years – I've made a special trip to buy chicken carcasses and vegetables, then watched them bubble away for a couple of hours, adjusting the heat so the pot remains at the gentlest of simmers, skimming and tasting.

At such times you enter a sort of trance state. Your brain is freed up to troubleshoot problems and resolve difficulties without the impediment of conscious thought.

This isn't to say everyone has to make stock, or wants to. There's a place for cubes, which are nothing to be snobbish about. Though if a dish depends on stock as its principal ingredient – soup, gravy, risotto – then you have to choose whether you want it to taste of a cube or chicken.

Gregory, today in maroon cords, pipes up to say he once made fish stock for bouillabaisse and neighbours reported him for smelling out the bin area. His Warwickshire pad is a flat in a converted stately home, where such things matter. Lilith, who has a rat problem, swears by a product called Whiffs Away. Melanie is about to join in, I do hope about stock rather than vermin, when her phone rings for the third time in ten minutes.

Vicky's hand goes up. She has traded yesterday's viper

outfit for a fitted leopard-print ensemble, more suited to a fitness centre than a kitchen. I'm not surprised the subject of stock holds appeal – a perfect time for her carefully curated collection of freezer bags, twist ties and stick-on labels to enjoy their moment in the sun. But no. 'There's a policeman at the door,' she says.

I press the button to open up and it's the uniformed female from earlier. The students look aghast.

She asks me to step outside for a minute and informs me in a low voice that they'll be calling the students out one by one for a few routine questions – names, addresses, that sort of thing. She's brought her pen along and sure enough she's clicking it.

'The students have no idea what's happened – all Mrs Hoyt told them was that there's been an accident.'

She ignores this, we re-enter and she explains the plan.

'What happened to Christian?' demands Lady B.

'I can't say anything at this time, madam. Mrs Hoyt has put her study at our disposal and given me a list of attendees, so I'd like to ask you to step up there one by one. Starting with . . . Mr Cartwright.'

Stephen stands and follows the officer out of the room.

After that, understandably, any hope of cooking is abandoned and the class descends into chaos. If the police have been called, there has obviously been some sort of foul play. Did someone hurt Christian? Was there a fight?

Meanwhile something creepy is starting to dawn on me; I look round the room and experience a sudden chill. Could one of the students be involved?

Of course, the likelihood remains that it was a break-in. The police will already be onto it: every street in London is now under the scrutiny of CCTV cameras.

Stephen returns, and the sergeant calls out, 'Ms De'Lyse.'

'It's just De'Lyse,' she says, and follows her out.

Lilith scratches her head. I see now her hair isn't just mauve, it's *multi-toned*, in shades of lavender, lilac, violet, purple and plum. How do they even do that?

'I heard voices,' she says portentously. 'Talking, arguing. I couldn't make out the words, but voices, late into the night.'

'So sorry if we kept others awake,' says Lady B lightly. 'That will have been Harriet and I, gossiping away.' Their bedrooms are on the second floor, across from Lilith's. 'So much to discuss: freesias or roses, how many tiers for the cake . . . and is Jason's sister too grown-up to be a flower girl?' Tinkling laughter. 'Eighteen and "fully developed" – I rather think so!'

'Quite an *intense* chat, it sounded like,' adds Lilith, frowning.

'Oh, you know what mothers and daughters are like when it comes to planning the happy day!' Another trill of laughter.

'I went out like a light,' says Melanie. 'So lovely and peaceful here, and a full moon over the square. Away from the cares of home and family.' Said with a sigh: the way her phone keeps ringing, they have no intention of letting her go.

Gregory, whose room is on the first floor, remembers nothing – he fell asleep plugged into a podcast about Schubert's Unfinished Symphony. His owlish eyes have a glassy look, as if he overindulged at dinner. On the same floor is Stephen – whom everyone has ignored until now. He was online till the early hours, playing a video game. He heard the locks of the front door spring open at about midnight.

'Just once, or did you hear them again later?' asks Lilith. 'If someone came in, they must have gone out.' He mutters a reply but I can't make out if it's yes or no. It's as if he has a quota of words each day and is frightened of running out.

'Anyone hear the breaking glass?' asks Vicky, who has evidently been saving up this revelation for maximum impact. Her room is at the back of the house, overlooking the courtyard. '*Smash – tinkle. Smash – tinkle.* Then footsteps. *Patter patter patter.*' She scampers her fingers across her bench, enjoying the drama.

'Are you quite sure?' says Lilith, feeling outdone. 'I'm a light sleeper. I used to sleepwalk when I was a child.'

'I think you'll find sleepwalking is associated with deep sleep,' comments Gregory; Lilith shoots him a look.

'I wouldn't make it up,' replies Vicky, with a patronizing little nod. Not the kind of pharmacist you'd want to get into an argument with about inappropriate purchases of cough mixture. 'Between five past and ten past seven this morning.'

After De'Lyse, it's Gregory's turn with the cops: he exits looking nervous, rubbing his palms on his corduroys. He's away longer than the others, and the female officer has a half-smile on her face as she escorts him back in. He's greeted by a nervous silence: we'd all like to know what kept him, but he's not giving anything away.

Next it's Melanie – she hops out skittishly enough, checking herself in the mirror on the way. When she returns she looks slightly flushed: 'What a *charming* young detective.' She's followed by Vicky, and then Lilith.

De'Lyse has been placed under strict orders not to post on social media about Christian's 'accident', and I feel sorry for her – it's as if they've taken her voice away.

'I'm not sure they can do that,' she says. 'Everyone will be saying: *What's happening with De'Lyse?*'

'I should phone my husband,' says Melanie. 'Ben's ex-army, he'd be round here like a shot if he thought we were in danger.'

'I don't think De'Lyse is suggesting that,' I reply. Although, now it's out there, what if we do have a psychopath in our midst, and they decide to go berserk again? No shortage of weapons in the Old Ballroom, and Rose's batty kitchenalia collection standing by in reserve.

At that moment the door whooshes open and Lilith bustles in with the detective in tow. 'I'm sorry this is taking so long, but we're nearly there,' he says, sweeping back an errant curl. 'Do we have a Harriet Brash?'

'I'm her mother,' announces Lady B, stepping forward. 'My daughter's not feeling well, but I'd be delighted to answer on her behalf.' She likes the look of him – they all do.

'We'll need to see her at some point, but you're next anyway, Mrs Brash.'

'*Lady* Brash,' she says, adding coquettishly, 'but you can call me Serena.'

When they've left, Lilith puts up her hand.

'I'm no expert, but if a lady is divorced from a lord, she isn't Lady Brash any more, is she? She's Serena, Lady Brash.' Another one who's been watching too much *Downton*.

'I think that's for envelopes,' says Melanie. 'You still call her Lady Whatever to her face.'

'Perhaps they're just separated,' says Vicky. 'Our son split up with his wife last year, and now they're back together again and trying for a family.'

'I'd say Serena is past child-bearing age,' says Lilith. *Meeow.*

Gregory gives a little cough. 'For what it's worth, I know she's divorced. There's another Lady Brash now.'

'Exactly my point,' says Lilith, who I've come to realize must always have the last word.

I decide when the interviews conclude that with the exception of Gregory, who is fidgeting even more than usual, the students have found the whole episode rather *fun*. I think they'll change their minds shortly. Meanwhile, we might as well get stuck into the coursework.

We make béchamel, first in the old-fashioned French way (Rose would approve), starting with a roux and slowly adding warmed milk; then as it's done nowadays, by tipping the lot into the pan and whisking like mad (she wouldn't). Then it's mayonnaise. The secret, I tell them, is to add the oil *literally* drop by drop until you see it thicken. I put Gregory in charge of whisking, Stephen of oil, and watch them at work. Gregory soon gets impatient, but Stephen perseveres: *Drip. Drip. Drip.*

Vicky puts up her hand and says that she remembers eating a fish and salad platter called Le Grand Aïoli at Christian's Brasserie. Could I show her how to make aïoli? (She pronounces it *oolly*.) Vicky hasn't mentioned before that she's such a keen member of the Christian fan club – indeed, I thought she seemed uncharacteristically retiring when he dropped in yesterday – but I'm happy to oblige. 'Mash your garlic with your knife, as I showed you yesterday.' It feels like a century ago. 'Then just the same as for mayonnaise, pinch of sugar at the end.'

After that I show them how to make hollandaise in a blender, another useful shortcut. Lilith obviously hasn't been watching because she asks if it's gluten-free. Vicky asks if you can freeze it and the funny thing is, if you whip a couple of egg whites to soft peaks and fold them in, you can.

I've laboured through the class as best I can, and to fill the last few minutes before coffee, I agree to let De'Lyse film me making a sauce. This will mean that as soon as she gets the go-ahead from the police, she has a video to post.

I offer her fashionable options such as chimichurri or gribiche, then realize I have a bottle of brandy sitting in front of me and my students might wonder why. How about sauce Diane? It's a bit retro, but De'Lyse says her mum is called Diane, so yes, please. Sweet girl.

The camera starts to roll, and I explain the recipe as I go along. Having made a croquembouche in front of an audience of 3,000 punters at Birmingham NEC, this is child's play. The most exciting bit is setting light to it. Pour a good glug of cognac into your pan, let it warm for a few seconds, then strike a match. *Whoomph!* De'Lyse loves this, and is further pleased when I glug and whoomph again.

As the flames die down, I think with a pang of dear old Christian; flambés were very much his style – he said you knew you'd done the job properly when you caught that strange smell of burning hair, once the flames singe the back of your hand.

I am finishing my performance, blowing kisses to De'Lyse's mum and reminding her followers round the world that every kitchen should have a fire extinguisher, when those wretched doors swing open again to admit the female sergeant. Would I accompany her, please, for a short word with her and her colleague?

I thought I'd been through this already – is it really necessary? While the students head off to the Pink Room for limp pastries and a cup of Suzie's poisonous coffee, I follow the cop to Rose's study. I might as well be marching to the scaffold; I feel suddenly afraid.

CHAPTER 12

The Shelley Room is a strange setting for a police interview. I wonder if they feel this, too, hemmed in by Rose's collection of Victorian cookware, and frowned down upon by framed lithographs of boiled rabbits and sphinx cakes. I wonder if they even know who Mrs Beeton is . . . or maybe that's unfair.

'Mr Delamare, we appreciate your time today,' says the blond detective. He even pronounces my name right – like the poet (though spelt differently), and not as 'Delamere', which is a place in Cheshire, or a service station on the M4.

They're gracious enough to offer me a glass of water, to which I boldly reply that I'd prefer a cup of tea. One of them goes off to make it and the other is called to the front door, which gives me a few minutes to calm myself and get my story straight. There is of course the small matter of my previous conviction.

Here is the background, in brief. The only person who knows about this is Julie; for reasons that will become obvious, it isn't something I put on my CV.

It begins with the death of my father in September 2009. He was a GP in a quaint Dorset market town – think honey-coloured houses and cobbled streets – and an important, respected figure in local life. Two years before he died, he arranged a six-month sabbatical from his practice in order to do a spell with Doctors Without Borders – something he'd long dreamt of doing. Subsequently he went on a second mission and managed to get himself killed by a car bomb in Baghdad.

After that my mother took her own life; it is not something I wish to revisit at this point.

I came into a modest inheritance – not nearly as much as it should have been, because I was stitched up by the partners at my father's practice; but I was an only child, and it seemed a lot at the time. And that's when I went off the rails.

At first it was harmless, just drinking and dancing until late, then sleeping it off the day after. Some Saturdays Julie would come along, which added to the fun. Although she's a few years younger than me (and ten times as wild), she and I were already best friends, a favourite joke being that we met through maple syrup and have stuck together ever since. It was a 'Maple of Canada' press launch, and I still have the spoon rest – carved from genuine maple wood – to prove it.

I already knew a lot of faces among the club-goers, but now I began to make friends. Everyone seemed to work odd hours (waiters, bartenders, musicians) so they didn't have to flog into an office the next morning. It was amazing to find myself part of the in-crowd, rather than always looking on in envy. I started hanging around seedy underground establishments in King's Cross or Mile End or London Bridge. I discovered that both the long – usually tedious – anticipation, and intense thrill when you actually 'scored', benefited from a chemical boost. It started innocently enough – a slurp of GHB never did anyone any harm. Or let's pop an E. Another line of charlie, why not?

There was a soundtrack to all this, and hearing certain songs now transports me straight back to those groggy, lust-filled months. 'Grenade' by Bruno Mars . . . Lady Gaga's 'Born This Way' . . . Katy Perry singing 'Firework'. Just a bar or two and a wave of nausea passes over me.

Julie fought me bitterly over the party drugs, and I stopped picking up her phone calls. That's when she started sending texts and emojis instead, which she's been doing ever since.

So it was that at four o'clock on the morning of 5 July 2011, high as a kite and longing for a cheeseburger, I drifted along Vauxhall Arches and straight into the arms of a pair of police officers. After a bit of banter, I decided to make a run for it and there was a scuffle. They were too fast for me, and before I knew it I found myself sailing along in a police car and deposited at Kennington Road Police Station; in handcuffs.

I've blotted out most of what happened after that, although I remember sitting for hours in a white-tiled cell that smelt of urine and feeling glad I wouldn't have to explain this to my parents or anyone else.

I was convicted for Unlawful Possession of Class A Drugs and given a suspended sentence and fine of £300. It didn't seem very much – less than I'd paid for the ecstasy tablets I'd necked earlier that night, plus the wrap of coke they discovered down one of my socks.

If my name ever did appear in a newspaper or online, I never saw it; certainly no one has mentioned it to me before or since. At the back of my mind, I sometimes worry there might be a criminal record hanging over me, but I've no idea how I'd check. Nor did it seem to matter – till now.

I couldn't summon the energy to go out and rekindle my career, so I stayed in and watched *The Simpsons*. I have a dense beard – my five o'clock shadow has been flatteringly compared to Don Draper's in *Mad Men* – and I need to shave every day: I started leaving it three or four days, then a week. I drank cheap Pinot Grigio, didn't change my clothes often enough.

I was saved by Julie. It might be thought she owed me a favour after the Estonia débâcle, when I rescued her from a 'romantic' seaside resort after being dumped and defrauded by a *soi disant* crypto millionaire. But that's not how our friendship works. We don't keep a tally.

After weeks of being ghosted by me, Julie broke in through a window. I had a long hard cry in her arms. Then, instead of 'snap out of it', or 'you need professional help', or 'it's all going to be OK', or 'let's make a plan', my ever-practical friend said: 'Why don't you start with a haircut?'

It seemed doable, and the following morning I found myself in a smart little hair salon on the corner of Chester Row and Bourne Street which caters for the high aristocracy. I am not high aristocracy, but my barber is an old friend and gives me the student rate (not that students ever go there). It's a laugh to be coiffed among the dowagers and dachshunds.

As fate would have it, sitting at the next chair was a businessman. He was deep in conversation with his stylist, not about hair length or conditioning products, but about frying pans.

'The handle snapped off last night while I was making an omelette,' he explained. A pleasant, confident tone – not one of those commanding boardroom voices but someone at ease with himself and the world.

I leaned back and angled my head to get a better look – after all, that's what mirrors in hairdressing salons are for. Debonair. Late forties. Sparkling blue eyes. Friendly smile.

Then I looked at myself. I may have been fifteen years younger than Mr Businessman, but the last few months had not treated me kindly: he was way out of my league. At least I could help with the pan.

Half an hour later we were in Peter Jones watching a sales assistant pack a gleaming black Staub with beechwood handle in layer upon layer of bubble-wrap and tissue.

'Pity I'm in a rush – got to be in the City for a meeting,'

my businessman said. 'You wouldn't, um, be free this evening? You mentioned cast iron needs seasoning – perhaps you could show me?'

I hesitated. Could this perfect specimen – this miracle of manliness and courtesy – possibly be interested in damaged goods like me?

'I'm Marcus, by the way,' he added, shaking me by the hand. 'Marcus Berens.' Then to the assistant: 'That's enough tissue paper, thank you – it's only a frying pan.'

'I'd like that very much. I'm Paul.'

'Wonderful. I'll be home by six thirty. Jubilee Cottage, off Skinner Place. We walked past it on the way here – green door, ivy up the front. Smallest house in Belgravia.'

CHAPTER 13

Once my tea arrives, the two officers ask me to go through it all from the beginning. Their mood isn't quite as warm and fuzzy as last time, and the blond detective keeps looking down at his notes. It's a well-cut suit he's wearing, perfectly pressed; maybe he's recently promoted and this is his first big case.

They reassure me this is just an informal chat, to fill in some background. Of particular interest are my movements yesterday night, between 11 p.m. and 1 a.m. Did I go straight home, or stop somewhere on the way? Did I return to Chester Square later on for any reason? What time did I go to bed? Was anyone with me overnight? (I stifle a hollow laugh.)

The detective is curious as to how I managed to avoid getting blood all over myself, given the state of Christian's kitchen. I've no good explanation for this, except that the blood was pooled away from where I fainted, and the death scene was so repulsive I had no desire to touch him or anything else in the room. (Thinking about it, I could have mentioned that I take particular pride in being clean and tidy round the kitchen, unlike many chefs, who regard it as a badge of honour to get daubed and splattered. Not that I'm comparing murder with cheffing, obviously.)

Now his colleague joins in, demanding to know exactly what I may have touched – worktops, table, the body, the murder weapon. She's clicking that goddamn pen again, and I try not to sound tetchy when I repeat that I didn't touch anything.

'What about the handrail up to the flat? Door handles?' she asks. *Click, click.*

They've caught me out. 'I may have used the handrail, certainly on the way down. As for the handles, I went in and out of the flat, and doors don't normally open themselves, do they?' I attempt a little smile.

'Not if they're already open,' she says.

I stop and think. 'Now you mention it, the front door was locked from the inside. I remember reaching in to open it so I could get in.' She writes this down.

Then the detective asks: 'Just to be quite sure, you didn't shatter the glass yourself?'

'Of course not! There was glass everywhere, it was some kind of break-in.'

'And you reached in with your hand?'

'What else would I do it with? My antennae? A tentacle?'

Not a hint of a smile.

'Was the door bolted, or locked with a key?'

'A key,' I reply. 'Though once the glass was broken, the door could have been locked or unlocked from the inside or the outside.'

'Obviously,' says the detective, with a dismissive shake of his curls. He continues: 'How about the door to the living room. Did you have to break into that?'

'Look, I didn't break into anything. It was ajar, so I may have pushed it, or touched the handle. I'm sure you'll take fingerprints, so you can decide for yourselves.'

The officers exchange glances. I've played this wrong – turned them against me.

'Did you touch anything in that room?'

'Probably. The wine bottle, for instance,' I reply.

'Any particular reason for that? You're aware you were tampering with a crime scene? Wilfully contaminating evidence is a serious offence.'

'That's ridiculous,' I protest. 'How was I meant to know it was a crime scene?' You can see how witnesses get tangled up when being questioned. 'Also, I picked something up from the floor, a lipstick, which I put on the table.'

Before they let me go, they ask my plans for the next few days. (I'm tempted by, 'Funny you should ask, flying down to Bogotá to catch some sun'; or 'Off to Algeria to join the Foreign Legion.') I tell them we're planning to carry on with the course, and they seem surprised, in a laconic kind of way.

'Was that your idea?'

'Absolutely not. It's what Mrs Hoyt wanted, and the students agreed. I don't know when you're planning to tell them it's a murder investigation, but that will probably add to the appeal. It's not every day you get to see one of those close up.'

They exchange looks of distaste, then the detective says: 'We don't think of ourselves as a sort of floorshow, Mr Delamare. You stick to cupcakes and profiteroles, and leave us to get on with the serious stuff. That will be all for now, except that it would be helpful to have your fingerprints. It's voluntary at this point, but will help us eliminate you from the investigation.'

The last time I had my fingerprints taken was in Vauxhall, and we know how that ended. The technology has changed – nowadays you press your finger down onto a small metal scanner connected to a mobile phone. All this in under a minute and I am dismissed.

I have twenty-five minutes till we're due back in class and I'm desperate to escape the hostile atmosphere inside the house. There's a young, friendly looking constable waiting by the front door and I ask him if I'm allowed out for a breath of fresh air.

'Very good idea, sir. First I need your name and when you expect to return.' I spell it out for him and he copies it down laboriously. I don't know whether it's all that fresh air, or the way they dress, but police officers look so healthy and appealing. As I watch him scribbling in his book, my curiosity gets the better of me.

'Do you write down everyone as they come and go, or just the suspects?' I ask, affecting a cheery smile. I've never had the slightest interest in police procedure, but it's different when you're caught up in it.

'It's called the scene log, sir. It records everyone who enters and leaves in the course of our investigation.'

'Interesting. Any idea how long you think we need to stay around? Before we're free to go?'

'You're free to go at any time, sir, unless you're under arrest. But if you mean how long the investigation is likely to take, that's very hard to say.'

'Ballpark figure?'

'In my experience, I would expect the scene of crime officers to wind up later today or tomorrow.'

'Have they found anything interesting, if you're at liberty to tell me?'

'I can't help you there, I'm afraid. But there's been lots of coming and going, and the boys have got big smiles on their faces, if that means anything.'

CHAPTER 14

Out in the fresh air, I check my phone: nothing from Julie. I can imagine her and the other section editors pacing about in dread, waiting for the shriek that summons them into Dena's emergency meeting. Her office is a 'loft-style' concept in high-gloss black and white designed to belittle and intimidate; visitors are consigned to slippery low-level sofas – last in, a gross PVC beanbag – over which she towers, enthroned on a monstrous leather chair. This has so many flaps and swivels that at the touch of a button she can fly out of the window.

To dispel this vision of horror, I set off for a walk. Chester Square was built to provide grand homes for stuffy Victorian financiers and lawyers, but it's loosened up over the years. As well as being a favourite address for politicians – such as Macmillan and Thatcher – Julie Andrews and Mick Jagger were unlikely neighbours for a while, and Yehudi Menuhin had one of the corner houses – selling a Stradivarius to pay for it. Fans would cluster outside in the hope of catching a trill or cadenza from his top-floor studio.

Nowadays it's mainly bankers, trustafarians, oligarchs. Still magnificent, but dead at the heart. There's a few people going in and out during the week, but come Friday, tumbleweed time. They're all away at their country houses, or skiing in Zermatt, or sunning themselves on their yachts in the Côte d'Azur. If you do see a gaggle of tourists, they're probably on a Lord Lucan walk. Poor Sandra Rivett was clubbed to death by the murderous peer just round the corner, and his wife Veronica ran bleeding to the Plumbers Arms, an otherwise pleasant local watering hole. Perhaps in future they'll add in a detour to the cookery school, to ogle the front door behind which a celebrity chef was beheaded.

I walk as far as Elizabeth Street, which over recent years has metamorphosed from the most boring street in London – estate agents, a dry cleaner, an electrical shop, a stationer – into a gastronomic honeypot. I don't know where the denizens of Belgravia did their food shopping previously, but now the pavements are lined with boulangeries, traiteurs, pâtisseries, chocolate shops, an organic deli, a wine merchant, coffee shops and tea shops, plus a cupcake parlour, painted baby pink and permanently under siege from Instagramming Japanese tourists. It's the closest thing I know to living in Paris, and if I were rich, I honestly believe I'd pick up a *plat préparé* every night and give up cooking.

My destination is a café-delicatessen on the corner. Normally I'd resent spending nearly £12 on a bacon sarnie, but right now I'd sell my grandmother for one. There are no chairs left outside, and it's packed inside, too: a mix of yummy mummies, buff young men (their personal trainers?) and tourists. I order mine to take away.

Shortly afterwards, my name is called out, and I realize I haven't chosen wisely. According to my mother, Diana Dors was expelled from the Rank Charm School for eating cherries out of a bag while walking down Knightsbridge, spitting out stones as she went. I hope I don't bump into anyone I know while I eat a bacon sandwich on walkabout.

There's no shortage of interesting windows to look in while I munch. A cashmere boutique, leather boots and handbags, French homewares, designer togs for children, a cigar shop and my personal favourite, the Belgravia Pet

Emporium. This is an animal lover's paradise, where you can treat your cutie to a handcrafted suede leather collar, the latest couture pet carrier, toile-de-jouy stuffed animals and – to curl up on after all the fun – a miniature button-backed sofa in tartan velour, complete with memory foam and scatter cushionettes.

I hear people saying, 'I'm a dog person' or 'I'm a cat person', but to me both are just as lovable, if you understand their funny little ways. One day I may have a cat or dog of my own; I think about it a lot.

The bacon is great – juicy and smoky and plentiful – and I am just rolling it round in my mouth, wondering if I should have treated myself to a slice of Tunisian orange and polenta cake to eat on the way back, when I see a shadow in the glass, of someone passing rapidly behind me.

You can feel when you're being watched – a sort of sixth sense prickling between your shoulder blades. I turn round smartly and see a familiar figure. Lean with short dark hair. Ripped denims, biker jacket – more Dalston than Belgravia.

Oh for God's sake! Him again. I was informed – promised – he was out of the country. South America . . . wouldn't be back for months. Last night, of course, told me otherwise.

I turn quickly and see him disappear into Gerald Road. As I do so, I note the bowed head and peculiar slouching gait, like a hound that's been kicked; the flash of a silver thumb ring.

For a second I freeze, unsure whether to flee or follow. Then I scrunch up the remains of my sandwich and walk swiftly to the corner. No sign: he's slid into a doorway or behind a van.

Next, I cross the street to the wine shop, and stare in at the magnums of claret and gaily coloured spirits. Sure enough, I can see his reflection creep out of Gerald Road and take up position outside the olde-worlde chemist shop on the corner. He knows that I've seen him – that's part of the game – and gives me the finger, before turning to look into the shop window, which is full of stranded sponges. Maybe he's weighing up whether real sponges are a sustainable resource. More likely, thinking how next to intimidate me.

The urgent question is how to get back into Chester Square without his following me. If he knows I'm working there, he'll somehow use it against me, as he's done before. Throw a brick through a window. Drop a parcel into the basement area and tell the police it's a bomb.

No choice, I'll have to make a run for it – and this time I *really* hope I don't bump into someone I know.

I take off at full tilt, racing around the corner, keeping St Michael's Church on my left; for a mad moment, it flashes through my mind to run in and claim sanctuary. But I sprint on into Chester Square and up the garden side, where the pavement is narrow and shielded by overhanging greenery. About halfway up I stop behind a removal truck and – *dammit!* – there he is, loping along behind me.

I pause for a second to think. He also stops, and coughs phlegm onto the pavement. Filthy habit.

I dash up the square – I can hear feet slapping on the paving stones behind me – until I'm outside number forty-one, under the very windows of the Shelley Room. What I'm not expecting is for Rose to be at the front door, seeing off a visitor.

A final, desperate idea flashes into my mind. Dodging behind parked cars as best I can, I hurtle past Rose and her friend – whom I seem to recognize for some reason – to the next corner, and sharply round this into the mews at the back of the house.

A few yards along I find the heavy black steel door Suzie

told me was used for deliveries. Yes, there is a touchpad. With shaking hand I tap in *1904* and say my prayers.

The door slides silently open – *thank you, God* – and I nip through the gap and out of sight.

I've shaken him off – here I am, safe and sound at last, in the haven of number forty-one.

With a sigh of relief, I look around me. The courtyard looks so different.

Now there's police tape everywhere, and big people in white overalls – like beekeepers – tramping up and down the flimsy cast-iron stairway, staggering under the weight of lights and camera equipment.

I'm crossing the courtyard towards the door that leads into the hall, wondering what Rose's connection might be to her visitor – who, it now dawns on me, is the mysterious ash blonde I saw talking to De'Lyse yesterday – when out steps the dynamic duo.

'In a hurry, Mr Delamare?' asks Ms Pen Clicker.

'We saw you from Mrs Hoyt's window,' explains the detective. 'Handy, the back doors on these large houses. If you want to come or go without being seen.'

CHAPTER 15

'Sorry to be late,' I say to my class, who have duly assembled in the Old Ballroom. It's only three minutes past two, but Vicky is studying her watch as if it's suddenly grown an extra hand.

They've obviously heard something, but is it the full story? Melanie has been crying, and Lady B is attempting to comfort her with a pack of tissues. Vicky's eyes are red and even more than usually bulging. Gregory wears a grim, set expression, and is tapping his fingers on his workbench. The Hon. Harriet, who has returned to class but probably wishes she hadn't, looks stricken, rocking back and forth on her stool while hugging a cushion she's found from somewhere.

I say, tentatively, 'Quite a commotion across the courtyard,' and Melanie emits a strangled sob.

De'Lyse jumps in. 'We're not dumb, you know – we've heard what happened. It's all online. Was it you who found him?'

'Maybe he'd rather not talk about it,' says Harriet, snuffling. (Thank you, Harriet.)

'Never good to bottle things up,' slings in Lilith. 'Tell us – get it off your chest.'

'So you knew all along?' says De'Lyse. 'You're standing there making jokes about lumpy gravy while the police are launching a murder investigation. Don't you think you should have said something?'

I take a deep breath. 'I'm genuinely sorry you had to find out like that, but we were instructed not to speak to anyone about what happened,' I say, stretching the truth. 'The police told me and Mrs Hoyt to wait for the official announcement.' Why am I covering up for Rose?

'Horrible way to go,' says Lilith. 'My mam's friend's husband had a piece of glass fall on him in Port Talbot. Sliced clean in half he was.'

'They're saying on Twitter that Christian's broken arm wasn't an accident, that he was beaten up,' continues De'Lyse. 'Do you think it's all connected?'

'It's an ongoing investigation,' I say, 'and I'm sure the police are considering all eventualities.' Listen to me! I sound like a public service announcement. 'So what do you all want to do? I can't believe that in the circumstances anyone's in the mood for cooking—'

'How long is the investigation likely to take?' interrupts Vicky, dabbing her eyes. She's distracted – hasn't been listening. 'I've got my train ticket booked for Thursday after lunch. It's hubby's birthday Saturday, you see, and I've stuff to prepare.'

'Ooh, I'm a Virgo, too,' says Lilith.

'Are you making a cake?' asks Melanie.

How can they be so trivial, at a time like this?

'I had an informal word with the police officer on door duty earlier,' I say, trying to restore an atmosphere of solemnity. 'He can't be certain, but he thinks the operation here should wind up tomorrow. So we could probably go home then, with any luck.'

Melanie says, 'I'm not expected home till Thursday afternoon. Until this all happened, I was enjoying myself.' This is rich, as all she's done so far is yak away on her mobile. 'I was rather looking forward to the chocolate class.'

'Have you ever had chocolate go all grainy when you melt it?' asks Gregory.

'Give it to the dog,' advises Lilith.

'Chocolate is poisonous to dogs,' Melanie says swiftly.

'Never heard that,' retorts Lilith. 'Betsy lived for Choc Drops and she made it to seventeen.'

'Unless we're being offered a refund, I think Harriet and I would be inclined to stay on,' says Lady B. 'Though naturally it won't be the same.' Everyone seems to agree, so for the time being the decision's plain: on we go.

Ghouls, the lot of them.

* * *

According to the timetable, we're meant to be roasting and braising this afternoon. Also – and it seems ambitious, to say the least – making bread *and* pastry. I can't imagine how Christian fitted it all in, unless – and this is likely – he skipped the tuition and spent the time reminiscing about his glory days.

The meats are soon dealt with, bubbling and sizzling away, though there's been a minor altercation involving (inevitably) Lilith. One of her coral-coloured acrylics has ended up in the short ribs. As if that's not bad enough, Vicky has taken the rap, after admitting she found it on the chopping board and put it somewhere safe (which turned out to be among the carrots).

Agitation is in the air, and I notice eyes flicking involuntarily in the direction of Christian's flat, and sidelong glances at one another. It is therefore a good thing that our next session is a calming one: breadmaking. A friend of mine has written a book about 'bread therapy', and I don't think there are many problems that can't be solved by a spot of kneading and knocking back. Doctors would do well to prescribe it instead of diazepam.

'If you're going to the bother of making bread, don't cut corners,' I announce. 'Organic flour and sea salt.'

'Surely we're going to sift the flour?' says Lady B. 'I was always told to hold the sieve high over the bowl and shake it.'

'Give it a good sieve,' chimes in Vicky.

'*Sift*,' I say, doing my bit to protect the English language. 'But it's nonsense. The flour goes everywhere.'

'It *aerates* it,' protests Lady B.

'Messy and pointless. Quick whisk in the bowl achieves the same thing – been scientifically proven.'

Lady B tosses her head in defiance and shakes up a flour blizzard, causing Lilith to run for cover. De'Lyse posts it on Instagram with the hashtag #winteriscoming.

'Now add the water. You can use it from the tap, but taste it first – it can be chloriney, specially in summer. Otherwise use filtered or bottled.

'Mix it in with a spatula if you want, but experienced bakers tend to use their hands, so they can feel what's happening. Keep mixing till the dough starts to come together into a shaggy mass. If you've got dry crumbs at the bottom, splash a little water over them to help gather them up.'

I move along the row and stop at Lilith. 'I bet you have beautiful water in Wales, don't you?'

'Liquid crystal,' she says. 'Makes tea taste like champagne.'

'If I may interrupt everyone for a second: you'll notice that Lilith has different ingredients from the rest of you because of her special dietary requirement.'

Lilith likes the way this is going, and looks round, smiling. Unbeknownst to her, I'm employing a psychological technique for dealing with annoying students. It takes a leap of faith, but you focus on the nuisance and make him or her the centre of your own and the class's attention. The theory is that by giving them what they (secretly) want, they eat out of your hand.

'Therefore Lilith is making soda bread, using gluten-free flour. It's much quicker than normal bread and we can get it mixed and baked in time for tea. The flour looks like normal flour, wouldn't you say, Lilith?'

'I'm still not touching it,' she declares with relish. 'Wouldn't take the risk.'

'Hmm. Well, you'll have to get it into the tin somehow. Shall I try and find some latex gloves?'

'No, it's my nails I'm worried about. After earlier.' She shoots a venomous look at Vicky, then adds with a simper, 'Please will you do that bit for me, Paul?'

I graciously agree and continue on my rounds. 'Now let's get down to kneading,' I announce. It's probably the most sensual kitchen experience of all. The way the dough metamorphoses from sticky to satiny under your fingertips, its visual transformation from pocky and beige to pale and smooth, the wholesome scent of 140 billion yeast organisms (that's per loaf) expanding and exhaling, the slapping sound of dough being pushed, pulled and stretched. Some breadheads even pull off a scrap and taste it, though I don't care for the fizz of raw flour on the tongue.

'Keep going, everyone,' I say. 'Give it at least five minutes – if you're doing it properly, you should feel warm and glowing from the exercise. Try and get a rhythm going.' Peace descends over the class.

When I come to De'Lyse she mentions she'd like to have a go at sourdough, which has become such a social media sensation. I suggest she try it out; some people love it, others find it a bore.

Vicky has been told bread dough requires less water in wet weather.

'Not that I've noticed – I think it's a myth,' I reply. 'On the other hand, if you have a barometer you may notice proving takes longer when the pressure is low.'

Stephen's dough is first to be ready. 'Looking good,' I say – I think it's the first time I've seen him smile. 'Attention, everyone. Once the dough is smooth, you can stop occasionally and throw it down onto the worktop, hard as you like. Try it out, Stephen.'

He raises the dough in the air, then pauses.

'Really?' he asks.

'Give it all you've got.'

With that, he takes a breath, leans back and hurls the dough down. It lands with a tremendous thwack – windows rattle, the class applauds.

'I didn't know you had it in you,' I say, genuinely surprised. For such a featherweight, it was quite a throw.

'And why do you do that?' asks Gregory. I hadn't noticed he wears hearing aids – expensive, practically invisible – which he now adjusts.

'The technique's called "crashing". It's a way of forcing the water into the flour. It makes for a more satiny dough and a better crumb.'

Everyone has a go, and soon the Old Ballroom is echoing to the sound of thwacking and walloping. I half expect the counterterrorism guys to rush in and tell us all to lie on the floor.

Lady B goes at it with fury, a woman with anger issues. Gregory doesn't look as if he has much power, but the timing of his release is perfect.

'Aha!' he says when I compliment him. 'I used to play cricket – fast bowler. Knew it would come in useful some time.'

There's a problem with Harriet. She has something I've encountered a few times in my career, which I call Sticky Hands Syndrome. The moment a sufferer touches bread dough, it turns to glue. There's an actual medical condition (palmar hyperhidrosis) which causes your hands and feet to sweat abnormally, but I suspect in Harriet's case it's just, well, nerves.

By the time I notice there's something awry, it's too late. There's gunk all over her clothes and in her hair, it's got into her handbag and she's trodden it into the floor. Lady B having disowned her daughter's ineptitude, I am left to clear up the mess with dishcloths, towels and a bucket of water.

I would have put Harriet down as a burster-into-tears, but she keeps her cool; indeed, there's something different about her today. She's still timid and jumpy, but with an undertone of defiance. The row with Mama – because obviously there's been one – has shifted the power balance in her favour.

The dough fiasco also brings out something unexpected in another member of the class. De'Lyse warm-heartedly takes pity on Harriet and offers to share her dough with her. We place our efforts in the fridge to prove overnight: this being the compromise I have come up with to rescue the absurd lesson plan I have inherited.

Here I am, thinking ill of the dead, when my phone buzzes.

OMG!! Just heard about Christian! ru OK? 📞 me asap.
Tell me you weren't the one who found him.

CHAPTER 16

As we make our way to the Pink Room for tea, it's clear that we're in the epicentre of an official crime scene. Dustcloths have been laid across the carpet and there are police wherever you look. The door into the courtyard has been propped open with a crank-handle butter churn (oak, mid-nineteenth century: Rose won't be happy) and a hi-vis tent has been set up adjacent to the cast-iron stairway. Is Christian still lying up there? What else did the police find in his flat?

Rose graces us with her presence as Suzie pours the tea. Her appearance has taken a quantum shift for the worse, with untidy hair and pearls awry.

'I'd like to thank you all for your – forbearance,' she says, sniffing. Melanie steps forward and they hug stiffly.

I circulate among the students, doing my duty, and finally succeed in getting Rose into a quiet corner.

'I'm finding it really hard, keeping this going,' I say, under my breath.

'A difficult time for all,' she agrees. 'At least I have reclaimed the Shelley Room. My desk is covered with ring stains from mugs of tea, or whatever police people drink.'

'It doesn't make for a very conducive atmosphere – police swarming round the place. Stop-and-search if you want to go out of the front door,' I say.

'I asked them if they could hurry things along. *Twenty-four-seven operation, as long as it takes*, they said. In other words, overtime, charged to the taxpayer. I did request that they shouldn't come through the house, use the mews entrance, but oh no, they have to ruin the carpets with their heavy boots. They've been up and down the stairs, poking about in the attic, rummaging in bins, knocking on neighbours' doors. I can't imagine what they expect to find.'

'Are they still insisting the students hang around? You'd think they'd want the place clear so forensics can do their thing.'

'Everyone to stay until further notice,' she replies frostily.

Duly admonished, I move away and help Suzie, who is shovelling the remains of Lilith's leaden soda bread – which doesn't appear to have been favourably received – into the dumb waiter.

'Did you hear the latest news about Christian?' I ask under my breath. She stops clinking cups and saucers. 'They're saying he was beaten up,' I continue. 'Didn't fall down an escalator.'

She resumes her stacking. 'None of my business, but I did wonder.'

'Any reason in particular?'

'He claimed he'd fallen down an escalator on the Tube, right? But he went about by cab – didn't use the Underground.'

'What baffles me is, who would do it? He's— He *was* pretty easy-going. Not the sort of guy who had enemies.'

She pauses and looks at me. 'I wouldn't be so sure.'

'Meaning what?'

'Oh, nothing really.'

'If you know something, you should tell the police.'

She hesitates – wishes she hadn't started.

'It doesn't matter now – but he didn't go about the place making friends. If you must know, he even tried it on with me.'

'I beg your pardon?'

'Crept down here one Sunday afternoon when I was on

my own – brought me some chocolate thing he'd made with marshmallows on top. Ugh.'

'Oh dear,' I say. 'How embarrassing for you. So you're suggesting that he might have harrassed some poor woman, and was called out for it?'

'No, not at all. All I mean is that maybe he wasn't always Mr Nice Guy and there are some bad people out there who might have had it in for him.'

* * *

I return to the Old Ballroom to find the students clustered round De'Lyse's iPad.

'OK, what's the latest?' I say.

There are a handful of new developments. It's been confirmed that Christian was beaten up in West London last Saturday, and his arm broken by three thugs – a gang of some kind. The assault was captured on CCTV outside the gym where he worked out. It's also online that his death occurred at approximately midnight.

There's much sorrowful shaking of heads, but still they want the class to continue. And so it is that we throw ourselves into the last lesson of this surreal day – pastry-making.

It seems absurd to be faffing about with something so ephemeral when the world has lurched on its axis, but in better circumstances it's a class, like bread, that I'd enjoy teaching. Indeed, if things had played out differently, I might have become a pâtissier. Pastry chefs are set apart from the rest of the kitchen brigade – more precise and independent-minded – and their scientific approach appeals to the geek in me.

I divide the class into pairs. Each will make a different type of pastry. I put De'Lyse with Stephen (shortcrust), and Melanie with Gregory (flaky). I team Lady B up with Vicky (choux), and ask Harriet to join me for the big one – puff. I'm still determined to get to the bottom of her whispered exchange with Christian.

Where's Lilith – the new, tame Lilith – in all this, you might ask? Well, in view of her wheat phobia, and adhering to the student-from-hell principle, I appoint her to make all the fillings: lemon cream for the shortcrust, ham and leek for the flaky, crème Chantilly for the choux, and Mediterranean vegetables for the puff. Quite the worklist, and I hope she doesn't get the flavours muddled up.

'Thank goodness for Lilith,' I declare out loud. 'Where would we be without her?'

It's an action-packed ninety minutes. Cracks soon appear in the Lady B–Vicky partnership, each accusing the other of mismeasuring and sabotage.

De'Lyse starts off in charge of the shortcrust operation, rubbing in with rather too much vigour, then Stephen subtly takes command. He sprinkles just enough water over the crumbs, then patiently brings the dough together with his long, cool fingers. He swears he hasn't done it before, but it seems to come naturally.

For Gregory and Melanie's flaky pastry, I've suggested they freeze the butter and grate it into the flour, which will bake to form pockets of golden crunch. He snatches the butter out of Melanie's hands – at which I see her bare her pointy little teeth – and slams it against the grater. You need to pay attention when grating, and soon enough there's a yowl. Suzie arrives with blue plasters to patch up his shredded knuckles.

Meanwhile, war has been declared between Lady B and Vicky: they're going to throw away what they've done and go their separate ways. We're going to end up with a lot of éclairs.

'You're doing really well,' I say to Harriet, toiling quietly away at her workbench.

'Thanks,' she replies, her brow knitted in concentration.

'How are you feeling about Christian's death? It's a lot to take in.'

'It's terrible. I still can't believe it.' She rolls faster, her jaw tight.

'He wasn't the easiest, but he always meant well.'

She lowers her voice: 'I'd rather not talk about him. It's bad enough Mummy going on and on.'

'Sorry – I didn't mean to upset you. Everyone's still in shock,' I add.

After a few moments, she stops and looks me in the eye. 'I know Christian was your friend,' she says cautiously. 'Did he confide in you?'

'We'd pretty much lost touch – I've hardly seen him for the last couple of years. Why do you ask?'

She looks relieved and turns back to her work. 'Oh, no reason in particular. Am I using too much flour?'

'Dust it off with your pastry brush,' I reply. Lilith interrupts to tell me her lemon cream has curdled and I'm drawn away to rescue it.

All pastry doughs benefit from overnight chilling – yes, even including choux paste – so we transfer our efforts to the fridge. We seem to have accumulated quite a backlog to bake, but tomorrow is, thank heavens, another day.

By the time I've tidied up and the students disappeared I notice a wallet on Gregory's bench. It's very much a gentleman's wallet, probably from Bond Street, and monogrammed *G. F.* Hmm. Not the initials of Gregory Greenleaf – a name that's still bugging me.

Maybe the wallet isn't Gregory's at all. I take a quick look. A wodge of sterling, another of euros and half a dozen business cards from France. A ticket for *The Comedy of Errors* at Stratford in two weeks' time. He splits his time between

France and his native Warwickshire – the wallet must be his. And what's this? Two condoms.

Well, that's embarrassing.

I tuck the wallet safely in the drawer of Gregory's workbench. After all, if we have a murderer in our midst, maybe there's a thief about as well.

CHAPTER 17

An hour and a half till the glorious Chester Square dinner is served, with more treats from Chef Suzie.

I'm certainly not going to risk going back to Jubilee Cottage, not with the very real prospect of being shadowed or jumped out at, so I decide to find somewhere quiet to think things through. I remember how, as young commis chefs, Christian and I would curl up in the common room between shifts, draping ourselves over chairs and sofas or under tables, like kittens taking naps. That's exactly what I feel like doing now.

I wander along to the front hall. The young cop from earlier has gone off duty, and his replacement has set himself up with a small table to sit behind, a bit like a concierge. He looks up from his copy of the *Evening Standard* and smiles at me.

'Stepping out?' He reaches for his ballpoint.

'Not till later. Have we hit the headlines?'

'Small piece on the front page about a death in Belgravia,' he replies. 'There's a press briefing tomorrow first thing, so that's when we can expect the real fun to begin.'

'Well, if it's OK with you,' I say, 'I'm going to tuck myself away in a quiet corner till dinner.'

'You go ahead, don't mind me.'

Across the hall from the Pink Room is a door marked Strang Room, which has been intriguing me. I push it open to reveal a stiff, square drawing room occupying the front corner of the house, with the same tall sash windows as the rest of the ground floor and stiff silk curtains in gunmetal grey. I imagine it's intended as a place for students to relax in, but it reminds me of my dentist's waiting room, and I could swear it has the same mouthwashy smell. There's a Broadwood grand piano, high-backed chairs, a brocade-covered sofa, and dozens of portraits staring down from the walls, but still it looks sparse and under-furnished. A slab-like marble fireplace, probably not lit since 1950, adds to the funereal chill.

The Strang ancestors look like a miserable bunch. A couple of military men, a bishop, some banker types. They were evidently not drawn to society beauties either: the wives look like they've been drinking vinegar. As I walk about, I feel myself followed by a hundred beady eyes.

I don't come from a grand or important family, but I can't imagine it's much fun for Rose to be endlessly scrutinized by her ancestors, stretching back to the days when Captain Cook and Napoleon were hogging the headlines. Does she feel it her duty to pace up and down these echoing corridors until she too is reduced to an unflattering oil painting? Is her goal in life to pass the problem on – all four stuccoed storeys – for the next generation to deal with? I'd be tempted to cash in the whole shebang and buy a villa in the south of France.

Meanwhile, whether Rose likes it or not, Mistress Scandal is a-knocking at the door. Even if it turns out Christian's death had nothing to do with the school – even if it turns out he was decapitated by a random serial killer or aliens – I cannot see how she and her business will survive. Imagine the strain she must be under. I resolve to make more allowances for her, be kinder to her.

My exploration leads me next to a mahogany door marked LIBRARY. I'm guessing this was originally some kind of service room – a hang-out for the butler, perhaps – as it's invitingly small and dark. By Chester Square standards, it's cosily furnished, too, with leather chairs, a squashy Chesterfield, low tables and a sideboard set up with a kettle and jars of tea and biscuits. Best of all, the walls are lined with shelves overflowing untidily with hundreds and hundreds of books. Cookbooks!

I breathe in. There's nothing like the smell of books, paper and ink – a sweet, musky scent, with top notes of coffee and chocolate. I could spend hours looking through this lot – especially the technical and reference section – though I've more than a thousand of my own at home.

At Jubilee Cottage, the kitchen-dining room is in the basement, and the walls are entirely lined with cookbooks. It's cosy down there – books make great insulation, even if, as Marcus pointed out, they reduce the room size by ten per cent and suck up most of the light.

It's been ten whole months since he died, but I still can't stop thinking about him. What I miss most is his dry humour, his reticent charm, but I remind myself it wasn't all a bed of roses for us, particularly to begin with. My arrival dropped an atomic bomb on his family life. And don't underestimate the personal sacrifice I made myself, when I discovered I'd fallen in love with a man who hated garlic.

I select a particularly comfortable-looking wing chair in the corner, adding a couple of cushions from the window seat for extra luxury. I don't think I'm going to be disturbed, so I pull over a footstool as well. I'd love to nod off for half an hour, but no chance. I can still feel the day's fight-or-flight hormones pumping through my body.

What I'm absolutely busting to do, of course, is talk to Julie, but I've missed my moment. Tuesday is her orchestra evening. Yes, you heard that right – Julie is a keen musician and plays with a group called the Putney Pops Orchestra. It sees itself as the amateur equivalent of the John Wilson Orchestra.

At the moment, PUTPO is currently rehearsing for its biggest concert of the year – *Magical Christmas Mystery Tour* at the New Wimbledon Theatre. I went to an unforgettable panto there two years ago with Julie and her niece and nephew; unforgettable not because of Lesley Garrett as the Fairy Godmother but because Noah ate too many M&Ms and was spectacularly sick in the interval. In Technicolor.

To look at Julie, you'd probably guess she was a contralto, or played the trombone or cello; something voluptuous like that. In fact, she's a clarinettist. She went to music college, and could have had a professional career, but changed her mind after training to go into magazine journalism instead. It's as a musician that we see the real Julie: assured, confident, master of her instrument.

When I first got together with Marcus, she was acting the usual cautious best friend, determined I wouldn't be taken for a ride, or chewed up and spat out.

'If he's mean to you, I'll smash his face in,' she said, although she is the kindest, gentlest, most lamb-like person you will ever meet.

This went on for months, till I happened to mention that Marcus loved classical music.

'What sort of stuff?' she asked, suspiciously.

'Piano music, that sort of thing.'

She narrowed her eyes. 'Which composers?'

If I'd replied Liszt, Hindemith or Boulez, she would have fired him on the spot.

'Mozart and Schubert.'

'Good. And?'

'Chopin, Rachmaninov. And he's very fond of Ravel,' I replied.

'Why on earth didn't you tell me this before? He's *perfect* for you.'

After a while, I get up from my chair arrangement and toddle over to the sideboard. If I wish hard enough, maybe a bottle of lightly chilled Amontillado will materialize, but when it doesn't, I put on the kettle.

My mind wanders from Julie to the magazine, and thence to Dena and her temper tantrum. From past experience, she normally calms down in a day or two. If Julie keeps her head down, maybe this one will pass.

Right on cue, I feel my phone buzz in my pocket. It's Julie. And not one of her idiotic texts but a call, on FaceTime.

'I don't believe it,' I say. This evening she's swept her hair back, ballerina style, with a huge red peony pinned at the side. 'Your house is on fire. You've fallen down a sinkhole.'

'Shut up! I want to make sure you're OK.' I hear musical instruments in the background, that silly burbling sound of bassoons and flutes and trombones warming up. 'I've got exactly ten minutes. It's been on the evening news – what on earth's going on?'

I run her through what happened as succinctly as I can.

'A *cleaver*? That's horrific! That's not what they're saying officially – just death in "suspicious circumstances". And you must have been questioned by the police?'

'Twice, but only informally. I just happen to be the person who found him – not a suspect. But what about you? What news on the Christmas shoot?'

'It's not what you want to hear, but Dena's gone berserk.'

Being editor of a glossy magazine sounds glamorous, but the truth is rather different. Dena's life is spent bickering about budgets, juggling deadlines and fretting over sales figures, with that editorial Antichrist known as 'the publisher' eternally breathing down her neck. In this case that is one Richard Buzz, proprietor of Buzz Publications.

Richard Buzz went to Harvard Business School – that's what they all say – where he picked up the idea that if you have competitive products in your portfolio, you play them off against each other. He takes particular pleasure in fanning the flames of hatred between *Escape* and its sister publication *Lovely*, edited by Dena's arch-rival Tammy; his current Buzz-phrase is 'smart-sizing' – a euphemism for laying off staff and screwing freelancers.

Yesterday Richard announced to Dena he's going to merge the *Escape* and *Lovely* cookery teams into a 'foodstyle hub'; whichever mag sells best at Christmas will be the team to survive.

As a further blow, later that morning Dena's mole on *Lovely* secretly pinged over the rival magazine's Christmas layouts. One by one Dena opened the contraband PDFs and her heart lurched: how in hell's name did both mags end up with the same freakin' *Nutcracker* theme? In the same insipid blue and silver colourway? To cap it all, the Identikit (blue and silver) Christmas tree with same bandana-ed French bull-dog dribbling underneath it?

For the rest of the day, Dena locked herself in her office to rework budgets and wrangle with finance. This morning, she screamed at production until they gave in and extended the print deadlines. And while I was pummelling dough in the Old Ballroom, Dena was breaking the news to Julie that the entire Christmas section had to be reshot by end-of-play Thursday. Object number one: bury *Nutcracker*. Object two: pulverize *Lovely* at the newsstand.

'You know I wouldn't embroil you in all this if I could possibly help it,' Julie says. 'But I need you. If we mess this up, I'll be out of a job and you'll come down with me.'

'Julie, darling, it's impossible – the police have ordered us to stick around. But you've directed shoots before – you can do this! You *must* do it.'

'Oh, come off it – just bowls of fruit and ten ways with a slice of toast. Hardly the same.'

'You're always putting yourself down. You know how to write recipes, style food for the camera, direct photographers – this is your chance to prove it.'

'Dena specifically said it had to be you. And you know how vengeful she can turn once she decides someone's betrayed her. Neither of us will ever work in magazines again.'

'Then we don't tell her.'

'What?'

'You direct the shoot but let her think I've done it. You won't have to tell any lies, just play her along.' I add the last bit because Julie is a Catholic, albeit a loose one, and I don't want to lay unnecessary guilt on her.

'I wouldn't know where to begin.'

'You've got to start believing in yourself. You were there with me on the Christmas shoot – you know exactly how to go about this. I'll come up with some ring-a-ding-ding ideas and we'll talk them through later on.' Magazine editors love a theme, because it holds the editorial pages together and provides continuity amid the dross of advertising: thinking them up is the problem . . . which is probably how the team ended up cracking nuts.

There's a clattering of music stands and I hear her call, *Won't be a second!* I track her as she weaves her way among the instruments – double basses, tubas and a bassoon.

'It's impossible,' she says hurriedly to me. 'Call me the minute you get home.'

There's a tapping sound followed by a sudden hush – the conductor calling the musicians to attention.

Julie whispers urgently: 'One more thing – and listen carefully. This situation with the police. You're caught up in it whether you like it or not. You were first at the scene of the crime – you're suspect number one. You have to prove to them it was nothing to do with you. Promise me you'll do that – don't let them pin it on you.'

'OK, I promise,' I say with a weary shrug.

'Keep your eyes and ears open. Don't trust anyone – especially the police. And now I've got exactly sixteen bars before I come in. Goodbye.'

A promise to Julie is a golden pledge: I can no longer sit on the sidelines, hoping for the best. She knows much more than me about the police and the way they work, and if she thinks I'm in the firing line, I'll do exactly what she says.

Also on the line, it would appear, is my livelihood.

CHAPTER 18

Before I know it, the gong crashes and we're summoned to dinner. Word has come from on high that we are expected in the Pink Room earlier than usual, because Rose would like to speak to us. It feels a bit like a royal address.

She's already there when I arrive. I don't know whether it's in Christian's honour, but she looks very much the part of grieving former lover in a long black velvet dress buttoned to the neck and worn with yin and yang pearl earrings, black one side and white the other.

She beckons me in with a long raised forefinger and indicates for me to close the door.

'Before the others arrive, I wish to thank you for entrusting me with your secret,' she says in a doleful whisper.

'What secret?'

A puzzled look crosses her face, then she resumes. 'I wish you to know that I have seen dark hours, and that *I understand*. I too have ambled down the boulevards of despair.' She glances heavenward. 'Supped with the gods of sorrow.'

I blink. What's she talking about? A flicker of doubt passes across her face, stopping halfway, but she sticks to her guns.

'I am honoured that you think of me as . . . a friend in need.' She puts her hands together, as if praying. 'Estella to your Pip, if I may make so bold.'

Miss Havisham, more like. 'Look,' I say, alarmed. 'What's all this about?'

'Why, your phone call of course!'

'I didn't phone you. You must be mistaken.'

'My dear boy,' she says, laying a hand on my arm. Her fingers are freezing – she must have a circulation problem. 'My darling aunt had cancer. Treatments have improved so much – radiotherapy, chemotherapy, sophology—'

'Rose.' I pull away. 'Snap out of it. I was downstairs – why would I phone you? And Sofology sell sofas – nothing to do with cancer.'

'But . . . just an hour ago you were pouring out your heart to me! Weeping down the phone. Wailing like a baby!'

Aargh! It's him! He's done it again.

I take a deep breath. 'Rose, think back, did the caller address you by name?'

She thinks for a moment then shakes her head.

'Did he mention anything specific – about the course, or the school?'

'Now you ask, I think not,' she replies. 'You said – the caller said – that you'd had bad news from the clinic and your cancer had returned.'

'I'm deeply sorry, but it seems you've been the victim of a malicious hoax. It's not your fault. This has happened before.'

'But why would someone do such a thing?' she asks, outraged.

'His name's Jonny,' I begin tentatively. 'He's very . . . troubled.'

'Oh, please!' she declares. 'I do not wish to be dragged into the netherlands of your private life.'

'I think you mean netherworld.'

She sails on. 'Piled on top of all else, I now find myself subjected to a cruel and inconsiderate act of deception. I would respectfully beg you to take more care in future over the company you keep.'

'He's not a boyfriend, he's—'

'—absolutely no business of mine,' Rose concludes. She puts her hands to her ears, determined to hear no more.

'Just out of curiosity, did you tell the others about . . . this cancer thing?'

'I was going to announce it after dinner, so as not to dampen the gaiety,' she says, as if chewing a mouthful of starch.

Gaiety? 'So were you planning to send everyone home, or teach the rest of this blighted course yourself?'

'In times of crisis, it is all hands to the pump.'

'Well, at least you know your way round the curriculum,' I snap back.

With this she straightens up and fixes me with her eyes. 'Number forty-one is meant to be a wholesome place, Paul. Since you arrived, it has turned into a Chamber of Horrors.' All true, although if Netflix takes up the option she can at least rent them the location for a fortune. 'Furthermore, I believe the worst is yet to come.'

'You mean the press?' I say, and she nods. 'Always kept well clear of them myself. So have you had to deal with them before?'

'In my experience, they'll soon get bored and go home.' She examines her nails to signal that the matter is closed.

Undeterred, I try another tack. 'The police certainly seem to be throwing themselves into the investigation. How did your interview go?'

Her face twitches. 'Why do you ask?'

'No reason. The rest of us were comparing notes about where we were when it happened, that's all.'

'No need to pussyfoot, Paul. I was in my private quarters.'

I wait. Never underestimate the power of silence to draw out the truth.

'Doing my accounts,' she says at length. 'Until the early hours.' I imagine her poring over a candlelit ledger, spiking receipts on a steel spindle. 'Mundane, I know, but even at Chester Square we have to pay VAT.'

She shakes her head sorrowfully, wheels round and almost knocks over Suzie. People here appear so suddenly and noiselessly; like ectoplasm.

'Dinner's ready, Mrs Hoyt.'

'Lay another place, Soo-Zee. Mr Delamare has made a miraculous recovery.'

* * *

I stand beside Rose at the sideboard as the students filter in. She's written out the menu on a card: despite saying she thought it cheapskate to serve the food cooked in class, the main course bears an uncanny resemblance to the roasts we made earlier.

I'm not sure whether it's something the students agreed between themselves or a spontaneous reaction to the grave events of the day, but they've dressed for dinner. In my denims and crumpled shirt, I now feel totally out of place, like when you're on a cruise and no one told you that when the ship's at sea, it's tuxedos at dinner.

While pretending to examine the menu, I focus on the female guests' make-up, specifically their lipstick. I'm trying to see if anyone's suddenly switched colour, on account of having dropped 'Old Flame' at the scene of the crime.

Rose counts heads then tinkles her cowbell to announce she wishes to address us. It's such a pretty, musical sound that it deserves a backdrop of Alps and meadows rather than the set of *Arsenic and Old Lace*.

'Good evening, everyone, and thank you for being so prompt.

'It has been a dreadful day for all, and I would like to

extend my sincerest gratitude for your patience and sensitivity. This is not how things normally happen at Chester Square Cookery School. In particular, I must ask you to overlook the fact that our cleaning contractors were not allowed onto the premises today, for obvious reasons, meaning that beds were not made, floors not polished, et cetera.'

Murmurs of sympathy and understanding all round.

'I hope life may return to normality over the next day or two, but for now let us try to enjoy a calm and civilized evening in one another's company. As a modest *remerciement*, I would like to offer you wine tonight with the compliments of Chester Square Cookery School. Soo-Zee, perhaps you will be so good as to pour it now.'

Suzie jolts into action. 'It's that annoying stuff with corks in,' she says to me under her breath. 'Would you mind?' She hands me a corkscrew.

I open three bottles of white and two of red. The white is a Bergerac, the red a *vin de pays* from Languedoc – nothing out of the ordinary – but it's free, and the students line up for their bounty. While I pour, I notice Suzie transfer the discarded capsules and corks to the dumb waiter. Even if she's not the most inspiring of colleagues, she keeps things tidy.

'I'm sorry it's not a fine Bordeaux,' I say to Gregory under my breath as I pour him a glass of red.

'Fear not,' he replies. 'I took the precaution of packing a couple of bottles of Margaux, in case I should find the Chester Square cellar wanting.'

The alcohol has the desired effect, and the room warms up.

The loudest voice, as usual, is Lady B's. Elegant in draped royal blue silk jersey, she is reminiscing to Gregory about the Bath branch of Christian's Brasserie, converted from an old bank.

'So tragic – we used to see him there constantly. Harriet and I were "groupies", weren't we, darling?' She has that shouting-at-foreigners tone, even when speaking to her own offspring. 'Harriet, I'm telling Gregory about Milsom Place.'

Her daughter, dressed sacrificial-virgin style in white broderie anglaise, has taken a glass of free wine but only seems to be toying with it. She has a faraway look about her. 'Yes, Mummy, we saw him two or three times. He was always very charming.'

Gregory emits a noise that sounds like a snort and takes a sip of wine. He is resplendent in scarlet trousers; side by side, the three of them look like the Tricolore flag. He says, 'Christian will be fondly remembered. I like to think that in a small way I played a part in his success.'

'How so?' says Lady B, wrinkling her forehead in faux-concern. *This sounds interesting*, I can almost read there.

Gregory looks rather as if he wishes he hadn't started and adjusts a hearing aid. I hope there's a setting for shrill voices at close quarters. 'Only that . . . I spent a lot of money with him, one way or another. Not that it—'

'Not overcharged, I hope,' hoots her ladyship, before gabbling on. 'We were once on the Amalfi Coast and a restaurant tried to make us pay the bill from another table. It was a set-up – the waiters were in on it. Much as one treasures the Neapolitan landscape—'

'Gregory's trying to say something, Mummy,' interjects Harriet.

'No, no, it's nothing,' mumbles Gregory. 'Do carry on.' He takes another sip of wine and bows his head.

Lady B tries to resume her verbal onslaught, but Harriet isn't having it. 'Go on, Gregory, we're listening. Tell us.' Her mother frowns at her.

He blinks slowly. 'Ahem, it's only that in the past I may have invested in one or two of his enterprises.'

'Oh-ho!' cries Lady B. 'So did he know you were coming on the course? Or were you planning to spring it on him?'

'Oh, he wouldn't remember me – I was a small player.'

'You sly dog,' says Lady B, tapping the bridge of her nose archly. For an erstwhile member of the aristocracy, there's something decidedly coarse about her. 'Did he remember who you were, or cut you?' Maybe I was the only one to notice, but there was something distinctly odd about the moment when Christian and Gregory encountered one another at dinner; for Christian at least, it seemed a nasty surprise.

'Mummy, Christian wasn't like that,' says Harriet. 'Remember that super-polite letter he sent us when Bath closed, telling us how much he appreciated our custom?'

Lady B looks daggers at her daughter. 'You're a sweet girl, Harriet, but that was a circular, sent to all and sundry. I've told you before – you're far too trusting.'

Gregory closes his eyes and looks like he wishes he could curl up under a stone.

Rose and Melanie are talking quietly in a corner and I top up their wine so I can catch some of the exchange. For once it's not about Christian.

'The problem with Cressida is she wants what she can't have. She takes one look at her father and thinks: if he can drive a Porsche, why can't I? If he can afford to chuck a couple of thousand away on a horse at Newmarket, why can't I have a Loewe handbag?'

'It's a problem of our day – materialism,' says Rose. I can imagine these two old friends, given an evening to themselves and a couple of bottles of vino, chewing up the modern world and everything that's wrong with it. 'Ben's well, I hope?' she adds.

'He sends his love.'

This appears to stall the conversation, so I move on to Vicky and Lilith, already on their third glass. At some point someone must have suggested to Vicky that animal motifs suited her, or maybe she picked up the idea of a 'signature look' from TV makeover shows; anyway, tonight it's zebra. No surface has been left unstriped: dress, tights, shoes, bag. There's a coquettish zebra bow in her hair and zebra beads and earrings. It's quite an effect: look too long and the lines start to pulse and vibrate like op art.

As for Lilith . . . I do not claim to be an expert on ladies' fashions, but I cannot believe that ruffles are recommended for the fuller figure. They are soft, they are pretty, you want to reach out and touch them, you might even in certain circumstances wish to bury your face in them, but alas they add volume, even where volume is already present in abundance.

As far as I can tell, Vicky has let something slip.

'So you went to them *all*?' Lilith asks, tucking her hair behind her ears so as not to miss a word.

'Well, yes. There were just the five, in fact,' replies Vicky, on the defensive.

'*Five!* But they were all over the country. You must have been travelling for *days*,' says Lilith.

'It was less than an hour to the one in Cambridge – on the train.'

'But was it to see Christian, or just to eat his food? Or maybe you wanted to eat *him*!'

'You should wash your mouth out, Lilith. But I suppose you could say I'm a fan. *Was* a fan.'

'Fixated, more like,' huffs Lilith. 'So when you traversed the country in the hope of a glimpse of him, was he there?'

'I always checked he'd be cooking when I phoned up and made my reservation. I like this wine, don't you?'

I have managed to find a diversion to keep me within close earshot, in the form of a dangling curtain pull requiring urgent attention. Lilith, fortunately, is not letting her victim off the hook.

'So you *did* get to meet Christian, then?'

'Of course,' replies Vicky. I can see her reflection in the

window as I fiddle with the cords and it is going unmistakably red. 'Three times. Maybe four. Let me see: Cambridge, as I mentioned . . . Oxford . . . Winchester – twice, I think . . . Bath – lucky I didn't bump into Lady Loudmouth.'

'So let me get this straight. You keep turning up at his brasseries, sitting in the corner on your own, picking away at a salad. Longing for him to come and say hello to you. Maybe even touch him, look into his eyes. Didn't he think it a bit odd?'

'It's perfectly normal for business people to eat on their own nowadays. Don't you find it draughty here by the window?'

'It must have been hurtful – not being recognized yesterday, I mean,' says Lilith, peering at her prey intently.

Vicky rallies back. 'Who's to say we didn't exchange glances? You were so busy pawing at him, you didn't see. He was looking at me very meaningfully.'

'I bet he was! Did he take out a restraining order against you, then?'

'Don't be ridiculous. I'm no stalker.' By now she is vermilion in the face.

'What does hubby think?'

This is just getting interesting when I'm forced to quit my observation post by De'Lyse, who's beckoning me over (somewhat imperiously) to join her and Stephen, talking near the door. They're the youngest members of class, but so different: Stephen with his babyish look – shaven head and whispery voice – and De'Lyse exuding confidence and glamour in a gold-sequinned top and black trousers, worn with an elaborately tied checkered head wrap and big hoop earrings. There's something rather touching about the way she's taking the trouble to chat to her confrère; although I'm not sure their conversation is a mile a minute.

'We've just discovered we're neighbours,' says De'Lyse. 'Me, I'm Tooting born and bred.' She nods at Stephen.

'Crystal Palace,' he mumbles.

'I used to go to a gym in Chrissy Pally,' says De'Lyse; I make a note to call it that in future. 'Taekwondo.'

'Karate's more my thing,' replies Stephen, with a chopping motion of his hand.

'Glad you're enjoying the cooking,' I say to him. 'Bit different from gardening.' He looks down, in the evasive way of a teenager reminded to do their homework instead of playing video games. 'And I hope you're both managing to learn something, despite the . . . disruption.'

'I like it best when we're doing stuff, rather than watching,' says De'Lyse.

'A woman of action,' I say, and she chuckles and turns away.

I snatch another look at her lithe physique and find myself wondering how much strength it would take to overpower Christian, specially with one arm in plaster. I've never investigated martial arts, but I know there are techniques that enable you to throw someone twice your size across the room, should you feel the need.

CHAPTER 19

I notice Suzie indicate to Rose that the food is ready, and prepare myself for the musical chairs moment while we work out who sits where. Your placement on such occasions determines whether you will have two hours of gaiety or gloom, and if I play it right, I may even get a chance to ask some useful questions.

Because of Jonny's prank call, only nine places have been laid at the table, which gives me the chance to choose where to put the extra setting supplied by Suzie. I select the optimum spot for tuning into conversations in every direction, plonk down my wine glass and drag over a chair.

By this time most of the students have helped themselves to the starter, which is a dish of smoked mackerel pâté (I would have sprinkled it with chopped capers, anchovies and herbs to lift the colour). As usual, Lilith asks if it contains gluten, then without waiting for a reply, helps herself to a huge grey dollop.

'What happens if you eat gluten?' asks Vicky; Lilith glares at her. 'By accident, I mean. For instance, if you had a big thick slice of toast for breakfast. Or a chocolate muffin.'

'You don't want to know,' sniffs Lilith.

'I know that bloating is common,' perseveres Vicky. 'And churning.' She makes a pumping motion with her fist. 'Have you tried charcoal capsules?'

'As we say in Wales, *cau dy geg*.'

By good fortune I find myself with Melanie on one side and Harriet on the other. I've hardly exchanged a word with Melanie so far, and much prefer Harriet to her loudhailer mother.

'Would you like some bread?' I say to Harriet. She takes a slice and butters it lavishly; it's the first time I've seen her eat anything. 'Gosh, I thought normally brides give up eating and the dress has to be taken in.' That comes out all wrong – did I just imply she's being piggy? – and I receive an odd look in return. Still, while we're on a bridal theme . . .

'What colour palette are you going for?' I ask. I love those mood boards wedding planners do nowadays, so the bouquet matches the stitching-on-the-dress matches the marquee lining. You may as well start married life in perfect harmony, even if it doesn't stay that way.

'Oh, do you mind if we talk about something else?' she says.

Whoa! A bride who doesn't want to talk about her wedding? Move on *fast*. 'I'm rather looking forward to seeing how our bread comes out tomorrow,' I say, without missing a beat.

Melanie cuts in from my other side, eager for attention. 'We could go and take a look after dinner. Check progress.'

In the circumstances, I think it would be better not to go tiptoeing around number forty-one in the dead of night. 'Better let sleeping dogs lie,' I reply, which comes out sounding odd. Suddenly I have a brainwave. 'You look very eye-catching tonight, Melanie,' I say. It's no exaggeration: she's in a green silk shirt with flared sleeves and a close-fitting black fishtail skirt.

'Oh, thank you. Kind of you to say.'

'I'm always in awe of the wonderful things women do to make themselves look bewitching.'

'Believe me, I'm a beginner compared with some people,'

she says, glancing rather obviously towards De'Lyse. 'But I try my best.' She flicks a glance at me, eyelids narrowed speculatively. Surely she must realize?

'You know what I love?' I say, hurrying to shatter the moment. 'They call women's make-up such funny names, like Pinkissimo, or Devil-May-Care, or Sex Kitten. For instance, I bet your lipstick is called something daft.'

'Ha! You make me laugh! I haven't worn this one before – I must have dropped mine somewhere, so Rose gave me one of hers. Let me look. You're right – it's called "Dark Deed".'

'I meant to ask – how are things in Tite Street? It must be strange, staying just down the road.' I'm angling to find out why she's always on the phone.

'Chester Square feels like another world,' she says, dreamily. 'I was enjoying it so much until – you know what. But the family are all fine. While the cat's away!' I notice her eyes have a habit of darting nervously about. 'In fact, they probably both have a better time without me. I know my husband started the day with a full English, which he certainly doesn't get when I'm around.'

I always think there's something aggressively heterosexual about a full English breakfast. It's not that I'm a chia-porridge-and-kale-smoothie sort of guy, but all that fatty stuff plays havoc with my sugar levels so I crash mid-morning; it must be different for beefy rugby-player types.

'And I expect Cressida and her friends have ordered in pizzas,' Melanie continues. 'Or gone to the pancake place.'

'Cressida's your daughter?'

'Stepdaughter. She's seventeen.'

'I'm sure they're missing you. Have you found the course useful so far?' I ask.

'Lots of fresh ideas, thank you. Makes me feel like throwing a dinner party, which we haven't done for ages.'

'You could invite Rose – show off your new skills.'

'I don't really think so. Ben's not . . .' She lowers her voice. 'Between you and me, he's not keen.'

'Why's that?' I ask.

'He was rather put off by the Christian business, apart from anything else.'

'What do you mean?'

'Rose's affair – I'm sure you know all about it.' I nod and check she's not listening in. 'Ben thought Christian behaved like a scoundrel – deserved a good whipping. And that Rose let the side down getting involved in the first place. It's not as if either of them was committing adultery, but he's a bit old-fashioned about these things.'

'Did your husband know Christian, then?'

'Only by reputation.'

'How about you? Did you remain on friendly terms with him?'

'With Christian? Oh, I only met him once or twice. He certainly wasn't the reason I came on the course, if that's what you mean.' Her eyes don't quite meet mine.

Interesting.

After this, she strikes up a conversation on her other side, which gives me the chance to observe Rose. She's sandwiched between Lady Brash and Gregory and appears to be enjoying herself more than usual.

'Oh, we'd love that!' shouts the human megaphone to one side, while bird man pecks his approval on the other.

'We shall see what we can do,' says Rose. 'Of course, it's really up to Paul.' She gives me a magisterial wave and calls across the table. 'Your students have come up with a plan.' Uh-oh.

Things pick up for the main course, with meats laid out with jarred relishes and salad. I am proud to say that the rib of beef is the perfect shade of pink, the pork shoulder – rolled and roasted in the Tuscan style – rich and juicy, with a haunting note of rosemary. The lamb was in the oven for most of the afternoon, and is so tender it can be served with a spoon. I notice no one touches the braised short ribs.

Under cover of general conversation, I turn once more to Melanie. 'I know you and Rose go back a long way. Did something happen here in the past? Something involving the press? She mentioned it, but I didn't want to put my foot in it.'

She glances across to her friend, who is now being aurally bludgeoned by Lady B on the subject of contract cleaners. Apparently they ruin fine furniture by using silicone polish and chip skirting boards with their vacuum cleaners.

'Well,' Melanie says, under her breath, 'I'm not surprised she doesn't want to talk about it. It was a couple of years after I married Ben – so about ten years ago. Her husband had the most dreadful accident.' She narrows her eyes, deciding how much to tell me.

'I promise it'll go no further.'

'Alan was a financier. Rather aloof – didn't like parties or going out. A bit of an acquired taste, really, but that's neither here nor there.' She blushes faintly and fiddles with her napkin.

'Maybe he liked to keep Rose to himself,' I say. 'Some husbands do.'

Melanie looks at me intently for a moment, then continues the tale.

'Anyway, it was a hot weekend and the house felt airless. These huge places require a lot of ventilation, so he went to the top floor to open the windows, try and get a draught through. No one's quite sure how it happened, but a window must have jammed momentarily. He gave it a shove and fell out.'

'What an awful story!' I say, leaning in.

'Surely you read about it in the papers at the time? He went out head first and – I don't know how else to put this – impaled himself on the railings of the little balcony outside Rose's study. Died instantly.'

I take a swig of the *vin de pays* – not one of south-west France's finer efforts. Rose Hoyt, it seems, is one serially unlucky woman.

For dessert, Suzie produces tiramisu (sloppy – the savoiardi need to be dipped in coffee, not drowned). The only one who appears to enjoy it is Gregory, though I see Lilith has succumbed and is shovelling in spoonfuls under cover of eating a yogurt.

A mood of restlessness seems to spread around the table, and there are already murmurs of 'ready for bed', when a tintinnabulation rings forth.

'My ear has been bent,' Rose announces, putting down the bell and fanning out her hands like the Pope on Easter Sunday. 'As long as your tutor is happy with the idea, I will be honoured to give you a short tour of my historic collection of kitchenalia and culinaria tomorrow morning after breakfast. It's really only a few pieces passed down through the family—'

She's interrupted by a disturbance at the door, as if someone is trying to get in while unfamiliar with the working of a knob. After a second, it is thrown wide and in march two large men in suits, one dark, one fair. We all jump.

'Apologies for the disturbance,' says the older one in a deep voice, holding up a warrant card in a leather holder.

'Not wishing to ruin anyone's tea,' says the fair-haired one, looking enviously at the tiramisu. He's the curly blond detective from this morning.

'There is a gentleman here we would like to speak to,' says the first. There are three males round the table – if you count Stephen – so why is he staring at me? 'A Mr Paul Delamere.'

'Dela*mare*,' I say, as if this somehow lets me off the hook.

'Would you kindly step outside with us, sir?' As I reach the door, I notice the younger one cast a last wistful glance towards the remains of the buffet.

I am marched across the hall to the desk at the front door, where the older one announces himself – Detective Chief Inspector Something-or-other – then continues: 'Paul Delamare, you are being arrested on suspicion of the murder of Christian Wagner. You do not have to say anything but it may harm your defence if you do not mention when questioned something that you later rely on in court. We would like to question you about your movements on Monday night and you will now accompany us to Belgravia Police Station.'

Good God. I make a last desperate clutch at normality. 'May I put on my jacket? I, er, feel the cold.' I point it out on the coat-stand.

'Of course.'

That's better. Until the younger one asks me to put my hands in front of me and snaps on *handcuffs*.

Although it's years ago – and I was off my head at the time – I remember this from Vauxhall, the cold steel biting into my wrists. Can this actually be happening to me?

Julie was right, I've been too slow to prove my innocence. I want to protest it's all a terrible mistake, but then I decide to go quietly, cooperate fully and let them see for themselves. They've collared the wrong person.

CHAPTER 20

'This is a first,' I say. The most law-abiding person in the universe sitting handcuffed in the back of a police car, lights flashing. Two officers and a driver, just in case I try and make a break for it. Walkie-talkies crackling.

'You mean – first time you've been arrested?' asks a gruff voice from the front – the DCI.

'Well, first time for murder.' (*Drat!* Now they'll start tapping away on their little computers and find out about Vauxhall. If they haven't already, that is.)

I change the subject. 'It would have been quicker to walk,' I say. (*Smart alec*, they're thinking now.)

'Consider yourself lucky – it's starting to rain,' says the blond younger one, Detective Sergeant Something. It's a good head of hair, and he knows it. Lacquered to a non-stick finish with 'product'.

Three minutes later we draw up at Belgravia Police Station, a modern brick building on a corner of Buckingham Palace Road. To local outrage, they recently closed the front counter (now you have to head to Charing Cross if you lose your tiara or your poodle does a runner), but the backstage operation continues to grind away.

As I get out of the car, which feels clumsy as I can't grab hold of anything with my hands manacled, I'm relieved to see no one there to snap a photograph of me or jeer. The junior cop leads me by the elbow – gently, which I appreciate – into a sort of reception area called the 'Custody Suite', where my cuffs are removed.

Then there's a lot of tedious administration, which gives me some understanding of what a parcel or Amazon delivery must go through as it gets passed along, inspected, ticked off, stamped and signed for, on its journey from depot to destination. My jacket is borne away.

At length I find myself at a wooden table in an overlit interview room with a glass of water in front of me.

Do I want a solicitor?

Now this is a tricky one. I can hear Julie screeching in my ear: *OF COURSE you do!*

But I want it over with as soon as possible, not to wait around half the night. If I keep things light and friendly, we can get this over with, and I'll have a hilarious story to tell at dinner parties.

No, I don't need a solicitor.

Do I want to telephone someone?

No. (The only person I would *dream* of calling would be Julie, and think of the retribution that would unleash.)

The officers ask if they can call me Paul, but I wasn't listening when they said their names and I can't read their badges. Julie says I need to put on my glasses occasionally, though I don't know how she's such an expert as she wears contacts. Her eyes, as I'm always telling her, are one of her best features – bright, sparkling, a glowing shade of hazel I've never seen in anyone else. She has no idea how beautiful she is, and if she were here now one bat of her eyelashes would secure my immediate release.

It's not entirely my fault my mind keeps wandering, because the younger detective is droning on in a monotone about my rights, reminding me that everything will be audio- and video-recorded.

I ask what happened to the woman police officer, the one with a pen from this morning; annoying as she was, there's comfort in familiarity. Apparently this is a Major Incident and I've moved up the police food chain. They check I've no objection to my phone being 'looked over', which can be done while we're 'chatting'. I have nothing to hide, so I unlock it for them.

At last we get down to it. The DCI starts, in a confident bass.

'So, Paul, there are a few areas we're interested in. Would you mind telling us once more exactly what happened after your arrival at Chester Square this morning?'

I know what they're doing: they get you to tell your story again and again till you get tangled up. After that, they go back over what you've said, dip into it, pick away, pull it out of order, try to catch you out. Like hummingbirds extracting the nectar from a recalcitrant lupin. Eventually, tired and confused, I'll make a fatal slip, and find myself on the way to Moscow as part of a spy swap deal.

The blond one keeps coming back to the cleaver. I can imagine the boss telling him beforehand: 'Keep asking about the cleaver till he makes a booboo.'

Yes, when I went into Christian's kitchen, I saw a kitchen cleaver. Yes, I saw that it had been used to cause a fatal injury. (Hardly likely to forget it!) No, the cleaver doesn't belong to me; bright red isn't my colour.

'Joking apart, did you touch this cleaver when you found Mr Wagner?'

'Of course not! Why would I do such a thing? I was shocked to death.' An infelicitous turn of phrase. 'I mean, I blacked out, I told you.'

They sit there looking at me, then the penny drops. 'Oh, I see what you're getting at,' I say. 'Fingerprints.' They exchange a glance – I'm right. 'But obviously you realize this is the cleaver from the cookery school.'

There's a pause. 'Yes, we're aware of that,' he says coolly. 'According to Rose Hoyt –' he checks his notes – 'it was kept in a drawer and she can't remember when it was last used. So tell us, Paul: why are your fingerprints all over it?'

'Suzie can't have washed it up properly.'

They look puzzled.

'But surely someone must have mentioned that I used the cleaver during the meat session?'

'Meat session, Paul?' says the blond one, leaning in and licking his pencil.

'The Noble Art of Meat Cookery,' I reply. 'That's n-o-b-l-e, not like Nobel Prize.'

'No need to be patronizing, Paul,' says Blondie.

The DCI gives a warning cough, as if to say: break it up, you two. 'Let me get this straight,' he growls. 'Now you're saying that you *did* handle the cleaver, and that this happened in class yesterday afternoon.' (Blondie's pencil goes to work. Probably: *Suspect inconsistent, contradicts himself.*) 'Any recollection what time that might have been?'

'About five o'clock – just before Christian made his entrance. He dropped into the class to say hello to the students.'

'Did he see you using the cleaver?'

'I don't see why it matters, but I doubt it. The students were swarming all over him.'

'Meaning?'

'As you know, he's a TV chef. They were practically ripping his clothes off.'

Blondie rubs his chin. It's super smooth – I bet he only has to shave once a week. Or maybe he waxes. Then he continues: 'Interesting you should bring that up. It's been suggested that you may be a little . . . *envious* of Mr Wagner, his fame and success?'

I practically jump from my seat. 'Who said such a thing? Blatant troublemaking!'

The DCI holds up his hand. 'All right, let's all calm down. We have information that suggests you were not on cordial terms with Mr Wagner at the time of his death. But let's go back to the cleaver. Who saw you use it, Paul?'

'Everyone! The whole class was watching. Ask anyone.'

'And you held it by the handle, Paul?'

If you're in a car crash, paramedics keep repeating your name like this, to stop you drifting into unconsciousness. It's maddening. 'No, I held the blade between my teeth and spun a cartwheel!'

'No need for sarcasm,' grunts the DCI.

He's right. This is going very badly indeed, and I mustn't lose my cool. 'I think I can see what's happened here,' I say, slowly and reasonably. 'You've found my fingerprints on the cleaver, which I handled in the afternoon. It should have been washed up after class, or even run through the dishwasher. I don't know why it wasn't.'

Stony silence.

'Although I wouldn't recommend it – putting knives in dishwashers, I mean. All that heating and cooling, and strong detergent – damages the blade.'

Blondie raises an eyebrow. He probably thinks he looks like Dirk Bogarde – practises in the mirror.

The DCI snaps straight back. 'Obviously we'll need to check this out with the witnesses.' He makes an elaborate study of his watch. 'Might have to wait till tomorrow for that.'

Keep me in a cell overnight? They can't!

'In the meantime,' says the junior detective, looking at his notes, 'there's something else we'd like you to refresh our memories about.' I can tell he's excited; if I'm right and it's his first real-life murder investigation he'll be desperate to prove himself. 'Would you be kind enough to run over what happened after you left Chester Square last night?'

Here we go again. I describe my walk home, coming in,

going to bed. I try and make it sound interesting, but there's not much to tell.

'So, on the way home, see anyone you knew? Any . . . *rendezvous*?' Lingering on the word.

If there's a cruising spot in Chester Row, it's news to me.

'Of course not!' I say. 'It was Monday night – very quiet. A few drinkers outside the pubs, taxis picking up and dropping off.'

'You appreciate that almost all London streets are covered nowadays by CCTV cameras,' says the DCI, shooting me a stern glance.

'So I've heard,' I say. 'And a very good thing, too.' While I don't like the idea of a police state, I'm pro-surveillance in all its forms; bring on identity cards and DNA registration for the whole population, crime rates will tumble. Marcus told me this point of view was naive and stupid, and Julie agrees, but as I'm not a criminal, I've always believed I've nothing to fear.

'OK, Paul, you said you live alone.'

'Yes, for the last ten months,' I reply.

'Nice little property you have there.'

'Thank you.'

'Valuable piece of real estate, I should think,' lobs in the DCI. None of their business!

'Any special friends . . . anyone you're dating, Paul?' asks Blondie.

What a dainty way to put it – 'special friend', like at infant school. 'I'm not seeing anyone at the moment, no.' I'm tempted to throw in something to shock him, along the lines of, *But I'm throwing a naked singles night on Saturday, if you boys would like to come along.*

'Did you arrange a get-together at your house for Monday night, by any chance?' says Blondie.

'Why would I do that?'

'We're asking you the questions, Paul,' says the DCI, a sharper note in his voice; he's getting tired – we all are.

I say nothing.

'OK,' says Blondie, savouring the moment. 'CCTV coverage from last night is starting to come in.'

'I'm very glad to hear it,' I say.

'Just say CCTV cameras happen to catch someone waiting around outside Chester Square Cookery School at 21.55 hours yesterday evening, who then leaves abruptly at 22.05. Same person is seen arriving at Jubilee Cottage at 22.14, rings the doorbell and goes down to the basement area. Then at 22.27, the person comes up the steps, and tries the doorbell again. At that point they accidentally knock into your dustbin, then leave. At 22.32 you arrive home and go straight down the basement steps, as if looking for someone—'

'*Of course!*' I declare. 'I'm *so* sorry. I honestly forgot about it – I can't believe I didn't mention it. My fault. Although obviously it's got nothing to do with any of this.'

They exchange glances.

'When I got home last night,' I explain, 'I found my bin overturned. Someone had been hanging round in the basement area. But they'd left by the time I got home – I didn't see anyone.'

'Who is this *someone* you forgot to tell us about, Paul?' asks Blondie.

'*Someone* you invited over for an intimate get-together,' throws in the DCI.

'Or *someone* who pops round when he feels like it, just like that,' says Blondie, snapping his fingers.

'Look –' I say – 'if it had been a friend, he wouldn't throw garbage all over the place, would he?'

'Maybe he was annoyed because you were late, or stood him up. But the interesting question is: what was he doing there?' asks Blondie.

'And who was he?' adds the DCI. I notice Blondie's voice gets higher as he gets more excited, the DCI's lower.

'I promise it's of no relevance.'

'Let us decide that, Paul,' says the DCI, hitting the bass notes. 'Would you like us to jog your memory, perhaps? We can show you a still from the footage, if that helps?'

Blondie produces a large, glossy photograph. I would have expected black and white – grainy with a lot of shadows – but it's full colour, surprisingly well lit. A figure is clearly revealed, leaning against my area railing, cigarette in hand.

'Jonny,' I say, through gritted teeth. 'His name is Jonny.'

'And who is *Jonny*? Someone you picked up? A lover?'

I roll my eyes. The second time tonight that's been suggested. What is wrong with people?

'Jonny Berens. And he's my stepson,' I say.

CHAPTER 21

My interrogators want to know all about Jonny, the works. In a way, it's a pity he's *not* involved in the Chester Square imbroglio, because he's such a thoroughgoing villain. The damaged childhood, getting thrown out of school, failing to stick at any job ever. I'm tempted to throw in a scar and a pet tarantula, to make him sound even more dastardly.

I mention the harrassment warning notice served on him earlier in the year – it was a last resort – and they want all the details. I don't really want to stir that up again so I keep it vague: attempted arson, broken windows, being pushed into moving traffic.

I tell them Jonny's phone number – which I know by heart – and suggest they call him right now. He currently lives in Earls Court with an Australian girl (whom I've never met but pity from the depths of my heart) and never goes to bed before three or four in the morning. Secretly, I'd love to see his face when the police ask him what he was doing hanging round my house last night.

'He's a very, um, erratic individual. I've no idea what he'll tell you, but I can assure you, he has nothing to do with . . . any of this.'

DCI and Blondie go off together to make the call – they seem to be joined at the hip – and I am left alone.

Ten minutes later they're back. I know they've talked to Jonny because they look . . . ruffled. I wonder if he used the opportunity to regale them with some choice examples from his rich vocabulary of expletives, or to share his forthright views on the Metropolitan Police. He has a way with words, our Jonny.

'It's a pity you have these memory lapses, Paul,' says the DCI.

'Waste of police time, Paul,' chimes in Blondie.

'We'd love to send you home, call it a night, but just for everyone's peace of mind, we need to sort out this cleaver business. Of course, we'll have to corroborate this with the students.'

'Who are all in bed by now,' says his sidekick.

Then, out of the blue, it comes to me. 'Have you finished with my iPhone?'

The DCI gives a weary nod. The phone is fetched and arrives back in an evidence bag. More unnecessary plastic that will end up choking dolphins.

I turn it on and tap Instagram. Ignoring the yawns of my interrogators, my fumbling fingers key in 'Callaloo and Bammy'. Up comes De'Lyse's smiling face and a reference to her 18,971 followers. I don't have to scroll down far to find a thumbnail of an apron-clad figure waving a red-handled cleaver in the air.

No one likes watching themself, so I hand my phone to the DCI. 'Video from yesterday afternoon,' I say, unable to hide my satisfaction.

They pore over the little screen. A figure – unmistakably mine – capers about brandishing the cleaver, and there are two bumps as the pigeon heads land in the bin. Then I hear, in a jaunty voice I recognize as my own, 'First rule of butchery – off with his head.'

The police officers look up at me with distaste, then Blondie notes it down. 'Anything else you'd like to tell us?' he asks.

'Yes,' I reply, and take a deep breath. 'You've got the wrong man. A friend of mine was murdered last night in cold blood. I would ask you not to waste your time on people like me, who are plainly innocent.'

The DCI shrugs dismissively then concludes: 'OK, Paul, we're releasing you without charge. The detective sergeant here will now see you out and deal with the paperwork. I hope I'm being helpful when I say you come across as a bit, well, foggy. If we need to question you again – which is likely – try and get your story straight. Interview concluded at 23.38.'

'Just one final thing,' I say. 'I'm not going to find myself all over the newspapers, am I?'

'We have no plans to release your name. Not at present, anyway.'

We drive home through heavy drizzle. I hope my neighbour doesn't spot me stepping out of a police car.

I'm drained, and so is my phone. I plug it in to charge and head for the shower.

Under the hiss of hot water, I go over and over my disastrous interview. I've had a narrow escape, and antagonized the police. Besides which, someone seems to be feeding them false information – pointing towards me.

ENTRÉE

<u>New Year's Eve 2008</u>

WHAT A YEAR!

Another TV series commissioned – my second Michelin star – National TV Award – and now this £££ contract with Emirates (fingers crossed) . . . I know I can cook, but who would have guessed?

My agent sent me to a wealth advisor (never dreamt I'd need one of those) who wants me to invest while the cash is rolling in. Yawn. You only live once. Money's for enjoying.

Next week I'm catching some rays – Barbados – then it's back into the kitchen, where I belong. At the moment I'm going through some French classics, and this is my take on 'chicken in half-mourning', which is a dish they do in Lyon with slices of black truffle under the skin. The truffle is a waste of space in my opinion, so my version has two sauces: one black, one white.

I phoned Barbara to say Happy New Year. She was surprised to hear from me.

POULARDE DEMI-DEUIL

Put a couple each of onions, celery, sliced garlic cloves, 5 bay leaves, a bouquet garni, handful of peppercorns, half a sliced lemon, seasoning and a nice fat chicken in a stock pot and cover with water. Poach covered for 1¼–1½ hours, till cooked, and cool in broth. When cool enough to handle, remove the chicken (use broth for soup) and remove and shred flesh, keeping white and dark meat separate.

For the white chicken, melt 25g butter with 300ml cream, simmer for 3–4 minutes till slightly thick then add the juice of a lemon quarter and seasoning. Add white chicken meat just to heat through.

For the dark chicken, whisk up 3 tablespoons of oil with 2 tablespoons of Dijon, mango chutney, Worcestershire Sauce and a good pinch of cayenne till gloopy. Coat the dark meat in this and grill till spotty in places, 3–5 minutes.

Serve light and dark meats side by side. A feast for 4, rice goes nicely.

CHAPTER 22

Wednesday

I wake far too early to the sound of rain lashing my bedroom window. My first ritual of the day is to check my barograph. I don't understand our island climate any better than anyone else, but happen to be the proud owner of one of these old-fashioned meteorological instruments used to record atmospheric pressure.

The mechanism is made of brass and has a nib, containing a tiny reservoir of ink, which over the course of a week draws a wavy line on a chart affixed to a slowly rotating drum. The line has been going down all week and is currently stuck at the bottom of the chart. Wet and thundery: autumn in the air.

My mood is further lowered by the knowledge that I've let Julie down in her hour of need: I swore I'd phone her back last night and I failed her. Right on cue, in comes her first message of the day.

> Hope U had a good zzZ and that 2day turns out 👍.
> Been 🤔 , 🗣 l8r if you get a mo? ⚫ ⏪ in 🐑 = calm
> b4 the ☔

In her position, I'd have texted something vitriolic – *Call yourself a friend? Thanks for nothing!* – but she isn't like that, which makes me feel even more of a rat. She hopes I slept well and wishes me a good day; she has been thinking and would like to speak later. Then the usual astro-garbage – Mars retrograde in Aries (fluffy white ram), calm before the storm.

I feel a stab of panic – I promised her a corking idea for her reshoot and the only ones I've come up with so far are terrible: *Round the World Christmas. Sustainable Christmas. Metaverse Christmas.*

Praying inspiration will strike before it's too late, I divert myself by assembling my props for class. Today's session is *A Pinch of Magic*. Ignore the twee name. It's about herbs and spices, and that is a fascinating subject.

My livelihood depends on my senses of taste and smell. About one in four of us is born a super-taster, with more tastebuds than the rest of the population. Your sense of smell, on the other hand, is something you develop. Ever since I can remember, I've been storing away olfactory experiences.

There's one super-talent I don't have, alas. Very few people – and women only – are born with a genetic mutation that enables them to see up to 100 million more colours than the rest of us. (I wonder what they'd make of Lilith.)

Especially for today, I've pulled out Dad's old medical bag – the one he used to take on home visits. It's a proper old-fashioned Gladstone bag in tan leather, with all sorts of pockets and flaps – probably some I've never even discovered. This makes it ideal for tucking in the few dozen small jars, pots, drums and boxes that comprise my collection of aromatics and my Peugeot grinders (amazing pieces of engineering – they also make cars).

* * *

By the time I reach number forty-one, the weather has brightened up a bit but the rain is still lashing down. I can see that last night's constable was right – the locusts have arrived. A swarm of reporters, photographers, sightseers and police is clustered around the building. It's so bad that they've closed off Eccleston Street, which will play merry hell with people trying to get to work; unless you happen to be on a bike or scooter, in which case traffic regulations do not apply.

Some of the spectators are holding umbrellas, others getting drenched, including a handful of sodden, unhappy-looking police officers. I catch the eye of the least unfriendly, and she barks some instructions into her radio then takes me by the arm.

'Stick close – we're going through.'

It's horrible! Everyone turns to look at me, cameras start snapping and selfie sticks are raised in the air. Now I know what it must feel like to be a cabinet minister. 'Was it you who found him?' 'Paul, look over here!' 'Are you Paul Delamere?'

Dela*MARE*, I want to shout back, but how do they even know my name?

As we go up the steps, the front door mercifully opens and I am propelled by my minder into the haven of the front hall. Sitting at the table is a new constable, this one so young he might almost be a cadet. Someone at police charm school has taught him the art of looking suspicious while receiving a polite greeting.

He has drawn himself a neat little grid to record who comes and goes, and I feel sorry that my arrival is going to sully his handiwork. He inscribes my name then *7.49 a.m.* alongside it.

'Much happened overnight?' I ask.

'Only just come on duty,' he says. He flips back a page to reveal that his predecessor was keen on doodling.

'May I just wriggle behind you for a moment to get to the umbrella stand?' I say. 'I'll try not to drip all over you.'

As I do so, I sneak a glance over the PC's shoulder. The

name is obscured by daisies and cobwebs but I can make out that *someone* left and returned at 12.11 and 01.48 respectively.

* * *

Punctuality is something I learnt late in life – I would recommend it to anyone – but this is getting out of hand. More than an hour and a half till class begins, rattling around this gloomy place, reliving yesterday and worrying. And who's the midnight prowler, who sneaks out when everyone else has gone to bed?

I lug myself and bag down the hall to the Pink Room. Here's the plan: I'll brew myself some *proper* coffee then whizz round to check if there's anything I've overlooked.

Although it's à la mode to drink espresso, made in a great big shiny machine, I prefer good old-fashioned filtered coffee because of its clean, light taste. Three tablespoons of coffee (very finely ground is my preference) to three hundred millilitres of water is easy to remember, heated to just over ninety celsius. My expert friend tells me that the French press, because of its coarse filter, allows a wider spectrum of flavours through than paper, but I find the result thick and muddy.

These Belgravia houses are built like fortresses. While I wait for the kettle, I hear bumping noises from overhead, and the muffled sound of voices. The Pink Room is situated directly beneath the Shelley Room. Who's clomping about in Rose's study at such an unbusinesslike hour?

I go back into the hall, under the stern eye of the young copper. Looking nonchalant, I cross to the Grand Staircase and ascend. Halfway up, I stop to admire a painting of a shipwreck, complete with drowning sailors: I am still being watched. Once he can no longer see me, I tiptoe along the landing and put my ear to Rose's door.

I hear shouting and the thump of something heavy falling over – a chair? a person? – then a tinkling sound – broken glass? Why did Victorian carpenters have to make their doors so thick? It's not fair on the eavesdropper.

I can make out the voice of Rose – something along the lines of 'No, I will not!' – and another voice, shriller – 'You have no choice!' A third – also female – cries: 'Let's try and be reasonable!' Next, heavy footsteps. They're on the move.

Interspersed with the display cabinets on the landing are a few freestanding pieces, including a vast butcher's block (oak, French, early twentieth century), and an ornate silver-plated carving trolley (Edwardian, with domed lid and lion's head handles). You can quite imagine a moustachioed maître d'hôtel wheeling it up to your table, then swinging it open with a flourish to reveal a glistening saddle of lamb or haunch of venison.

Quick as a flash, I dash behind it. I'm in the shadows, and the glitter of the silver will distract the eye of anyone who glances my way, but what about my head sticking up at the back? I'm flat against the wall, so I have no choice but to lift the dome, poke my head into the void and gently close the cover over it until it's resting on my neck.

It's not as uncomfortable as it sounds, but it still feels odd to be bent double with your head in a chafing dish, like a joint of meat waiting to be carved. There's a lingering smell of roast beef and gravy; then my thoughts wander to Salome, who had John the Baptist's head served to her on a platter; then with ghastly inevitability to Christian.

It seems like for ever, but eventually I hear Rose's door open, someone emerge, and the door slam behind them. Footsteps stamp their way along the landing, passing within inches of the carving trolley, to the top of the staircase. I lift the dome a crack, just enough to see two figures marching downstairs. Leading the way is the ash blonde from the garden – who is she, and why does she keep turning up here? She is followed by De'Lyse.

It takes me a minute to winkle myself out of my hiding place. I stand up, rubbing my back. Just when I think my ordeal is over, I find myself staring into a familiar pair of blue eyes, beneath a familiar halo of golden hair.

'Well, look who it is!' exclaims Blondie, looking even more pleased with himself than usual. Today he has a bodycam clipped to his top pocket. I see him adjust it to ensure the moment is captured. 'I just popped in to catch up with Mrs Hoyt, and who should spring out from behind a dessert trolley?'

'It's a carving trolley,' I squawk.

'I beg its pardon. I need to speak to Mrs H then I'll see you downstairs and you can tell me what this is all about.' He adds with a smirk, 'You've got five minutes to think of something convincing. Wouldn't want to have to re-arrest you, now, would we?'

CHAPTER 23

By 9 a.m. I still haven't had my coffee, so I'm forced to brave the Pink Room for breakfast with the students. I've made my peace with the DS, having decided to make a clean breast of my espionage operation. Maybe it will help him to know that Rose hosts early morning catfights with a mysterious visitor in a power suit and five-inch heels.

As if I'm not sufficiently on edge, my thoughts keep turning to Julie. Within the next hour the team will be presenting to Dena – if she's not satisfied she'll gouge their eyes out – but has anyone come up with an idea? I certainly haven't.

To the accompaniment of rain drumming on the windows, the students drift in, eyeing me curiously. Melanie comes up to me and lays a sympathetic hand on my arm. If I had beautiful antique rings, I too would flaunt them; emeralds and diamonds.

'Everything OK?' she asks. I nod: no way am I going to give them the blow-by-blow on my evening from hell.

'We saw you being driven away in the panda car,' says Vicky. I can imagine her glasses hugging the window, breath misting them up with the excitement of my downfall.

'Armed guards and all,' says Lilith.

'Nonsense,' says Vicky. 'Those motorcycles were pizza deliveries, I saw the boxes on the back.'

'Undercover,' says Lilith. 'In case Paul jumped out and made a run for it.'

'In case he fancied an American hot with extra peperoni,' snaps back Vicky.

'And now the paparazzi have arrived,' cuts in a lofty voice. Lady B's hair has been spun and twirled like candy floss with the application of extra lacquer – perhaps she's planning to treat them to an Evita-like appearance at the front door.

'I, for one, shall be keeping a low profile,' mutters Gregory from behind a slice of toast. 'The investment community does not – ahem – care to find itself in the limelight.' He's puffy round the eyes again – too many podcasts.

I notice Suzie beckoning me into a corner and the others prick up their ears, hoping for gossip. They are about to be disappointed.

'You haven't any fish for *Spectacular Seafood* this afternoon,' she whispers. 'Delivery cancelled.'

'I can't say I'm surprised,' I say. 'The police are saying it's gridlock from Sloane Square to Victoria.'

'It's not that,' she replies. 'The seafood people have cancelled our account without further notice – no longer wish to be associated with the school.'

Poor Rose; something else she could do without. Then I remember I'm the one who will have to hold the fort, as per usual, with an hour-long class this afternoon and no fish with which to fill it. Or should that be fillet?

'I meant to ask you,' I continue, while I have her ear. 'Was there some kind of fracas in the Shelley Room this morning? I – er – happened to notice a young woman leaving in a hurry.'

'Some photos on Mrs Hoyt's desk got knocked over, that's all. There's always some kind of disaster when Milla comes round.'

'Milla?' I reply.

'Mrs Hoyt's daughter. Surely you've heard about her? You're the only one who hasn't – she's always in the gossip columns. One of *Tatler*'s "Twenty-five Women to Watch Under Twenty-five".' Then, acerbically: 'Although I know that's not your style.'

Ouch!

'Anyway, she's been a nightmare recently,' Suzie continues. 'Poor Mrs H is pulling her hair out.'

I'm about to quiz her on this when we're interrupted by the arrival of De'Lyse, demanding coffee. Suzie retreats to the sideboard to make another pot of her toxic brew. I notice Lilith whisper something in Suzie's ear, nudge her and point to Stephen.

I'm not sure if Rose has some celestial messaging system at her disposal, but word drifts about that we should assemble upstairs at 9.30 for the famous tour. I'll join for the first bit, then slip away and speak with Julie.

Before that, however, I give Suzie a hand loading the breakfast things into the dumb waiter so she can finish the story.

'What does Milla do for a living?' I ask.

'Works for a property developer,' she replies. 'She's angling to come back and manage the school. Says she could make a better job of it than Mrs Hoyt.'

'Really! And how is De'Lyse involved?'

'Oh, she's part of the plan. De'Lyse will be the school's new figurehead – young, female, huge following on social media. Then – well, this is my theory – the moment Milla takes control, she'll stab them both in the back, convert the place into ten luxury apartments and flog them for umpteen million apiece.'

I don't know why people always have to be fighting and doing each other down. Wouldn't life be simpler if we all just got on with our lives, instead of chasing after what we haven't got?

We're stashing the last of the breakfast things in the

compartment – it's surprisingly capacious – when it dawns on me how sad it must be for Suzie to have got herself caught up in all this.

'Don't you find it lonely living in this great big place when the students have gone home?' I ask her.

She pauses before answering. 'No one's ever asked me that. I sometimes wish . . . well, that I had someone my own age to hang out with.'

'You should make the most of London while you can. It's the most exciting city in the world for youngsters.'

'Not much fun on your own. Maybe if I had more money . . .'

On the spur of the moment, I decide to do a good deed for the day. As well as improving tonight's dinner prospects, it will give me a chance to ask her a few more questions.

'Suzie,' I say, brightly, 'there's this new delicatessen on the corner of Elizabeth and Ebury Street. Fancy coming along to check it out? You might find it interesting from the student meal point of view . . . get some fresh ideas.'

'Are you saying you don't like my cooking?' she says. To my relief, a smile is hovering on her lips. 'To be honest, I only know the basics. I told Mrs Hoyt that when I joined. If she wants some fancy-pants chef, she'll have to pay a lot more than minimum wage.'

At which point, she hits the DOWN button and the dumb waiter embarks on its stately descent into the bowels of the Old Scullery.

* * *

On the dot of nine thirty, everyone is clustered in the Shelley Room. It's a tight fit, especially with Lilith barging round, peering at everything as if it was an exhibit in a murder trial. I take the opportunity to check out the photographs – the ones that didn't get smashed – on Rose's desk. They include a group of debs in white ballgowns draped round a staircase, and a black and white studio portrait of Rose, very Condé Nast. If I were her, I would put these away: they must remind her every hour of what she's lost.

Melanie sidles over. 'That's me,' she whispers, pointing at the ballgown next to Rose.

Rose is describing the history of number forty-one as if she's reading a sermon: '*The room we're standing in is named in honour of Mary Shelley, of* Frankenstein *fame, who lived a few doors down at number twenty-four and used to be seen roaming the communal garden at dusk, dangling a reticule from her kid-gloved hand. Chester Square legend has it that it contained her husband's calcified heart, which failed to burn when the poet was cremated on an Italian beach in 1822.*'

'Too gruesome,' mutters Lady B . . . under her breath; Stephen seems to find it funny.

Longing as I am to hear the next instalment in this spell-binding saga, I have by careful increments managed to manoeuvre myself to a position near the door. Under cover of a desultory patter of applause, I slip out to freedom.

* * *

'Julie! Thank goodness you picked up!' Thank goodness too for FaceTime, so I can see her lovely face. You can tell when she's nervous because she licks her lips, and she's doing it now. 'Tell me what's happening.' I've slipped into the library – and by a miracle, managed to get Julie on the first ring.

'Well, we're going in to present to Dena in half an hour. If I run through my list, will you tell me if I've forgotten anything?' She holds a spreadsheet up to the camera. 'Photographer, tick. Location, tick. Props stylist, tick. Decorations, tick. Props, tick. Food stylist, tick. Home economist, tick. Food order, tick. Models, tick. Chaperones, tick. Transport, tick.'

Big photoshoots are monstrous to organize – certainly comparable to moving house or getting divorced. Overshadowing this one is the knowledge that if we don't get it right, Julie and I will be out of a job. 'And you've remembered the schools are back, so the traffic will be terrible?' I say.

'Definitely. All the pick-ups have half an hour traffic delay built in, plus I've warned everyone it's going to be a very full day – eleven shots, plus reportage. No slipping off early to avoid the rush.'

'You must have been up all night,' I say. It would have taken me a week to organize that lot, and I'd still have forgotten to order something vital, such as the turkey. 'I was delayed yesterday, didn't want to call too late.' I could never lie to Julie, but this is sailing close.

'Don't worry – you deserve a bit of down time. How are you feeling, by the way?' she continues. 'No more run-ins with the police?'

'Hello? Hello?' I say, pretending the Wi-Fi's dropped out. 'Sorry, lost you there. So, did you sort out the recipes?'

'I've reworked them as best I can,' she replies. 'Now *Nutcracker*'s died the death, we thought it safest to take out all the nuts. You know what Dena's like – if she spots a chestnut in a spoonful of stuffing, she'll turn anaphylactic out of pure spite.' It breaks my heart to think of all my work going down the pan, but you can't work in magazines and be sensitive.

'So what's the theme?' I ask, hoping against hope that the team has come up with something.

'Well, we've been racking our brains –' more licking of lips – 'but we haven't really got one.

'For the festive homes section, Lucinda says she could respray the toys, wrap hessian around the swags, and cover everything else with wraps and throws, to hide the blue and silver.' Lucinda is *Escape*'s Homes Editor, recently poached from a posh decorating magazine; like most people connected with interior design, she thinks she's a cut above the rest. 'She keeps going on about Nordic nesting, whatever that means.'

'Hmm,' I say. Lucinda may have been at school with Pippa Middleton, may even have played in the same hockey team, but she has yet to experience the Wrath of Dena . . . which I fear is heading her way. 'What about fashion?'

'Spencer's not happy: he loved *Nutcracker* – all the frogging and epaulettes.' (I bet he goes down a storm at Vault 79 on uniform fetish night.) 'He wants to pitch a boots and belts story.'

'Doesn't sound very Christmassy,' I say. Another fetish night, if anything.

'He wants to call it . . .' I watch Julie's face contort as she tries to hold the laughter back.

'What? Tell me!'

Between guffaws, she manages to squeak, '*Puss in Boots*,' before we both crack up.

I consider the fashion industry – along with social media and online gambling – as a curse of modern life, but that's not the point: Dena won't buy it – not in a million Nordic winters.

Julie starts licking her lips again in earnest. 'We were all banking on you to save the day – a big idea. Except . . . the meeting's in twenty minutes.'

My heart sinks into my shoes. A nightmare vision flashes before my eyes: Julie queuing in the rain at a Jobcentre, me begging in the street with a piece of cardboard saying HUNGRY AND HOMELESS.

I hear the students shuffle along the corridor outside. On

my way to close the library door, I see Lilith sail past, upholstered this morning in a phantasmagoria of turquoise, fuchsia, scarlet and lime.

'Julie!' I say, blinking. Colours swirl and shimmer in my imagination, kaleidoscopes spin.

'What? What is it? Have you thought of something?'

I grip my phone as if my life depended on it. 'OK: here's exactly what you need to do . . .'

CHAPTER 24

On my way to the Old Ballroom, I look into the courtyard and see rain sheeting on the diagonal; it's getting windier. The forensics people are still bustling about in their white outfits, going in and out of their little tent. I'd like to imagine inside a cosy garden-shed set-up – pots of tea, Radio 2, a blow heater – but all I can see is a white table and plastic boxes.

Meanwhile I throw myself into preparing for class; at least it'll take my mind off the Dena situation. This morning – assuming Rose at some point releases her captive audience – we can 'bake off' our pastry. (I blame TV celebs for introducing the nation to horrible chef-speak – baking off, frying off, roasting off, sautéing off, fridging off, caramelizing off.) That leaves this afternoon, which I'll worry about when I get to it.

I know it isn't good for my nerves, but I check the news on my phone. The police briefing has just happened.

There are some new developments. It's been ruled out as a terrorist incident. Plus the police have discovered that Christian was in debt to the tune of several hundred thousand pounds, which must be how he got himself beaten up by the West London mob.

Who would have guessed?

If he was mixed up in that sort of thing, maybe he had other secrets too. My eyes drift across the Old Ballroom to his locker.

I wander over and give the handle a casual tug. Breaking and entering is not my forte, but it would be easy enough to get in if you had the right tool, and where better to find such a thing than a kitchen?

I try jimmying it open with a palette knife, which will unfortunately never again be much use for frosting a carrot cake. A plastic spatula and cake slice also bite the dust. Abandoning brute force, I succeed in sliding a metal bench scraper into the gap, give it a sharp tap and . . . ping! The lock springs open.

It's an anti-climax. An apron and a ball of socks. A Spanish phrasebook and a metal tape measure. I'm about to give up when – *what's this?* – tucked underneath the rest, I find a small dog-eared notebook, the type with an elastic closure to keep it from flapping open.

It feels intrusive to look at something once so personal, so private. It's a sort of 'recipe diary' going all the way back to 2003. The entries are sporadic – usually a few lines plus a recipe. I recognize some of the latter immediately – those cheese biscuits the world raved about, and no one ever quite managed to replicate. That poached chicken dish with two sauces.

I wonder if Christian one day intended to turn this into a cookbook? A *real* cookbook, rather than the TV spin-offs that were churned out under his name. Maybe I'll even find some clues to help me work out what happened.

I'm flicking over the pages when I hear steps coming up the ramp. I slide the notebook into my pocket and slam the locker shut, but something drops onto the floor.

The doors whoosh open, and in walks Melanie. 'Forgot my charger,' she says, eyeing me up and down. 'Looking for something?'

'Er, I found it,' I reply, brandishing the bench scraper.

She continues to look at me oddly, perhaps because one of my feet is glued to the spot.

'Well, see you at coffee.'

'Won't be a minute,' I reply. She glances back suspiciously before leaving the room.

With a sigh of relief, I move my toe to reveal a laminated pink and yellow card. It must have been tucked between the diary's pages – possibly acting as a bookmark – and says across the top: *HM Armed Forces Veteran*.

Underneath, in small print:

D192969E
C S Wagner
Expiry 17 Jan 29

CHAPTER 25

You think you know someone and then something like this slaps you in the face. All those years of friendship, through thick and thin, and he never bothered to mention he'd been in the army. I head for the Pink Room, nodding distractedly to the constable at the front door.

I find it all laid up – including boring biscuits and a yellowing apple for Lilith – but no students. I call down the back stairs for Suzie, hoping she'll know where they are; no reply.

The basements of these grand London mansions have histories just as rich as the upper floors, and I've been dying to have a look at this one. And so I step through the green baize door and wind my way down the spiral staircase to the Old Scullery. The varnished treads are rickety and slippery, not even a handrail: I can't believe it passed a risk assessment.

I remember being taught in history that the spiral staircases of medieval castles were built clockwise, so that those defending them could more easily slash with their swords, or at least could if they were right-handed. I notice this one runs widdershins.

At the bottom I'm greeted by mouse-coloured paint and a mushroomy smell. Every surface is encumbered with Rose's kitchenalia, including a pine dresser overflowing with vintage china.

Its shelves are stacked with a random miscellany of blue

and white plates, ginger jars, sauceboats, tureens, and a Wedgwood cake stand. Peeking out between the china are figurines – a baker carrying a sack of baguettes, a woman taking vegetables to market.

Whenever I see this sort of display, my mind turns – rather prosaically – to dusting. Is it left to poor old Suzie?

Then a door opens, and out she steps.

'Oh, it's you,' she says, surprised. 'Is there a problem?'

I mumble an apology – sorry for invading her space.

'No one normally comes down here,' she explains. It must be odd for her, passing the hours in this twilight zone, cut off from the rest of the world, soundproofed from the street. Like living in a cave. Troglodyte: not a word you get to use very often. 'But it's nice to see a friendly face.'

'Do you sleep down here as well?' I ask.

She indicates the room from which she's just emerged and flicks a switch to reveal a tiny, windowless cell containing a narrow iron-framed bed, a chair and small table with a TV on it. Another word springs to mind: anchoress.

'Hardly the Ritz,' I say.

'I've lived in worse,' she says. 'According to Mrs Hoyt, some of these places have whole families of Filipinos crammed in under the stairs, or in converted coal cellars under the pavement. Besides,' she adds, 'I get a bathroom all to myself, and my own private launderette.'

I follow her past the groaning dresser to another door. The first thing to assail me as she opens it is a gust of detergent, bleach and fabric softener; next a low rumble; then the light flicks on automatically to reveal an entire gleaming wall of washing machines and tumble driers, stacked in formation. One machine is busily churning away.

'The stupid thing is that most of the school stuff goes off to laundry service, so these machines are hardly used. Handy for me though, whenever I want a clean T-shirt or a pair of socks.'

On my way out via the kitchen she notices me examining an interesting wall display of skimmers, slotted spoons and those wire ladles that come in so useful when you're deep-frying, known as spiders.

'People have too much stuff,' she says. Then pauses, as if building herself up to say something, before she comes out with: 'By the way, I didn't mean to be unfriendly earlier. Delis aren't usually my thing, but I wouldn't mind taking a look at this new one you mentioned, if you don't mind me tagging along. I was wondering about lunchtime, if you're free.'

* * *

Eventually the students crocodile back to the Old Ballroom. They have that glazed look people get in art galleries, from standing and staring. The rain is making a din, pounding on the flat roof above us.

I daresay they're still curious about what happened last night, but I'm not going to let them dwell on it because we have work to do. And, rely on it, I'll be watching them carefully.

First job is to blind-bake De'Lyse and Stephen's shortcrust. His floured fingers wiggle deftly round the tin and I'm glad to see him press the pastry into each indentation, neatly and evenly; she goes at it like a child modelling clay, pushing and shoving.

From a skills point of view, she's hopelessly underqualified to head up a cookery school. I hope that still matters; or maybe it's more important that she looks fabulous, with her flawless complexion and smoky eye make-up. How did she get mixed up with someone like Milla Hoyt?

Soon the Old Ballroom is filled with the unmistakable

nutty, buttery aroma of baking. I note that Vicky has gaffer-taped her oven door shut to prevent any act of vandalism on Lady B's part – but otherwise peace and goodwill prevail.

Lilith's moment of glory is approaching. She's set out her fillings on trays, and found from somewhere a steel trolley, so that as soon as an oven timer pings, she trundles in like a juggernaut, shoving all asunder.

It's so exciting that we forget about lunch until Suzie arrives to remind us. The students drift off to the Pink Room while Suzie and I tidy up.

'Is Mrs Hoyt OK about your popping out?' I ask.

'The students should be able to manage without me just this once,' she says. 'But just in case Her Majesty does a tour of inspection, Stevie has agreed to tidy things—' Then a baking sheet crashes to the floor. She stoops down to retrieve it and licks the tips of her fingers. '*Ouch!* I didn't realize it was hot!' Beginner cooks are very sensitive to heat – one becomes less so the older and more experienced one gets, I find. When I pick up the baking sheet, it doesn't seem at all hot to me.

We make our way to the front hall, where the police cadet is looking bored. From the windows we can see the throng outside is thicker than ever, but at least it's stopped raining.

'Is there any way we could use the back door instead?' I ask, as I put on my coat.

'Sorry, sir. For the time being everyone has to use the one entrance.'

We make a dash down the steps and manage to break through the crowd before they're aware what's happening, then I grab Suzie by the arm and we fast-foot it to freedom.

'Can we slow down a bit?' she says. Maybe she wants to savour the unfamiliar fresh air and daylight, or is worried about slipping on the wet pavements. 'No need to rush.'

'Fine by me,' I say, slowing my pace. 'In fact, there was something I wanted to ask you.'

'Ask away,' she says.

'It was a real stroke of luck you turned up at Christian's yesterday morning – I might have lain there for hours, out for the count. I just wondered what brought you across.'

'Oh, nothing really. I thought he might have overslept. After a late night.'

'Late night?'

'You know what he's like – sorry, *was* like. He probably invited someone up for a drink. The bloke with the trousers – I think I saw him heading in that direction after dinner.'

'And you probably noticed the shattered glass, as I did.'

'That too. Yeah.'

Once we're in the organic deli, I steer her round a display of purple figs, wild mushrooms and striped aubergines kept fresh and dewy by a mist machine. Next we head to the cheese department, where a stack of Époisses and Reblochon de Savoie is pumping out a miasma of its own. She holds her nose. I cannot resist a whole gravadlax cured with beetroot, strewn with shavings of red onion. Despite the fact I'm buying it for tonight's Pink Room supper, Suzie doesn't reach for her purse, so I pay for it myself (£59, if you please) and keep the receipt to claim back from Rose.

No grand gourmet, our Suzie, but on the way out, I see her eyes alight upon a Valrhona chocolate mousse, adorned with white chocolate curls and *fraises de bois*, yours for £6.80.

'Let me buy it for you,' I say, generous to a fault.

'Oh, thank you! No one ever buys me anything. May I have two?'

If not a gourmet, a glutton!

We set off on a scenic route back to number forty-one via Ebury Mews.

'It's a horrible feeling, having the police breathing down our necks all the time,' I say. 'I felt like a criminal, having my fingerprints taken.'

'Me too. I didn't really mind, but it's not as if I touched anything up there.'

'How did your interview go?'

'Didn't have much to tell them,' she replies.

'My alibi sounded a bit thin: I just went home and fell into bed. How about you?'

'I was streaming a film on my laptop—'

'Oh, what? I love films.'

'*Terrifier 2*. The only thing is, the cop lady borrowed my laptop to check my history – just a formality, she said. It's a bit boring till I get it back.'

'I'm glad they're being thorough. If I had a spare laptop, I'd lend it to you.'

'Thanks,' she says, looking genuinely touched. 'I said you were different from the others.'

At snail-like speed, we trail back to the door of number forty-one. She holds back, as if dreading going in.

'I meant to ask,' she finishes. 'What's the deal between you and this Jonny character?'

'Oh that – it's nothing really. He's just a bit, well, troubled. Why do you ask?'

'Only because Mrs Hoyt was talking about it earlier. She said you were a bit cagey about him.'

'Well, not deliberately. It's not as if I'm trying to hide anything.'

'I'm sure she means well. She's under a lot of pressure – having a hard time of it at the moment.'

We turn to go inside and I glance up at the house. Framed in an upstairs window, Rose stands looking down at us, her face in shadow.

CHAPTER 26

I make my way across to the Old Ballroom, tap in the entry code – and *bam*!

I always said those blasted doors were a menace, and now they've swung straight into poor Stephen, on his way out.

'I'm so sorry!' I cry. 'Are you all right?'

He's on the ground, holding his head, and in my panic all I can think of is the personal injury claim he'll launch against me. *Have you been injured in an accident that wasn't your fault?* I'm ashamed to react this way, but it's what the world's come to.

After a few seconds, he stands up. Thank goodness – though he could still have internal injuries, or delayed concussion.

'Didn't know the doors were about to open,' he mumbles.

'It was all my fault,' I reply, remembering too late that you must never admit liability. 'Do you want to sit down? Glass of water?' What was he doing here anyway, skulking around on his own? He seems to read my mind.

'Just came over because I'd, like, forgotten something. The others are in the Pink Room finishing lunch.'

With that, he limps off, and I'm on my own at last. I pick up my phone and tap 'C S Wagner D192969E' into Google.

Why didn't he tell anyone he'd been in the military – the Royal Regiment of Fusiliers, no less? He looked like a soldier – always held himself upright, and had that confident, alert look about him that comes from military training, and which women (and some men) find it impossible to resist. And it would have explained the missing years before he started cheffing – he was ten years older than the rest of the commis, and never told us why. You'd think he'd have been proud of it.

Next I type 'christian wagner royal fusiliers' into the search bar and up pops a news story from the archive of the *Wiltshire Times*. In the very first paragraph, another shock. What's this? Christian Wagner married – and a father?

Never to have told me about having a wife and kid . . . It makes me wonder whether I really knew him at all.

And indeed, there's worse to come. In 1999, it seems, his poor wife died accidentally in their army accommodation in Tidworth Camp, south of Marlborough, and Christian was put on trial for manslaughter. He was acquitted, but in a terse statement delivered on the courtroom steps, blamed the army for letting him down. How did the tabloids never dig this up?

I'm so shocked by this revelation that I have to sit down to absorb it. Setting aside the bitter sense of having been betrayed, it dawns on me that these terrible events are likely to have had repercussions down the line, and ruined other lives as well as his.

I need to find out more about his early life and career – and fast. There's one person who may be able to help with some deep background on Christian, and that's Jerome.

* * *

All too soon the students file back in. Stephen looks OK – no sign of whiplash – and I'm informed De'Lyse will be ten minutes late because she's offering leftover morsels from lunch to the police team. I hope they'll be impressed by our efforts.

News of Christian's untimely death has travelled far and wide, and we find ourselves in the eye of a tornado. #RIPChristian is trending on social media, and the twenty-four-hour news channels are looping eulogies from leading lights of the food world, including two dames and a rash of CBEs. A dozen chefs are claiming he was 'like a brother' to them, including one whom I know for a fact he never met. The Savoy, where he worked for two disastrous months in 2003, has declared a week of mourning and the students of a catering college he never attended or visited are holding a vigil.

To the disdain of Rose, soggy bouquets are piling up along the railings of number forty-one faster than the funeral director can remove them.

Who would have thought it? When I go, will I be lamented by friends I never had?

Despite the careful packing of my Gladstone bag this morning, everything's got jumbled up, so I ask teacher's pet Lilith to lay the spices out in alphabetical order on my bench.

'Why do so many begin with C?' she asks. Good question, and one to which I've never found an answer. We pass them round, rubbing and sniffing.

De'Lyse, arriving with a glow about her (I daresay she had the SOCOs eating out of the palm of her hand), says she and her mum buy spices in large packs from a shop in Peckham. They're a household of five (including three younger brothers – what a handful) and use spices in huge quantities.

Eventually we get to pepper. A nub of wisdom passed down through the Delamare family – probably since we arrived in this country as Huguenot refugees in 1685 – is 'pepper flies', so should always be added at the end. At mention of the word, Harriet starts squeaking uncontrollably – what's known as the 'pixie sneeze', as favoured by the upper classes.

'Breathe into a paper bag,' says Lilith.

'Rubbish, that's for hiccoughs,' says Vicky. 'Say "watermelon", then keep repeating it.' To general amazement, this works.

After that we move on to herbs. I get wistful at the mention of them, because I don't have a garden, and with the exception of a bay pyramid and a couple of rosemary bushes I keep in pots on the front step, have to buy cut herbs at outrageous expense from the supermarket or farmers' market.

Needless to say, Vicky wants to talk about frozen herbs. I can see some of the others looking down their noses at the idea, but I've tried them and they're acceptable, so long as you stir them into dishes, rather than scatter. Last-word Lilith trumps the rest of us by announcing you can freeze fresh herbs in ice cubes, though I can't think of many things improved by having ice cubes thrown into them, unless you count a gin and tonic.

At this point, a buzzer goes off and it's time for our bread doughs, all plump and risen, to go into the oven. While the students score and glaze I creep into a corner, because I want to make a sneaky call and can't wait a moment longer.

'Jerome, it's Paul.'

'Dear boy!' he shouts back – he's become rather deaf over the years. I can hear operatic music surging in the background, which can't help. 'I've been enjoying a rather fine luncheon – just the thing for a rainy day. Smoked salmon from that place on the Somerset Levels, with a glass of Meursault.'

A glass or three, if I know Jerome.

'I say!' he continues, coming too close to the mouthpiece, which distorts his voice. '*Deeyooeeraboutkareesa*?' I take this to mean – did I hear about Christian?

I can't face going into the details now, not with Lilith creeping about, ears flapping. So I just reply, 'Yes. Simply terrible. In fact, that's why I'm—'

'Aaspo-ooeeemosaadaay.'

'Jerome, please hold the phone further away. I can't hear what you're saying.'

'Is that any better? I was just saying, I spoke to him on Sunday, I think. Yes, it was definitely Sunday, because my neighbour was coming over for a pre-prandial, only she cancelled at the last minute because of a crisis involving her daughter. The one who's married to a vet.'

I don't know who any of these people are, and really don't care. But interesting that he and Christian spoke so recently.

'Yes,' Jerome continues. 'He phoned me, quite out of the blue, saying he'd broken a limb of some description, and could I think of anyone who could cover his job for him at short notice? A cookery class for Belgravia ladies. He said he'd gone through his address book from A to Z and not a bite. I wish I'd thought of you, except you're such a busy boy nowadays.'

I suck in a breath; not quite how Christian sold it to me.

'Jerome,' I say, 'I need your help.' I cup my hand around my phone, aware of a purple presence pulsating just behind me. 'I need to track down Christian's family, or anyone he knew before he came to London. It's urgent. Can you help?'

Jerome Marnier is a much-loved fixture of the food world, harking back to the days of the gentleman host, when dilapidated properties could be picked up cheap and transformed into country house hotels, and TV chefs were despatched to Tuscany for a month to knock out a couple of Chianti-soaked cooking shows. The early nineties were his glory years, when money was pouring in from books and part-works; the first time the Queen Mother ate in a public restaurant, she chose Jerome's in Camden Passage.

He dissipated his fortune as quickly as he accumulated it, buying and losing a riad in Marrakesh, a flat in Paris and a villa on a Greek island, since when he has depended on the kindness of munificent friends and patrons.

Ever since I've known him, he has lived in a gracious home with ample supplies of everything, but this is perhaps because every year or two, when a patron's generosity wears thin, he moves on. (I wonder if there is some kind of register of rich, grand people willing to sponsor the needy and deserving, and if so, whether I can put my name down.) Jerome's current abode is an exquisite Regency hunting lodge overlooking the Teign Estuary in South Devon, on the estate of the Marquess of Somewhere-or-other.

Christian was one of Jerome's protégés, and although from such different worlds and backgrounds, they found much to enjoy in each other's company. Jerome was drawn to Christian's charm and dash, to say nothing of his dazzling looks; Christian to the older man's repartee and limitless fund of funny stories, mainly about the rich and famous. I was a bit of a bolt-on, and never felt Jerome found me interesting enough.

'Christian . . . early life? Not that I know of,' he replies. 'He was from Wiltshire – not my favourite county, not by a long shot. Wild and windswept. Druids. Mind you, Salisbury Cathedral is rather fine – I hope you've read *Martin Chuzzlewit*?' I feel as if I'm trapped in a Spirograph set, where your pen goes round and round creating lovely shapes, but you forget why you started.

I hear a scraping sound and turn to see Lilith wedge herself behind the recycling bin in a crouching posture.

'Jerome, can you remember anything at all about Christian from his pre-London period? Any friends or contacts?'

'Hmm,' he says, lingeringly. 'Well, long, long ago there was a sister, but they were non-speaks. Hmm . . . Let me rootle about for my address book. Mrs Vobe will keep putting my things where I can't find them – she's my *femme de ménage*. Has a withered arm, like in the Bible. Don't go away.'

I am left listening to the music, Callas singing 'Vissi d'arte', with Jerome booming along in basso profundo. Hours later, there is violent clunking and he's back. I hear a puffing sound, then the crack of a lighter.

'Sorry, cigar went out. Here it is. Under the Ws.' Pages rustle. 'Didn't our Christian move around a lot! Here we are – Barbara. Did you know that *Barbara* means "bearded lady" in Latin?'

I write down the address. 'Thanks, Jerome. I really do have to dash.' I cover my phone and yell out, 'Harriet – rolls are ready!'

'What are you having for dinner tonight?' Jerome asks. 'I've got some rather nice lamb cutlets that I'm going to . . .'

When I finally extract myself, I swing round to find a new drama unfolding. For a second I think Melanie's face is contorted with laughter, then I realize she's sobbing; it's strange how one can muddle up the two. Lady B has an arm around her, and Gregory is urgently straightening the utensils on his workbench, embarrassed.

'I'm so sorry,' she says, when I approach. 'Cressida's been on the phone again. Ben . . . well, we're not sure where he's gone.'

'How long has he been missing?' I ask.

'Since Monday night, according to Cressie.'

Hmm. So much for his full English yesterday morning.

'Is this a regular thing of his, disappearing without telling anyone?' asks Lady B down her nose.

'It's happened before,' admits Melanie, mopping up the tears.

'Is there somewhere he ought to be? Does he have a job, I mean?' I ask.

'Absolutely – he's head of security for a fine art dealer. The Strebi Gallery in Old Burlington Street. It's been going so well for him too over the past few months. This time, I really thought . . .'

'Don't you think you should go home?' suggests Lady B.

'Obviously that's what Cressida wants. She always . . . blames me. But coming away like this – it was a big thing for me. I'm worn out by running everyone's life for them. I just can't do it any more.' She starts weeping in earnest, and I turn away.

The tension of this stressful afternoon is further racked up when a pair of female police constables march in; they have a bustling, rambunctious traffic warden look about them, as if they've caught you on a double yellow.

They take up position with backs to the double doors, hands on hips, ready to prevent a getaway; a dangerous place to stand, but that's their own look-out.

'No cause for alarm,' says the larger of the two, though the look in her eyes means *don't anyone try anything*.

The other, half the size of her colleague, pipes up in a thin, reedy squeak: 'We would like to speak to a Missus – er . . .' Gregory adjusts his hearing aid while she peers down nervously at a piece of paper. 'A Mrs Lilith Something – I'm not sure how you say it.'

The beefy one glares at her and snatches away the paper. 'Lilith Mostyn. Let's be having you.'

All eyes swivel to Lilith, who has turned bright pink beneath her violet thatch.

'Concerning what?' she asks. I've never seen a puff adder, but I bet this is what one looks like when it's cornered.

The bigger cop's eyes sparkle: maybe she'll get to use her Taser. 'Come along quietly now, madam. We have a car waiting.'

At which Lilith, humphing and tutting, is marched off into captivity.

CHAPTER 27

The students are flabbergasted, and so am I. Who'd have thought Lilith was mixed up in all this?

As usual, I ask if everyone is happy for the course to continue, and as usual they accede. I think this is more because they can't imagine how else they might occupy themselves than because they really want to learn about the finer points of cooking with chocolate. I choose not to remind them about the cancelled fish class, in case they start clamouring for refunds; meanwhile, the breads have all been baked to shining glory and the smell is intoxicating.

De'Lyse takes lots of pictures but I'm not sure if or when she'll be posting them on social media. This morning she posted photos of her lemon tart and they didn't go down well. 'Shame on you, De'Lyse – some people have no 🖤' commented one of her followers, after which they piled in like lemmings about her callousness and lack of respect. She shrugged it off, saying that in a few hours it will have blown over.

I suggest to the students that once the breads have cooled, we can freeze them to be taken home tomorrow. This is music to Vicky's ears, and from nowhere she produces a Tupperware box of freezer supplies, including multicoloured Sharpies.

At last it's time for tea. 'Join you later,' I say as they head off, Melanie trailing along behind, glued to her phone.

* * *

It's a highly inconsiderate husband who just vanishes on a whim, so I decide to run a quick check on this Ben Hardy-Powell character. Considering he was a commissioned officer in the military, there's surprisingly little on Google. The Strebi Gallery specializes in the style known as 'neo-realist' – dancing couples, curvaceous dolphins, scantily clad women against ocean backgrounds. Not to my taste, but absolutely no mention of Ben. Nothing on Facebook either.

I hope to have more luck with Barbara Wagner. What if she goes by a married name, and Jerome simply scribbled her down under Christian's name in his address book? It would be typically careless of him.

I tap in the name and the first entry that comes up is for a Brazilian choreographer. I add 'Swindon' and get nothing, then try 'telephone number'. Nothing. With some reluctance I open LinkedIn (too corporate for my taste) and learn it has 500+ Barbara Wagners (which I doubt), the queen bee being a Director of First Impressions (head receptionist?) at a motel in Nevada. Which leaves Facebook, where I find a dozen Barbara Wagner Somethings, including lots in Germany, and then . . . *eureka*! A Barbara Wagner Edwards, of Swindon.

As fast as my heart jumps, it plummets. I know about this awful Facebook phenomenon that when someone dies, their relatives spend the next five years locked in combat with Mark Zuckerberg to get their page taken down – and I'm guessing that's what's happening here. The last post from Barbara herself is dated autumn 2019 – a photo taken with her dog in front of a lake – after which the only posts are from friends and family, saying they love and miss her.

I can see the resemblance to Christian – particularly around the lips and cheekbones – but she looks older than her brother ever became and has a troubled, careworn look; perhaps she was dragged down by illness.

How is one ever to know what private turmoil is going on in a stranger's life? A friend was going through a torrid divorce when one day she found herself in the back of a taxi being driven by a rude, miserable cabbie: she became so angry with him it turned into a screaming match until they reached Paddington, at which point the taxi driver turned round to her and apologized, tears streaming down his face. He'd just heard his wife's cancer had returned. He wouldn't let her pay the fare, and they wept in each other's arms on the station steps.

Someone called Isla Edwards has commented about 'missing our dear mum' so I call up her profile. Late twenties, sharp features, beauty therapist. I send a short message, asking her to contact me urgently about her uncle.

* * *

Our class is called *Well-tempered Chocolate*, the purpose of tempering being to give chocolate gloss and 'snap'. From a scientific point of view, what you're doing is causing the cocoa solids to crystallize in a specific, orderly way, rather than chaotically. To achieve this, you warm, cool, then rewarm the chocolate to specific temperatures. If it sounds tricky – a bore, even – it is. Professional chocolatiers can do it in their sleep, but I make an executive decision. We're not going to bother.

On the other hand, 'seizing' – when melted chocolate goes all thick and grainy – is worth knowing about. It feels like the end of the world when it happens, so as an experiment that is useful on more than one level, I want to see how my students react when such a disaster strikes.

I ask everyone to measure out chocolate chips and melt

them, using their usual method. At all costs, make sure it doesn't seize.

'Why chips?' demands Lady B. As they put it in the Old Testament, this is a woman who 'sits in the seat of the scornful'.

'Because it's so messy chopping it up,' I reply. 'Unless of course you've got servants.' This puts her in her place.

She and daughter set up pans of water and rummage about in the cupboards to find Pyrex bowls. Vicky and De'Lyse race for the microwave. Stephen and Gregory, who have evidently never melted chocolate in their lives, pour their chips straight into saucepans and flame up the gas.

I'm interested in conjuring, and familiar with the concept of misdirection. As I patrol the benches, muttering words of encouragement and comparing notes about the weather, I surreptitiously flick water into bowls, crank up the gas and switch the microwave to 'boost': surefire ways to ruin good chocolate.

First casualty is Vicky, who opens the microwave and declares: 'What the heck . . .?' Lady B blames the Hon., who I'm glad to hear answer back for once: 'Oh, put a sock in it, Mummy. It's because you keep shouting.' At which point Harriet, realizing her chocolate has seized too, shrugs and plonks herself down on a stool.

In the brouhaha, I watch from the corner of my eye as Stephen slips his pan, complete with coagulated chocolate, into the nearest bin, finds a new one and without a word starts over: not exactly playing straight. Gregory slams his pan against the bench. 'Something wrong with the chocolate, I fear.'

At this point I own up. 'Seizing can happen to the best of us – you need to know what to do next.' They don't seem particularly amused, but I show them how to make it smooth again by – counterintuitively – beating in cold water, a teaspoon at time. 'Or you can just use it as it is – for instance, in choc-chip cookies.'

My eye is caught by my Gladstone bag, still on the workbench in front of me. 'Anyone heard of tonka beans?'

* * *

Small and leathery, like wrinkled black almonds, tonka beans are produced by a tree native to South America called *Dipteryx odorata.* It's hard to describe their potent fragrance – a mix of vanilla, pear drops, spice and furniture polish. They're one of only two spices that inform you of their presence in the kitchen even before you open the jar. (The other being asafoetida.)

You can grate tonka into custards, creams or ice creams, as you would nutmeg, and it also sings in harmony with coffee and nuts. Today we grate about a quarter of a bean into our chocolate-chip cookie mix, to give a vaguely tropical spiciness. I pass the rest of the beans around the class, for everyone to smell.

'I'm not sure I care for it,' announces Lady B. 'Don't sniff it, Harriet, it's not for you.'

She inhales deeply. 'Lovely,' she says, glaring back at her mother.

What adds to the general thrill – I can't help but notice Vicky in particular prick up her ears at this point – is that tonka contains coumarin, a powerful poison, and must be used sparingly.

'How do you define sparingly?' asks Gregory.

'Go by flavour,' I reply. 'If it tastes too strong, you've used too much.'

'Absurd,' he says. 'You're saying the only way to find out if it's poisonous is to be poisoned by it.'

I continue, 'If you like the smell of tonka, there's a fragrance based on it. It's a bit of a collector's item, but I'm sure they sell it at the perfume shop over in Elizabeth Street.' This gem of a shop sells hundreds of rare and limited-edition scents – people travel from all over the world to visit. 'It's a cologne called Après un Rêve.'

I have a personal reason for being attached to it, but I'm certainly not sharing that with the class.

When I ask for the tonka beans to be returned to me, I find I'm a couple short. I recall something similar happening at school – a parents' drug awareness evening where all the samples disappeared. Two beans are enough to make someone extremely ill, administered properly. Or maybe someone just likes the smell.

* * *

The cookies come out of the oven and we end up with far more than we need. De'Lyse arranges the most shapely on plates and skips off to share them with her new police friends.

The students use the pause to check their phones, as do I. A quick scan of my emails shows that word is out about my involvement in the current calamity. I've more or less lost touch with my friends after so long in the wilderness, so I suspect some of those messaging are more interested in tasty gossip than 'how I'm doing'. I'm about to log out when I notice a message via Facebook . . . from Isla. My heart jumps.

> Never met him but saw it on the news. Mum and him didn't speak. Why have you contacted me?

I don't expect others to polish their sentences to the same lapidary perfection as I do, but it's a bit abrupt. On the other hand, she's the only lead I've got, and she's left the door ajar. I message back:

Please will you phone me about Christian?
I promise it will only take ten minutes.

Then I add my number on a new line.

As I hit send, the doors fly open and in gallops De'Lyse.

'You'll never believe it!' she declares. 'Not in a million years!'

We gather round, agog.

'You know the guys in the white coats – forensics? Well, they loved the cookies, so I ask the friendly one: what's the story on Lilith?'

She has us in the palm of her hand.

'He said not to go telling everyone – obviously you're not everyone, we're friends now, after all we've been through. They found something up there.' She gestures in the direction of the courtyard, and Christian's flat.

The anticipation is unbearable. Lady B claws at her workbench and I can see Gregory's Adam's apple jumping up and down.

'And you know what it was?' asks our tormentor.

Get on with it!

'It was a hair, a human hair. Long and fine – likely a woman's. But there was one thing about it that was very strange. It was purple.'

CHAPTER 28

I find London strangely beautiful as darkness begins to fall, most of all when it's raining. I love the way the street lights and headlamps reflect in the puddles, the gay glint and twinkle of shop windows being illuminated, the cosy glow of domestic life peeping out before blinds are pulled and curtains drawn.

Tonight I've decided to go home between the end of class and dinner: I've got enough time, and if the students are going to deck themselves out in full finery again, the least I can do is put on a clean shirt. I've also booked a Zoom call (or rather, efficient Julie has) for half past six.

I'm in a world of my own as I pad along Chester Row, mulling over another astounding day of shocks and surprises. It seems unbelievable that yesterday started out as just a normal morning, and look where we are now.

I cast my mind back to Christian's flat, and the murder scene itself. Did I miss anything, among the strange, apparently random scattering of clues? The lipstick and lingering perfume . . . the open bottle of wine . . . The scarf, unwrapped but never tried on . . . The folder on the coffee table. And now, this incriminating hair.

I stop briefly a couple of times, once waiting to cross South Eaton Place, then outside the Duke of Boots, where they've posted up their new autumn menu. My other local is the Fox and Hounds in Passmore Street, which has a real coal fire and where you're likely to bump into actors from the Royal Court.

I'm sure it's me being neurotic, but each time I stop, I look back in the direction I'm coming from, and a dark figure with an umbrella stops dead.

At the corner of Skinner Place I stop and look back a third time, steeling myself for an encounter with my nemesis. The figure produces a key and lets himself into a house in Caroline Terrace. Not Jonny, but some poor fellow wearing a surgical boot. It's got to the point where I'm hallucinating.

Arriving at the green front door of Jubilee Cottage, I ask myself, as I always do, what I did to deserve to live here? I'm the son of a country doctor – people like me don't live in Belgravia. The police last night couldn't work out how I could afford to live in such a prestigious place, and they were right: I'm an imposter.

Except I'm not. This is my home. I live here and I intend to continue doing so until my dying day. Not only that: I have a legal right to do so.

* * *

At the time I entered Marcus's life, he was emerging from two years of the most appalling stress and upset; part of me still believes this is what triggered his final illness, even though the doctors said they doubted it.

The upheaval was caused by his divorce proceedings, which started after his and Olinda's silver wedding anniversary. They had married rather young – when Marcus was twenty-one – but managed to carve out a satisfactory life together for all those years. Marcus was always discreet with me about his marriage, commendably so, but from what I can tell, they made it work by living in parallel. He threw himself into his career as a corporate lawyer, and Olinda . . . Well, she pleased herself.

It would be easy to paint my partner's ex as a vain, selfish, petty, vindictive, pointless kind of person . . . because that's exactly what she is. But let's dwell on the positives: she plays a good hand of bridge and arranges flowers like an angel.

In the late nineties they bought a great big mansion in Hampshire and that's when the relationship started to unravel. Oddly enough, Jubilee Cottage was the final nail in the coffin. Marcus bought it on a whim, without telling his wife, from an old friend who was moving to a retirement home.

By this time Marcus was based in the City and the idea was that he would spend weeknights at Jubilee Cottage, and Olinda would take the train up and join him whenever she wanted to see friends or do something in town. He honestly believed his wife would be delighted with his acquisition, and boast about it to her friends.

For her first visit – as a surprise – Marcus pushed the boat out. Pulbrook and Gould came in and filled the place with flowers. Mosimann's supplied supper (turbot en croûte with sauce mousseline). Krug on ice. Candles everywhere.

Whether it was premeditated or just a random act of malice, Olinda breezed in, surveyed each room (which can't have taken long) and announced she hated it. Marcus was ordered to summon a cab which, it later transpired, conveyed her not to Waterloo, but all the way to West Meon, at a cost of £478 charged to his credit card.

Obviously, I can't talk about Olinda and Marcus without mentioning their son Jonathan, or Jonny as they always referred to him. The first thing to state is that he is only two years younger than I am, which must be difficult for him on all sorts of levels.

As I understand it, however, he was bad from the get-go.

His parents were probably too young (he arrived a couple of months after they were married), then Marcus started travelling and the boy's upbringing and education were left to his mother. What with the stealing, and the bullying, and the knives, and the drugs, it came to a point where the education system gave up on him altogether, and it's a wonder he can read and write.

I should add, in fairness to him, that he's apparently not all bad. He's a talented mimic (he does a brilliant Paul Delamare, as I know to my cost) and can draw (he's a graphic novelist). I believe he also keeps a house rabbit – an American chinchilla – which some might find endearing.

It interests me that a lot of Jonny's early problems concerned money, of which, ironically, there was never any shortage. His bullying took the form of extorting cash from those weaker, smaller or younger than him.

The real crunch came, inevitably, when Marcus died. Before then Olinda had procured for herself a staggeringly generous divorce settlement. There was some dubious collusion between the legal teams – both QCs, so they should have known better – and she ended up with the country mansion, half his investments, half his pensions, a guaranteed income for the rest of her life, and – this made me laugh – a lavish educational and training budget to equip her to make her own way in the world. Throw in a car, plus half the value of Jubilee Cottage, and you can see why Marcus, flogging into the City each morning and working his guts out, might have been just a shade resentful of his former wife, whose only responsibilities were to check how many 'smiles' she received on eHarmony and get her nails done before lunch.

One of the arguments put forward by Olinda's legal team was that Marcus had over twenty years of working life remaining during which to restore his financial situation. This explains why, at the time of his death, he had precious little in the bank, and why I currently find myself in the situation I do. We should have married, but by the time we got round to discussing it, he was already very ill and it felt unseemly.

When he died, he left me a life share in Jubilee Cottage – what used to be called in olden days 'usufruct'. I can live here (so long as I pay all the bills) but I can't make alterations to the property, sell it, or rent it out. Before the end, he also begged me to be kind to my stepson, and if he was ever in distress, do what I could to help him.

Of course, Jonny went ballistic when he found out about Jubilee Cottage. 'Why should I slum it in a rat-infested basement in Earls Court while fag-boy lounges about in *MY* house?' was how he charmingly put it.

The first thing he did was challenge his father's will, which gobbled up a large chunk of his inheritance. After that, he came over all nice guy, took me out to lunch and told me Marcus had promised him Jubilee Cottage, so why wouldn't I do the 'right thing'? Since then, he's decided to make my life here such hell that I'll pack up and go.

A month ago, when Marcus's probate finally went through, the solicitor let slip that Jonny had gone to Brazil – would be away till at least Christmas. No such luck. Now he's back, I know it's all-out war.

* * *

Whenever I tell the story of Marcus, I know people wonder how he can have been married all those years, and had a son, if he was gay? These are delicate areas, and I never thought it my place to wade in and demand answers from him. He certainly loved Olinda when they married – in photographs he kept, you can see it in their eyes. He was also thrilled to become a father.

I believe he stuck with the marriage until he could bear it no longer. At some point he realized he was attracted to men, but did nothing about it until the day he was having his hair cut and was struck by what he described as a thunderbolt. What an honour that it happened to be me he fell in love with.

When Olinda found out that her ex-husband had a *boyfriend*, she was, in her usual perverse way, pleased. ('So it wasn't my fault, after all,' she clearly told herself, before phoning all their mutual friends to share the gossip.) Jonny, considerably less so.

I feel Marcus's presence in my life even though he's gone. I wear his wristwatch. People don't seem to wear watches as much nowadays – a pity, as it's a more elegant way to check the time than peering at a phone – but this is an Audemars Piguet, understated steel with a blue dial. I can't begin to imagine how they squeeze an automatic mechanism into such a wafer-thin case.

On his desk in front of me now is his tortoiseshell fountain pen, alongside a bottle of Diamine ink. I have a knack for remembering people's handwriting – part of me wishes I'd trained as a graphologist – and I remember the first time I saw his swift, flowing italics, the graceful way he wrote a simple word like *Paul*.

And in every room, there's the whisper of Après un Rêve. If you look it up, the perfume house tells you it has top notes of liquorice and coffee, middle notes of sandalwood and iris and base notes of tonka, patchouli and musk. For a time I started wearing it myself – there's a huge bottle of it in the bathroom – but then I began to stop noticing it, which made me even sadder.

My introspective mood is lifted by the sound of my computer coming to life, which must be Julie's call coming through. Please let it be good news.

CHAPTER 29

Julie bought me this circular lamp that clips onto your computer so you're flatteringly lit when making a Zoom call. It has four different 'tones' and half a dozen degrees of light, but on-screen I still look like Banquo's Ghost.

She, on the other hand, doesn't need artificial assistance to look gorgeous. Glossy hair, flawless skin: she doesn't have to spend a fortune on La Prairie and Covent Garden hairdressers – it just comes naturally. She has brought her laptop into the *Escape* meeting room, a fish tank in the centre of the editorial department, with magazine people scuttling about with layouts, contact sheets, flat-plans and clipboards on the other side of the glass. You'd think they'd tuck a meeting room away, so the people in it had at least an illusion of privacy, but no. Probably something else Richard Buzz picked up from his time at 'Harvard'.

'You'd find it better if you fix the Zoom lamp lower down,' advises Julie. 'It's making your head look shiny.'

I do as I'm told. 'Tell me everything,' I say.

'You first,' Julie counters.

'Business as usual,' I reply. 'That's what Rose and the students seem to want. Meanwhile the school is under siege by paparazzi and riot police. How was your rehearsal?'

'Oh, you're sweet to ask. Our new conductor wants us to do this Glenn Miller choreography, where you stand up when you get a solo and blast it out, which is awkward for me because of the angle of the clarinet's mouthpiece. Anyway, I said I'd try it out in "I Am The Walrus" but I overbalanced and landed on top of first trumpet. Everyone had a good laugh, as you can imagine.'

Julie is nimble and graceful, but you wouldn't want her landing on you. I think the fact she refuses to aspire to a size zero is one reason why Dena refuses to acknowledge her talent.

'So tell me what happened at your meeting,' I say. 'Are we out on the street?'

'Well . . .' She scans her eyes around to check there are no listeners glued to the glass walls. 'Do you want the good news or the bad?'

'Good news, just for a change.'

'Well, I did what you said and dragged Lucinda and Spencer off into the beauty cupboard.' Magazines have these cavernous walk-in spaces where they store samples and props for editorial meetings and photoshoots. You may remember the fashion cupboard in *The Devil Wears Prada* but beauty cupboards are even bigger because of all the freebies. 'I told them our only hope was to work as a team and present a united front to Dena.'

'How did they take it?' I ask.

'You can guess. Lucinda started waving about these peculiar decorations she'd called in from the Swedish shop – gnomes and mice made of felt, wooden snowflakes, beige baubles . . . And Spencer had obviously made a quick phone call to his ex, the one who's on *RuPaul's Drag Race*, and was brandishing a pair of thigh-length platform boots.

'So I put on my serious look and said that in less than a quarter of an hour Dena was going to go berserk – might even kill someone – if we walked into her office with Scandi Blah and *Real Housewives of Cheshire*. That's when I told them your idea.'

'Well, we came up with it together, really,' I say, modestly. 'And did Dena go for it?'

'Go for it?' squeals Julie. 'She *loves* it. But that brings me to the bad news . . . She said that if the shoot comes off and we survive the headcount massacre, she's going to take us both to lunch.'

At this point I become aware of a weird gurgling, popping sound and a bluish fog creeps across the screen. Julie backs away gagging and a tiny, scarlet-draped blur comes into view, sucking on a vape. Don't look now, it's Dena.

'Paul!' she shrieks into the microphone, so loudly I almost levitate: she is proud of her caterwaul, having honed it during five cut-throat years on old Fleet Street. Then she comes right up close to the camera. Light bounces off her super-white porcelain veneers, causing the screen to flicker, and she waggles a crimson talon.

'Julie told me you've sorted the reshoot – great news! It would break my heart –' patting the place where, in a normal person, a heart would be – 'to see you both chucked onto the scrap heap!'

* * *

Julie keeps trying to encourage me to step out of my sartorial comfort zone, but so far I've resisted. My 'look' – if you can call it that – is grey or black trousers or denims; decent trainers; plus a proper shirt.

Marcus and I took the same shirt size, so as far as that goes, I've a lifetime's supply of the latter. By 'proper' I mean pure cotton, properly sewn – not overlocked with stubby seams and stick-out collars. He swore by Jermyn Street – smooth poplins or Swiss cotton, discreet patterns that never date.

In honour of the occasion, I decide on a cream shirt with pale blue and navy stripes plus some cufflinks Marcus gave me. His last birthday gift. To complete the look, proper leather shoes, which Julie tells me make me look like a gentleman. I feel different when I walk in them – more upright and assured.

I jump into the shower. Above the noise of the water, I can hear my phone ringing so I drip my way across the bedroom to my phone. The number on-screen starts *01793*, which I know to be the code for Swindon.

'Paul Delamare,' I announce. Long pause.

'It's Isla here,' she says. 'Isla Edwards.'

'Thank you so much for phoning – I'm very grateful.'

'So what do you want?' Her voice is tense, suspicious, as if she's had past experience of people trying to take advantage.

'I was a friend of your uncle's . . . of Christian's,' I say, trying to sound casual and unassuming.

'So you said in your message. Horrible thing to happen. You're not a reporter, are you?'

'No, just an old friend. The reason I got in touch is because I'm trying to track people down from the earlier part of his life, before he came to London. To let them know what's happened.'

'I expect they saw it on the news,' she says.

'Quite so. But there will be a memorial service later on. I can make sure they're invited,' I add, unconvincingly.

Silence.

'So, at this point, I'm just hoping for names and phone numbers.'

'Isn't that the sort of thing the police do?' she asks.

'They're working flat out on it, but as an old friend, I'd like to do what I can to help.'

'You know Mum passed a couple of years ago? Chris was her younger brother.'

'Yes, I did know that,' I reply, omitting to add that I found out via Facebook. 'Christian – Chris – didn't talk much about his family.'

'She'd have been gutted. She loved her kid brother even though they hadn't spoken for years.'

'Did you know him well yourself?' I ask.

'Not at all. He disappeared when I was five or six.'

'Disappeared?'

'Went off to London. Mum never saw him after that neither, though they kept in touch for a while. Do they know who did it?'

'As I said, the police are working on it. Is there anything at all you can tell me about his early life?'

'Not a lot. It was mostly before I was born. They lived in Dorcan.'

'Is that part of Swindon?'

'You've got Dorcan and you've got Covingham. That's where Mum lived. I'm in Stratton, up near the big Sainsbury's.'

'He was in the army, I think.'

'He was.'

'And there was that terrible accident involving his wife,' I add, implying that he confided in me about it, rather than failed to mention it for twenty years.

Isla pauses. 'Mum said it wrecked his life. Though in the long run things seem to have turned out OK for him.' Another pause. 'Till now, I s'pose.'

'I was hoping you might be able to put me in touch with your cousin.'

Her voice sharpens: 'I haven't got a cousin.' Another pause, then: 'Oh, if you mean Uncle Chris's kids—'

'Yes – of course, there was more than one,' I say. Children *plural*: something else I've just learnt, along with the geography of Britain's most boring town.

'I'm sure he told you – they were the reason him and Mum fell out. She was made their legal guardian – all done properly, a court order – but there was no money. She already had my kid brother and me, and she was on her own and working shifts. They had to be adopted out – there was no other way.'

Christian, Christian – what a sad and tangled web. And those poor children!

With that, Isla finishes the call as abruptly as she started it.

'I'm sorry about Uncle Chris, but I've no idea where the kids are now, and even if I did, it's none of your business. Don't contact me again.'

CHAPTER 30

Drinks tonight have been relocated to the grandeur of the Strang Room. The rain has started up again and provides a gentle background drumbeat. To add to the sense of occasion, Suzie has transferred the bedraggled flower arrangements from the front hall and laid out dishes of nibbles. Pringles and peanuts certainly have their place – for instance, if you're watching football – but it's a pity she didn't think to pick up a few olives or bits of charcuterie instead.

All talk is of Lilith, and De'Lyse – as self-appointed crime correspondent in chief – is at its epicentre.

'I thought there was something odd about her from the start,' she says, wagging a finger. She's resplendent in a shimmering silk cocktail number – like last night's sequins, gold – which appears to have been moulded around her supple curves. 'Why come on a course where you can't eat half the food?'

'She had a nasty side to her,' says Vicky. She too has pushed out the sartorial boat, though without similar success; a tiger-print top over some brown faux-leather jeggings, as I've heard Julie refer to them, that have the unfortunate effect of making it seem as though the big cat has moulted.

Even gentle Harriet joins in: 'Did anyone else see her when we were sharpening the knives? There she was, pretending to be interested in spatchcocking chickens, when all along she was planning—'

Lady B narrows her eyes. 'Don't be morbid, darling,' she says. 'I told you before, let the police do their job. It's bad enough what happened without picking over it like a vulture.'

Tonight, Gregory is in pink trousers, a sartorial step too far. 'I think what your mother is saying, Harriet, is that until we know the facts, it would be unfair to speculate. Although, speaking for myself, there is one thing I find highly intriguing. If the incriminating lock of hair—'

'It was a single hair,' interjects Vicky. 'No one said it was a tuft.'

'My apologies. I'm speculating as to whether the "single hair" in question was deposited in Christian's private quarters during the committing of the crime, or as a result of some, er, personal interaction between the two of them. After all, as is generally known, he could not resist the lure of the ladies.' He's twisting the stem of his glass so hard I'm surprised it doesn't snap.

'De'Lyse, did they find it in a pool of blood or on his pillow?' asks Vicky, not one to beat about the bush.

'They didn't say. But I can ask my forensics friend.'

'On the other hand,' says Vicky, 'can you really see those two – *together*?' She widens her eyes, an effect rendered nightmarish by the super-strength lenses.

This receives a harrumph from Lady B, who stalks off to speak to Melanie, sitting quietly in a wingback chair near the sepulchral chimneypiece, flaming hair arranged becomingly around her shoulders.

Stephen is also standing on his own, studying one of the portraits. Like the rest of us, he has made an effort tonight, in a light blue suit and white shirt buttoned up to the neck. For the first time I notice the faint shadow of a beard, so light it might almost have been brushed on for effect. It seems de rigueur for young men today to show off their facial hair – if they're lucky enough to have any – but there's never been anything wrong with clean-shaven.

I move to join him and glance up at the paintings. 'I hope my ancestors were a bit more cheerful than this lot,' I say, to break the ice.

'I think this must be Rose's great-grandfather, the one who invented the dishwasher,' he replies. It's a fair guess, as the forebear in question is holding a sort of turbine. And that's what I call a beard.

'I was sorry to have missed this morning's tour,' I say. 'What did you make of it?'

'Hmm. I'm not really into all that *stuff*. Handing it down between generations, like it's your sacred duty, because this wooden spoon once belonged to your grandmother. I don't think that's how things work anymore – you should be allowed to be yourself.'

'I see what you mean,' I say, trying to work out how to steer the subject round to my next question. 'After all, most of our existence nowadays is virtual – online, I mean.' He nods. 'You mentioned you were playing a video game the other night. I've never got into them.'

He eyes me curiously. 'It was an escape-room game called *Ghoulster*.'

'Do you play it on your own, or against other people?'

'Lots of us together. The winner is the first person to dig himself out of his grave.'

'I heard the police have been borrowing laptops, confirming where people were when . . . it happened.'

'They'll find it all there in my history, like I told them.'

At this point a hush falls across the room, signalling the entrance of Rose. She has pushed the boat out and wears a beaded black décolleté evening dress, with a creamy cashmere pashmina draped over her upper arms.

I realize I'm staring at her – though only in admiration – so I glance down, which makes it look as if I'm examining her cleavage. All I can think to say is how pretty the Strang Room looks at night.

After that we mingle about with our glasses of wine. I notice Stephen hoovering up the snacks, and hear the Hon. ask Gregory where he buys his trousers. The same place as Michael Portillo allegedly – a mail order company in Brighton – so this week's colour choices could have been even worse.

Rose is staying by the piano, schooner of sherry in hand, and it occurs to me that she might be waiting for someone to ask her to perform. In the past, there would invariably have been a pianist or two at any social gathering, with a *morceau favori* ready on demand.

'Do you play, Rose?' I ask dutifully.

'Oh, not for many years,' she replies, 'but visitors used to say I had a pleasing touch. How the hours would fly by under the spell of the great masters! My beloved Chopin, darling Debussy. Nocturnes . . . arabesques. But then life intervened – marriage, homemaking, bringing up a family. Care upon care – and now this.'

I know from Suzie that Rose has been asking questions behind my back, so I decide to go on the offensive and do some probing of my own.

'I hope to meet Milla one day. Having heard so much about her.'

'Is that so? From whom?'

'Oh, just generally,' I reply. What was it Suzie said? 'And, of course, I read about her in *Tatler*. Does she work in London?'

'Milla has fingers in many pies.'

'She must break a lot of hearts, judging by, er, what I've heard. Do you see much of her?'

'Her aunt left her a small flat at Brompton Cross. Perfect for a young girl about town.'

'She sounds quite something.'

Rose chuckles and taps me coquettishly on the shoulder, as if with a fan or a pair of those long evening gloves ladies used to wear. Then adds, wistfully, 'Of course, she's devastated about Christian. In some ways, he was a father figure to her: always kind, always firm. He was a good influence, I believe.'

I pause in hope she may clarify this, but she stares mistily at the cornice.

'I've enjoyed meeting your old schoolfriend,' I say, checking Melanie is out of earshot. 'Lovely that you've kept up over so many years.'

'Not *that* many years, if you please.'

'Oh! I only meant that she's been married twice and that –' might as well go for it – 'well, you were both close to Christian.'

'Quite so.' Aha, Melanie claimed she hardly knew him! 'We used to call him "the thorn between two roses". Melanie's second name is Rose, you see.'

'What a hoot!' I say. 'And you must know Ben, of course – I'm sorry Melanie's having such a tough time with him.'

'He's one of those men who should never have left the army,' she replies.

At that moment, Suzie, hovering in the doorway, catches my eye and beckons me over. She's normally so calm and expressionless that I can tell immediately there's something wrong.

'There's a problem with that fish you bought,' she hisses. 'It's raw! Don't tell me I have to cook it?'

* * *

I set off to fetch my knife from the Old Ballroom. It feels dark and lonely after the highs and lows of the past few days, the rain hammering on the glass above. I'm unbuckling my knife case when a noise makes me jump. It's De'Lyse – she must have followed me over.

'Hi there,' she says. 'Putting in some overtime?'

'I've got some slicing to do for our first course. Remember what I was saying the other day about always having the right knife for the job?' I lift out my filleting knife, and as an afterthought, my trusty old steel; strange that a lump of metal can invest me with such a sense of comfort and security.

'I heard you talking to Rose about her daughter,' she continues. 'How do you know her?'

It's the first time I've been alone with De'Lyse, and I realize she's one of those people who stands slightly too close, though she probably has no idea she does it.

'Oh, I don't. Someone mentioned her, that's all.'

'You were giving me the third degree the other night about the person I met in the garden,' she says. 'I didn't give you a straight answer.'

'I was just making conversation.'

'Well, it was Milla. Thought you'd be interested.'

'I see,' I say, sounding casual. 'Well, I did find out it was her, but only later.' I hate these situations where you get tangled up in your own improvisation. 'I mean, I saw her the next day and Suzie told me who she was.'

'You seem to have hit it off with Suzie,' De'Lyse says.

'I feel sorry for her. I give her a hand clearing up after meals and we chat. She doesn't seem to have any friends, and Rose doesn't pay her enough to go out and enjoy herself. You're about the same age, so you can imagine how difficult it is for her living in London on her own.'

'She's lucky to find someone she can confide in. In fact, that's what I was hoping to talk to you about.' De'Lyse looks towards the door, moves in so close we're touching and fixes me in the eye. 'I know Rose trusts you,' she says, voice lowered. 'I was hoping, purely out of friendship, and for her own good, you'd put in a word for me? With your experience of the food world – she might listen to you. She respects you.'

Really? 'So what am I meant to be telling her?' I don't like the sound of this.

'That it's time to hand the reins of Chester Square Cookery School to someone else. That I'd make a great principal.'

So crafty De'Lyse is trying to inveigle me into her and Milla's takeover scheme. How Machiavellian.

I think carefully. 'If an opportunity comes up, I'll certainly mention that you've been a, well, very active member of the class.' Trying to sound natural, I change tack. 'Oh, before you go, De'Lyse, we were all comparing notes about Monday night, what we were doing when it happened. Did you hear anything?'

'Checking my alibi?' she declares, laughing. 'But since you ask, we were having a family get-together on Facebook.'

'You keep late hours,' I comment.

'Not for my cousins in Trinidad,' she replies. 'Which reminds me – any idea when we'll get our laptops back?'

'No idea, I'm afraid.'

On her way out, she turns back, as if on a casual afterthought. 'There was something else I meant to say, too. A word of advice. No disrespect but I've noticed the way you look at Stephen. It's not a problem, I've got a younger brother who's gay. But maybe don't make it so *obvious*?'

CHAPTER 31

I love the way the carbon steel glides so effortlessly through the fish, reducing it to wafer-thin slivers. For prosciutto and charcuterie, there's an argument in favour of using one of those gleaming machines with spinning discs and flywheels, but for smoked salmon and gravadlax, you can't beat slicing by hand.

The table tonight has been laid out with name cards. I've been to enough weddings and formal dinners in my time to know that it's perfectly acceptable to adjust the *place à table* as long as no one sees you doing it. Thanks to some clever manoeuvring, I put myself at one end, so that I have everyone in view, with Vicky to one side of me and Melanie the other. Although the general assumption seems to be that the murderer has been caught, there's an unsettled atmosphere and wine flows freely.

I can see why women like wearing fur, on account of its being cuddly and come-touch-me, but it's not the easiest look to get right. Vicky's tiger top has a V neckline, fringed with brown fake fur. From the corner of your eye, and particularly viewed from the side, it looks like a hairy chest – a very hairy one.

I feel for her tonight, deprived of her usual sparring partner, though she's not holding back on the wine.

'I wonder if they're interrogating Lilith *seriously*,' she says with a marked lack of empathy. 'Shining bright lights in her eyes. Waterboarding.'

'I think the police in this country are a bit more civilized than that,' I reply, although it didn't exactly feel like it last night. 'By the way, I couldn't help overhear you telling Lilith you're a fan of Christian's restaurants. Did you ever go to the one in Oxford?'

She pauses for a moment. 'Lilith was trying to stir things up, but I've got nothing to be ashamed of. I went to all of them – some of them more than once.

'You know, the tragedy of it all is only just starting to sink in – the fact I'll never see him again.' For a moment I think she's going to burst into tears, but she manages to hold them back.

'Which was your favourite?' I ask gently.

'Tunbridge Wells. I made an overnight of it and stayed in a hotel. I booked for lunch *and* dinner *and* brunch the next morning, which I don't suppose many people do, and the head waiter person must have sent a message to the kitchen, because Christian came out and spoke to me. I'm not exaggerating, he sat with me for quite a few minutes. Then he had to go back, because they were busy. He would have loved to have spent more time with me.'

'He was very popular with the ladies.' This doesn't go down too well, so I rephrase it. 'I mean, how flattering to be on the receiving end of your admiration.'

'You know how it is when you feel you've known someone all your life – you don't have to say anything? That's what we had. We spoke with our eyes.' She swivels hers round in a way that I've only seen before in toads and lizards.

Gregory barges into the conversation, loud and overbearing as usual.

'Did I hear you mention Tunbridge Wells? That's where I

was born. We should really call it Royal Tunbridge Wells – as appointed by Edward VII.'

'No one's interested in the town,' says Vicky, curtly. 'There was a branch of Christian's Brasserie there.'

'I remember it well,' says Gregory, pouring himself another glass of wine. According to Suzie it's always free on the last night, though Rose is passing it off as another of her magnanimous gestures. 'A very tricky lease when the axe fell.' I shudder; he adds as an afterthought: 'Or so I read in the paper.'

At this point there's a rush to the sideboard for the remaining gravadlax, so I get Vicky back to myself.

'And did you first become, erm, interested in Christian because of *Pass the Gravy!*?'

'I have them all on DVD! And I went to see him at a food show. I don't normally like big crowds, but it was worth it.'

'Must have been quite an undertaking, travelling round the country.'

'I would say it came on gradually. My son had flown the nest by this time and hubby's business was taking off, so he was away a lot.'

I get the sense it is something of a novelty for her to find someone taking an interest in her life. I refill her wine.

'What does hubby do, if you don't mind my asking?'

'He supplies golf clubs to golf clubs. Well, that's his jokey way of putting it, but what it really is, he sells merchandise to golf pros and clubhouses. He's humorous, you see. And he must be good at his job, because as I say, he's away most of the time.'

'Don't you find it a bit boring, being on your own?' I ask. 'Lonely even? I live on my own, and I certainly do.'

'Don't get me wrong, He's very generous. He won't touch my salary from the pharmacy. Says, "Vee" – that's what he calls me – "what you earn is yours. Go spend it." I admit it got out of control at one point, what with all the trains and hotels. He lost it, and things haven't been the same between us since.'

'Oh, I'm sorry to hear that. But you're still together, aren't you?'

'Yes and no. I'm telling you this in strictest confidence –' I notice Gregory adjust his hearing aid – probably zooming in – 'but hubby put two and two together, and found out I had this thing about Christian. Not that there was anything to find out, really. But hubby can get very angry, and it was all I could do to stop him marching down to London and having it out.'

'Does hubby know you're here now?' I ask.

'He phoned me yesterday morning – heard it on the news – and told me to come straight home. I didn't, as you can see. But to answer your question, yes, we do spend time together, though I never quite know when it's going to be. And I know you all think I'm obsessed with freezing things – I've seen you laughing behind my back – but if you had a husband who turned up any time of the day or night expecting a hot meal, you'd have a well-stocked freezer too.'

With this, she produces a pack of Kleenex, pulls one out and wipes tears away from her face and spectacles. I comfort her by laying my hand on her wrist, while an embarrassed Gregory decides she must want a glass of water, lunges for the jug and knocks Lady B's wine into her lap.

CHAPTER 32

As her ladyship is mopped down and pacified, I ponder for the second time today on how little we really know about what goes on in other people's lives. It's the story of my friend and the taxi driver all over again, except that Vicky is one of my students, and I should have been keeping a teacherly eye on her.

I notice accusing looks from the others, as if it's all my fault, so decide to turn my attention to Melanie, and see what more I can find out from her.

'I hope things have settled down at home,' I start off.

'Ben's resurfaced, thank heavens. I'm expecting him to call any minute, so please excuse me if I dash out to talk to him.'

'I'm sorry the course has been such a disaster,' I say.

'Oh, it's hardly your fault,' she replies. 'To be honest, I needed a break from the situation back home. I didn't expect to find myself in the middle of a murder investigation, but at least it's taken my mind off things.'

'Rose was reminiscing about your schooldays,' I say, checking she isn't listening in. She can't because she's under siege from Lady B, shouting some story about the time her bag was snatched on a Lisbon streetcar and she was strip-searched by the Portuguese police and asked out on a date, simultaneously.

'Really? I'm surprised. Yes, we were at Downe House together – she was a year below me. We were all a bit in awe of her, living in a huge house with a butler and cook, and someone to fold up her clothes at night and brush her hair. Of course, she wasn't the only rich girl at the school, but it was clear she considered the rest of us beneath her. Don't tell her I told you, but her nickname was "Strangler". Rose Strang, you see.'

'Ha! But didn't you say your parents were hippies?'

'Yes, they were – the rich kind. We lived in splendid squalor, or should that be squalid splendour, in Lincoln Street, just off the King's Road. When it was all boutiques and record shops.'

'The Swinging Sixties?'

'I hope you mean the Psychedelic Seventies. But you were asking about Rose. I remember this huge picture of her on the front page of the *Telegraph*, wearing a show-offy hat at Ascot. She could have modelled, too, except at the time, girls of her sort were discouraged from that.'

'I expect she misses it – high society, I mean.'

'Well, we all have to adapt, and it's not as if she's ever wanted for anything. Her husband made lots of money, of course, although most of that was gobbled up when he died.'

'Not if they were married, surely?' I am something of an expert on inheritance tax as it pertains to married and divorced couples.

'I don't take much interest in financial matters, but I know that after a year or two a lump sum came through, which Rose used to set up the cookery school. After that it dried up. Maybe the Hoyt millions everyone talked about never existed in the first place.'

'I hope the school can survive all this, for her sake.'

'On paper, she's a very rich woman, though I don't know how many years she has left to run on this place. These wretched leaseholds – it must feel like living in an egg timer with the sand running out. But what would she do instead? Number forty-one is her life.'

'What was her husband like? You seemed a bit cool about him when we spoke before.'

'Alan? Not at all,' she replies. With a proper blush this time. 'I meant that he wasn't everyone's cup of tea. Marvellous-looking, of course – rather like Jude Law – but an introvert: very deep – loved reading and listening to music. Totally different from Ben, for instance, who's more the larger-than-life type. They didn't get on, in fact, but . . . well, that's another story.'

Ben Hardy-Powell doesn't seem to like many people. I reply: 'You should write your life story – it's very unusual.'

Melanie adjusts her hair. 'Oh, I'm nothing special. I got married when I was far too young. I'm constantly telling the girls to wait till they're thirty.'

'Girls? Has Cressida got a sister?'

'I've a daughter from my first marriage. Jemima's just turned thirty-one and she remains unmarried, so at least someone listens to me.'

'You can't possibly have a child in her thirties!' I declare. Always goes down well and she beams at me.

'My first husband and I divorced quite a few years ago – he was an oil man. Guyana, Algeria, Kazakhstan. I don't know why oil turns up in such dangerous places.'

'And Ben? I think you said he worked for an art gallery.' My mind flickers back to those horrible paintings at the Strebi Gallery with the cavorting cetaceans.

'I suppose you could call it art. But yes, it gives him something to do. He's had a tough few years.'

'In what way?'

'Well, his mother wasn't easy and her death caused a bit of a crisis. He resigned his commission and ended up regretting it. If you've been in the military, you're used to being active. It's why I so much want this job of his to work out.'

'Anyway, I'm glad that all's well again at home,' I say.

'If only Cressida had told me earlier, instead of trying to cover things up. I didn't want to announce it to all and sundry, but apparently Ben jumped on a train and is now in Wiltshire. There's a group of them from his army days who like to meet up and drink themselves under the table.'

My ears prick up. 'Did you say Wiltshire? Christian was in the army once, you know, and based at Tidworth.'

'So was Ben – what a coincidence,' she says, a little too quickly. 'But the camp's enormous, according to Ben – ten thousand soldiers.'

'This will have been over twenty years ago. Christian was in the Royal Regiment of Fusiliers,' I say.

'Well, I never . . . that's Ben's old regiment. Surprising it never came up.' She shakes her head and fluffs her hair up with her fingers.

'Would you mind asking Ben if they knew each other? There may be old colleagues of Christian who remember him and can help us understand . . . what happened. Or maybe they'd like to put together a tribute, that sort of thing.' I know it's clutching at straws, but if he can shed any light at all on Christian's back story, I want to know.

'I'll certainly ask if I get a moment,' she replies, with an absent look.

At this point, there's a bleeping sound and she jumps up to grab her bag. 'Oh, I thought it might be Ben,' she says into her phone – I can hear the disappointment in her voice and someone wailing at the other end. 'It's Cress,' she mouths as she exits the Pink Room. 'Emergency.'

CHAPTER 33

In Melanie's absence I zero in on a conversation Gregory is having with De'Lyse. The wine has loosened him up and I get the sense he is showing off a little to his attentive young dinner companion. 'Oh, yes, over the years I've had properties all over the place. Rome, Scotland, Cape Cod. I used to rotate between them, following the sun. Which is why I'll miss Biarritz.'

'You ought to meet Rose's daughter,' says De'Lyse. 'She's only twenty-three, but already a successful property tycoon.'

'Oh, is that so?' says Gregory. 'Although I don't think I'll have much to invest for the foreseeable future.'

'Skid Row, is it?' chuckles De'Lyse.

Gregory pauses, then lowers his voice. 'You could put it like that. To be perfectly frank with you, I put my name to guarantees I shouldn't have done. I'll regret it to my dying day.'

'Strictly between ourselves,' De'Lyse continues, 'I think there's an interesting opportunity right under our noses – might suit you. My theory is, Milla's going to step in and manage the school, sooner rather than later, after what's just happened. She's going to need a financial director, someone with a bit of nous. Might pay to build some bridges.'

'Is that so?' says Gregory for a second time, thoughtfully.

I've been giving this De'Lyse–Milla conspiracy some thought. It's perfectly credible that an ambitious young woman like Milla would want to get her mitts on her mother's multi-million-pound mansion, but why involve De'Lyse? She's certainly a smart cookie – personable, determined, even ruthless – but does she really bring much to the party? I also wonder how Suzie found out about their plot. Mysteries wherever you look.

After a minute, I notice Vicky has bounced back and struck up conversation with Stephen, to her left.

'Part of me says – serves her right for having hair that colour,' she's saying.

Stephen is another one enjoying the wine tonight. 'I like it. Think how boring it would be if everyone was the same.' He's certainly coming out of his shell.

'I'm one for a more subtle approach,' Vicky continues. 'More *feminine*.' She runs her fingers through her chest wig. 'Don't bite my head off, Stephen – I know Generation Z think you can choose to be a man or woman, or anything in between. But I'm all woman and I always will be.'

'A femme fatale,' declares Gregory, who has been listening in, and Vicky titters.

Meanwhile, at the far end of the table, Rose has turned to the Hon. Harriet. She doesn't seem to clock that she's chosen the wrong subject.

'I remember my own wedding day as if it were yesterday,' she says, as if entering a trance. 'It was midwinter – a light frosting of snow on the rooftops – and to this day, if I catch the scent of daphne, it conjures up my bouquet.

'I don't know what you're planning in the way of bridesmaids, but mine were all tots, dressed in pastel shades. Imagine what mischief we all made in the vestry!'

This is a softer side of her that I haven't seen before; although it's easier to imagine her devouring children than frolicking with them.

'In fact, Rose,' replies Harriet, and I can see her exchange looks with her mother, 'we've put things on hold for the time being. Too much to think about all at once.'

'Very wise,' says Rose, still failing to pick up on the situation. 'Take things step by step. Start with the dress, because you don't want to hurry things there. Brides today tend to – how shall I put it? – display their wares in the shop window, whereas in my experience grooms' whistles are more whetted by a demure neckline and covered shoulder.'

Before Rose can dig herself in deeper, Melanie has returned from her phone call, and she's in tears again.

CHAPTER 34

She plonks herself down beside me and the table falls silent. I'm tempted to say, 'Talk among yourselves!' but too late because it all starts pouring out.

'Cressida's on the warpath again. How cruel these girls can be! Daddy's gone off the rails so of course it's all my fault. And then today, he tells her on the phone that the reason he bunked off was that he and I haven't been "getting on". The reason for *that* being his wretched drinking.

'I'm sorry, I don't know why I'm telling you all this. Ben I can handle, but when the two of them start ganging up on me—'

'Dump him!' declares Stephen. Everyone stares at him. His face was already pink from the wine, but now a dark blush stains it.

'*What* did you say?' gasps Melanie.

'I said, he isn't worth it. If you allow yourself to be abused, it will only keep on happening.'

'*Abused?* What on earth do *you* know about it?' cries Melanie. 'You don't say a word all week and suddenly you're accusing my husband of wifebeating?'

'There are different forms of abuse,' Stephen says slowly. 'Drinking is one. Taking sides against you is another. Next thing you know, he'll be—'

This outburst is interrupted by the arrival of Suzie who,

with much noisy clashing, starts clearing away plates and cutlery and ferrying them over to the dumb waiter, making further conversation untenable.

When it is able to be resumed, I try and take the heat out of the situation by telling everyone about my own step-problem, namely Jonny.

'I can't do anything right. And then his mother does everything she can to stir things up.' I don't normally care to talk about private matters in public, and I instantly regret it.

'His mother?' bellows her ladyship, clearly thinking: *This sounds juicy.*

'It would be indiscreet of me to talk about Olinda,' I say loftily. 'As for what you said just now, Stephen – of course you're entitled to your opinions, but I think you have to work at relationships, make allowances for people. You can't just "dump" them – they're not objects you put out with the household rubbish when you've had enough of them.'

'Well, I've certainly had enough of this!' he snaps, pushing back his chair. 'Goodnight, everybody.' And with that, he storms out of the room.

Just when I think the fireworks are over, it's Lady B's turn.

'That's *exactly* what I've been telling Harriet – isn't it, darling?' All eyes turn to her daughter, who is strangling a napkin between her fingers. 'I was explaining to her that when it comes to making the big, important decisions in life, it sometimes helps to listen to us – ha! – old-timers.'

At this, Harriet stands up so suddenly that she tips over her chair. Gregory hops up to assist, in a spirit of chivalry, but she waves him aside. With a glance at her mother that succeeds in combining scorn, fury and defiance, she follows Stephen out of the door. If she weren't so well-bred, I have no doubt she'd have given it a good slam behind her.

This has been an illuminating evening, but the best is yet to come.

In honour of the occasion, our main course is served in a huge dish topped by a silver cloche. This is lifted – a footman in white gloves would not be amiss – to reveal a lacklustre *cassoulet du jour*.

Although wars have been fought over which of countless variants is the 'authentic' cassoulet, I cannot regard it as one of the high points of Gallic cuisine: indeed, it tops my list of 'doomed dishes', which (in my opinion) never fail to disappoint. The beans suck up all the flavour while you hunt in vain for scraps of meat. (Also on the list, for various reasons, are clafoutis, fish pie, toad-in-the-hole, Cornish pasties, gnocchi, pains au chocolat . . . but we can argue about those another time.)

I am labouring over a recalcitrant morsel of cartilage and wondering what Suzie will do with all the leftovers – we're three down by now, so there'll be an awful lot – when the door shakes, as if being shoulder-charged, and lo and behold, it's Lilith!

Our mouths drop open in stunned silence – Rose clutches at the table as if she's seen a ghost – and a shrill, piercing whistle fills the air.

'Feedback,' says Gregory, fiddling with his hearing aids. 'Give me a sec. Apologies.'

Lilith, standing in the doorway with one arm raised like the Statue of Liberty, waits disdainfully for him to make his adjustments, then begins.

'Never in all my life . . . dragged off like a common criminal . . . paraded in front of . . . Bundled into a . . . The police will rue the day they ever tangled with . . . oh, you mark my words!'

'Please sit down and tell us calmly what happened,' commands Rose.

'Plenty of cassoulet, if you're peckish?' says Gregory.

'Was it like *Line of Duty*?' asks Vicky.

Seeing Harriet's chair upended, and another beside it empty, Lilith asks: 'Did I miss a fight?'

'Just a difference of opinion,' I say. 'Please sit down and tell us everything that's happened – we've been so worried.'

'Well,' she says, laying her hands on the table as if it were a ouija board and she Madame Arcati. 'Off we drive in the police car, flashing lights and everything, and I'm thinking, what on earth can all this be about? What have I done? And all the time the policewoman – the frightening one – is looking at me with these accusing eyes.'

'Arrested!' says Vicky, eyes dancing. 'In handcuffs?'

'If you're not going to listen, I'm not going to tell,' says Lilith. She lets that threat sink in, then continues. 'So we're driving along, with the rain lashing down, and I cry out, "Stop the car!" '

The rest of us look at one another in bafflement.

'You see, I never checked their ID – they could have been taking me hostage! Anyway, it turned out everything was in order so we drove miles across London and hours later arrived at the interrogation centre.'

'That'll be those new high-security custody suites at Paddington Green,' says Vicky. 'Or Scotland Yard, down on the Embankment.'

'Belgravia Police Station was the sign on the door,' replies Lilith haughtily.

'But that can't be far!' protests Vicky.

'Less than five minutes,' I add mischievously.

'Will you all stop interrupting! Then they take me to reception, where I hand in my bag and coat and sign some bits of paper. Then I'm shown into a little room, and I wait about till someone comes in and asks if I need the toilet, which I don't because of germs. Then, after a bit, someone new comes in, quite friendly, and asks, would I like a cup of tea and a biscuit?'

I'm beginning to wish we'd asked for a précis, rather than a blow-by-blow.

'Just when I'm giving up hope of seeing friends and family ever again, two men in suits walk in – detectives, the ones who popped in the other night to arrest Paul. They explain I'm not actually being arrested – they want to clear something up that's bothering them.'

'What an anti-climax!' cries Vicky. 'Not even arrested? They could at least have kept you in overnight.'

I notice Suzie slide into the room, drawn by the excitement. Seeing which, Lilith for some reason tips her a conspiratorial wink, then continues.

'So, it turns out that the forensics people found a woman's hair at the scene of the crime. Two in fact – one on his pillow, one on the bread board. No ordinary hairs – in toning shades of violet . . . and that made them think of me. One of the officers produces a plastic bag, which contains snippets of them, and says the remainder have gone off for DNA sampling, but don't I agree they look like mine? They definitely were, though I can't imagine how they got there.

'Next thing I know, the other detective – the nice-looking one with the hair – starts quizzing me about Christian: how well did I know him? Did I visit him in his flat?'

'You didn't!' squeaks Vicky, wriggling in her chair.

'I'm coming to that. This is what I said: I admired Christian Wagner's culinary prowess. I know many found him easy on the eye. He was undoubtedly a man of secrets.' At this point, she scans her audience with a knowing look, and adds sotto voce, 'I've worked a couple of those out for myself, by the way . . .

'But never – not in a million years – not till hell freezes over, or pigs fly – would you find me having a fling with a . . . *man.*'

We look at each other in confusion as her story reaches its climax.

'"So restore me to liberty!" I tell them. "Or you will arouse the full wrath of my wife, none other than the Reverend Dilys Mostyn-Cadwaladr, Archdeacon of Meironnydd."'

Having delivered this bombshell, she sits back in her chair and looks round at her dumbfounded audience. 'Any questions?'

Vicky jumps straight in. 'You mean to say, you weren't a murder suspect after all? And they let you go because . . . because you told them to?'

'It was all very friendly. You see, the older detective, the dark-haired one, went on holiday to Portmeirion last year. I was saying about the ice cream, though not everyone likes rum and raisin.'

'Hmph,' goes Vicky.

No one can think what to say, so Lilith announces she's tired after all the excitement, thank you very much, and sets off to have a long hot bath before bed.

CHAPTER 35

Whoever would have guessed? Not for the first time this evening, silence falls over the Pink Room.

'Cool!' announces De'Lyse. 'Wish she'd told us earlier.'

'Some people prefer to keep their private lives private,' says Rose. Even she realizes this sounds schoolmistressy, so she adds, 'But it's lovely to know she's happily, er, married.'

Melanie cuts in, 'I'm just relieved she had nothing to do with it.'

'On the other hand,' interjects Gregory, 'it means the killer is still at large. Possibly in our very midst.'

Vicky angles her wine glass thoughtfully. 'Say another of us planted Lilith's hairs at the murder scene . . . it would be easy enough to do. I had a bath after her yesterday – we've only got showers in our rooms – and I had to pick several purple hairs out of the tub. I think she may have a problem – you know, alopecia. But my point is, any one of us could have done it.'

'Vicky's right,' says De'Lyse. 'The hairs must have been placed there to incriminate her.'

This is met with a moue of distaste by Rose, or strictly speaking, a noue. 'The police know their job. If they felt we were in danger, they'd inform us immediately.'

Suzie arrives with an apple Charlotte – there's another doomed dish – but no one is interested apart from sweet-toothed Gregory, who tops a plateful with cream, custard *and* ice cream.

'Nice to see a man who likes his food,' comments Vicky. 'Hubby's on the portly side, too – on meds for his blood pressure.' The discouragement is too much for Gregory, and he pushes his bowl aside.

Melanie asks me, 'Did you know about Lilith? I mean, did she happen to tell you she was gay?'

It would be nice to think that gay women automatically reach out to gay men, or vice versa, in a spirit of mutual support and companionship, but alas, I think it's the opposite: if anything, we are mutually suspicious, and bristle when we encounter one another. Since it's out in the open with Lilith, however, there are things I'd be interested to know. Like: what does the Anglican establishment think of its female archdeacon having a wife? Is the mauve hair flaunted to shock the archbishop?

No one can face coffee, so I help Suzie load the dumb waiter and say goodnight.

Thank heavens the day is almost over. I remember this feeling from the years I used to work evening shifts in restaurant kitchens. There's a word for it – *banjaxed*; when you can't even summon up the strength to go home. And so it was that we hung about at the end of service, chefs and waiters together, chatting about nothing in particular, drinking espressos or glasses of wine, or puffing on more cigarettes to feel bad about tomorrow. Another hour would pass until we could summon up energy enough to head for the door, feeling sad and defeated. If you want to see what absolute exhaustion looks like, travel on a night bus or the last Tube and look into a few eyes.

In just such a catatonic state, I amble off to the Old Ballroom to put my knife away. All is quiet – the rain has finally stopped – so I wash and dry it carefully and stow it with the rest in the drawer.

To my annoyance, I realize I left my steel behind, and find

myself trudging all the way back to retrieve it. In only a few days it has become monotonous, this constant trekking up and down the endless corridors.

I hate it when someone suddenly looms up at you and you almost jump out of your skin – I'm sure a lot of heart attacks are caused by this sort of shock. So when I get to the green baize door of the Old Scullery, I call down softly: 'Suzie – are you there!'

Quick as a linty, she appears at the foot of the stairs.

'Sorry,' I say, 'but I think my steel must have got mixed up with the dinner stuff and come down in the dumb waiter. Can I just check before I go home?'

'Er,' she pauses, gripping the handrail. 'Look, I'm in the middle of something so not now, OK? I'll find it and give it back to you tomorrow. Goodnight.'

CHAPTER 36

Finally, I head home. The constable at the door must have gone home for the night, but on the table are the crusts of a sandwich: ham on white with a dab of mustard. I'm buttoning up my coat when I hear a soft muffled thud. Sound travels oddly in these high-ceilinged houses, and I'm guessing something heavy has come down on an upper floor, the noise muted by all the acres of carpet and curtains.

I cross to the foot of the Grand Staircase, just to check nothing's amiss.

Pinioned against the landing banister is an unearthly apparition, enrobed in a white sheet, arms windmilling. I blink in disbelief. It's Lady Brash.

She's barefoot, wearing a full-length white nightdress and a turban wound round her head. Her face is daubed in some chalky substance, like a kabuki actress, and under each eye, stuck on the diagonal, is a strip of tape. The only thing I can think is that the students are throwing a fancy dress party, and they've sent Lady Macbeth to invite me along.

'Serena!' I stutter.

'Come quickly,' she hisses.

'Why? And why do you look like that?'

'It's night cream – I was in bed asleep. Up here, it's an intruder!'

I follow her as she pads up one flight of stairs, then another.

We continue to the second floor. I've never been up here before, but through the darkness I can make out multiple doors leading off to multiple bedrooms, plus another staircase – steep and narrow – up to the attic level above.

Melanie and Harriet, pale and ghostly in the gloom, are cowering in their bedroom doorways. The former, in an old-fashioned rust-coloured dressing gown that makes her look like a giant ginger cat, has unplugged her bedside lamp to use as a cosh, and Harriet, in a frilly pink nightie, is armed with a pillow.

'Further up,' whispers Lady B.

I give my eyes a minute to adapt to the darkness. In my clubbing days this happened almost instantaneously, now it takes a bit longer. I make out a short flight of stairs rising up to a half-landing, then a second flight doubling back, under the eaves. There's something low down on the half-landing, flat to the floor.

'Whoever you are, don't move,' I shout, in my most manly voice. I turn to my audience and ask, rather lamely: 'Can someone turn on the lights?'

'Must have fused,' says Melanie.

I flick on my phone to act as a torch, then begin the ascent. The eyes of the others bore into my back as I mount the stairs, tread by treacherous tread, up to the half-landing. My heart thumps louder – fear pumps through my body.

At last I'm within touching distance of our uninvited visitor. Craning forward, I poke it with my forefinger, fully expecting it to leap up and stab me – or else a bomb to go off.

The object, however, is soft and motionless. From a mound of velour, waffle and quilting peeps a telltale shock of mauve.

'Oh no!' I cry.

First to my side is Melanie. 'Lilith! She must have fallen. Is she OK?'

I look down and see an eyelid flicker. Thank goodness she's alive – at least for now. 'What was she doing up here?' I ask.

'As Vicky said, it's the only bathroom with a proper bath in it.'

'She must have been on her way down,' adds Harriet from below. 'We were only saying yesterday how dangerous it is, with no proper handrail.'

'We mustn't move her,' says Melanie. 'I'll call for an ambulance.'

There's never a phone signal when you really need it, even though we're so high up we must be near the actual satellite. She goes off in search of one while I manage with some effort to locate a fitful heartbeat in Lilith's damp wrist.

'Can you hear me?' I lean down close to her head and say, 'Lilith! Stay with me!'

I see a tiny movement of her lips, but no discernible sound comes out.

While Melanie makes the call, I continue gripping that limp hand. She's mumbling away, trying to get something out.

I say to her, 'I'm listening – tell me what it is.' Then I put my ear to her mouth. She can only manage one word per gasp, as if the effort is squeezing the life out of her.

'I . . .' she wheezes.

'I . . .

'w . . .

'was . . .

'pushed . . .'

'What?' I whisper back. '*Who* pushed you?' There is urgency in my voice, but I don't want the others to hear. Harriet's hovering in her doorway and her mother stands transfixed at the top of the stairs, like an Egyptian mummy raised from the dead.

'Stay with me, Lilith. Tell me who did it.'

But the effort has been too much for her and she drifts into unconsciousness.

From nowhere Vicky arrives, dressed in a velour puppy-pattern onesie and bearing a duvet, which she tucks solicitously around the inanimate figure. Then she quietly kneels down beside her, takes her hand and bows her head. I realize she's praying.

Only now does it dawn on me that the person who pushed Lilith must still be hiding in the attic. 'Don't move,' I tell everyone.

I know it's foolhardy, but my blood is up. There are five more steps leading to the attic floor. I take them slowly.

At the top are three doors, all closed. The first is marked BATHROOM, and as I push open the door wisps of steam from Lilith's recent soak are caught in the torchlight. My nostrils are filled with the fragrance of summer fruits.

I pull the light cord – it comes on. Modern white fittings, roll-top bath. But there's no one here.

Next is a box room, with a bed in it and nothing else.

Finally, a storeroom with two built-in cupboards. So this is where he's hiding.

'Come out!' I yell at the cupboard doors. Nervous squeaks from the guests on the floor below. I snatch open the first cupboard, expecting a hooded figure to leap out, but all it contains is a rocking horse.

'I've got a gun!' I yell at the other door, yanking it wide. Inside is an ancient doll's house. Very Hammer House of Horror – but no assassin.

I descend the treacherous little staircase, passing the *Pietà* of Lilith and Vicky, and announce to the three below that we need the police as well as the ambulance.

'Who were you shouting at up there?' demands Lady B.

I ignore her. 'Was Lilith on her own in the attic?'

'As far as we know,' says Lady B.

'Did anyone else come down? Did you hear or see anyone leave?'

They look at one another through the gloom, shaking their heads. 'We were here all the time – absolutely not,' says Lady B.

I'm making my way downstairs, puzzling over how Lilith could have been pushed if there was no one there to do it, when I hear footsteps racing up towards me. It's Suzie.

'What happened?' she asks, reaching me, out of breath. 'Is someone hurt?'

I suggest she wake Rose. Stephen emerges from a nearby room and asks what all the noise is about.

Ten minutes later, an ambulance arrives, followed by the police. I'm amazed by the effortless way the paramedics sweep in and take command of the situation, leaving the rest of us feeling like useless bystanders. Vicky asks if she can accompany her friend to hospital, and weeps when she's told no – unless she's family.

A stretcher materializes and Lilith is borne downstairs and into the open doors of an ambulance. It's raining again.

We're a mournful group gathered in the front hall to wave her off – all the students bar Gregory, who is probably plugged into a podcast. De'Lyse, iridescent in her gold silk still, offers to knock at his door, but we agree to leave him be. Of them all, Vicky seems most stricken.

'I feel so guilty,' she says. 'All those horrible things we were saying about her butchering Christian, and now this.'

At which point Rose sails down the Grand Staircase, still dressed for the ball in her black gown.

'Is the spectacle over?' she asks, sorrowfully. It's an odd way to react. 'Another terrible accident to stain the reputation of number forty-one.'

I look round at the students, wondering if I'm the only

one who knows this was no accident, my head racing with questions.

What did Lilith say or do tonight that made someone decide to do away with her?

Who can have pushed her, if she was the only one on the attic floor?

GARNITURE

Saturday 9th June '18

Just back from three weeks filming 'Pass the Gravy Stateside'. Why have the Brits got it in for American food? This is the sort of grub I love – it's Mormon, believe it or not. The funny name is because you throw it in the back of your Chevy and take it to a wake.

The Christian's Brasserie project looks like it's a goer. We took a look at a possible site in Pimlico Rd and I bumped into Paul. He invited me back to his place for a drink and I finally met the boyfriend. Posh but seems like a good bloke. For years I've been telling Paul to loosen up, not take life so seriously, and finally he looks (almost) happy.

I too have news on the dating front. When I first came to London all those years ago I did some catering jobs for this rich lady with a GREAT BIG house in Belgravia. There always was a bit of chemistry and now we've hooked up. If it weren't for Milla – her pain-in-the-ass daughter – it would be the perfect set-up.

FUNERAL POTATOES

Fry a chopped onion in about 25g butter till softened, then stir in 2 tablespoons flour and cook till golden, a minute more. Slowly whisk in 200ml each of chicken stock and milk or cream and cook till smooth and thick. Stir in a 640g pack of frozen hash browns. Cook till thawed and broken down (7–8 minutes, turning occasionally) then stir in 100ml soured cream and 85g grated cheese. Add a dash more milk if it seems thick.

Pile into a baking dish, top with crushed cornflakes (or cheese and onion crisps, even better) and bake for about half an hour at 160°C fan, until golden and bubbly round the edges.

CHAPTER 37

We sit around in the Pink Room drinking tea while a pair of police constables stomp up and down the stairs, then set themselves up in the Shelley Room. They interview us individually, and although I was the one who insisted they be called, I'm left till last.

I describe the events of the evening carefully, ending with Lilith's whispered accusation; about which they seem remarkably blasé.

'But don't you see – someone tried to kill her! Attempted murder – you need to investigate,' I say.

'Duly noted,' says one of the officers unenthusiastically. 'Although you said that there was no one on the top floor, so she can't have been pushed.'

'How can you be so sure?'

'Three witnesses confirm that no one was seen leaving the scene. Lady Brash says she had her door open all the time, and no one went past. The woman with the glasses says there's a squeaking floorboard on her landing, and she didn't hear a thing. We went and looked for ourselves, and there's no way anyone could have got down without being seen.' He crosses his arms and leans back. 'Unless you're suggesting they abseiled out of the window.'

I ponder this.

'Look, Lilith told me she'd been pushed. I'm not making it up.'

'You stated she was semi-conscious when you found her. She probably had no idea what she was saying.'

'So I just go home?' I say, tetchily.

'We have your number if we need anything else.'

'I'm not at all happy about this. Please ask one of the detectives on the Wagner investigation to phone me. Say it's important.' As I turn to go I hear him mutter: 'Hoity-toity.'

I trudge my way home through a fine soft drizzle, what is known technically as a 'sea fret'. The wind catches it occasionally and blows it in my face, and the pavement feels slick underfoot. I keep my eyes down.

All the lights are out in Skinner Place. I think of my cosy bed waiting for me upstairs. I don't often treat myself to hot chocolate but tonight I deserve it.

I get out my keys. Like all city-dwellers, I take security seriously, and six months ago – thanks to Jonny – upgraded my locks. At the same time I had something known as a London bar installed, which reinforces the frame and makes it harder for intruders to kick the door in. You need to feel safe in your own home.

I'm meditating whether to add a tot of brandy to my hot chocolate, maybe even a scoop of mini-marshmallows, when I realize my key won't go in the lock. I try again. Then I try the other keys. I switch my phone to torch and examine them.

Squeezed deep into each mechanism is blob of whitish glue. What is *wrong* with that evil bastard? Last time – when he hammered nails into them – it cost me nearly four hundred quid. I feel like bursting into tears – what the hell am I meant to do?

I make an executive decision and call Chester Square. After at least twenty rings there's a clunk and a pause. Rose is no doubt thinking – what now? A chemical warfare attack about to be launched on the school?

'Hello,' says a spectral voice. I know that in polite society it isn't done to admit your name or number when you pick up, and Rose is, as in every other way, old school.

'Rose – it's Paul. It really is this time.'

Another long pause, then she says, slowly and suspiciously: 'Identify yourself.'

'Paul Delamare. Your course tutor. Standing in for Christian.'

'Anyone could have read that in the newspapers,' she snaps. 'Don't call again.'

I think desperately, flailing about for something only I would know. 'The Wi-Fi code – *LobsterThermidor.*'

'We have been warned about hackers. I'm ringing off now in order to call the police.'

'Rose, give me one more go. Your nickname at school – it was Strangler.'

There is a long pause. 'Who on *earth* have you been talking to?' Then, after working it out, she asks stiffly: 'So, why are you calling?'

'It's an emergency. The locks on my front door have been vandalized and I can't get in.'

I wouldn't have expected it, but her response is gracious and sympathetic; maybe somewhere in that human iceberg there is after all a soul. She'll ask Soo-Zee to sort out bedding and towels and show me to the 'room at the top'. I must forgive her for not greeting me in person, but she's *en deshabille.*

* * *

The room in question really is at the top. Up and up we go, groping our way up the unlit section of straircase where Lilith took her possibly fatal tumble, back to the attic, nestling under its mansard roof.

I now see that opposite the bathroom door is a framed full-size poster of Hitchcock's *Vertigo* – blood red with a dizzying white vortex in the centre – hanging somewhat crooked. So I'm to sleep in the box room.

I turn to Suzie. 'Really?' I ask.

'It's not just *any* room. This one's got a history.' I detect a faint smile as she says goodnight.

From the goodness of her heart she's left me a toothbrush, so I go into the bathroom. *Scrub scrub scrub scrub*. Some of my best ideas come to me while I'm brushing my teeth, but none tonight.

My window, which has no blind or curtain, looks out over Chester Square and its leafy garden, a bird's-eye view that in happier circumstances I would enjoy. Hardly any lights on – what a lonely place to live. Jubilee Cottage may be a hovel compared to this, but it's a lot more lively. I try and imagine myself in my own bed at home, being lulled to sleep by the rumble of trains and the noise of happy partygoers heading home. Instead, heavy silence.

It's stuffy up here, so I decide to open the window. In general, these grand Cubitt properties have sash windows, but this being the attic, it's a casement. I lift the catch and give it a shove – probably hasn't been opened for decades – only to realize it opens inwards. Taking great care, I lean out for a better look.

Far, far below I espy Rose's balcony and its jagged fringe of railings. A sudden thought clutches at my heart.

This is the window from which her husband fell to his death.

CHAPTER 38

Just thinking about it makes me shiver, but as I look out, there's something else. High as I am above the street, I catch a whiff of bonfire-scented smoke. I look down to see an orange dot glowing erratically and a dark figure slouched against the railings.

What's he doing here? The cops said he was hanging round the school on Monday night, and now he's back. Is he waiting for something – a signal from a window? Or did he watch me fumbling with my locks and trail me back?

I'm tempted to yell '*Jonny!*' – make him jump – but I'm not going to give him the satisfaction. Let him stay there all night and get drenched.

On cue, a flash of lightning fills the bare room with its weird quivering light, followed by a soft rumble of thunder. I smile to myself, wait half a minute and then check again.

Just as I thought. He's raced off to take cover in the Tube. Like Emperor Augustus, Jonny is an astraphobe: terrified of thunder and lightning.

I take off my shoes and lie down on my pallet. I always try and put a brave face on things, but this is testing it to the limit. The police don't believe a word I say, and I'm imprisoned in a house of riddles. A killer is at large – and it feels like I'm being set up to take the rap.

I pick up my phone, praying that I'll get a signal. *Yes.* I tap 'hoyt death belgravia' into Google and soon enough 'Alan

Hoyt Financier Death' pops up as a suggested search. At the inquest into the financier's death on 27 August 2014, the coroner recorded an open verdict.

Melanie told me he fell while trying to push the window open, but she's mistaken – or else lying. The window opens inwards. If he forced it, he'd have fallen *into* the room. No: he was pushed – or jumped.

I lie down again, tingling all over at this new realization. The thought of suicide stirs up unwelcome memories. Neither is murder the stuff of sweet dreams.

It's a bad habit, tapping away at your phone after you've gone to bed, but I keep thinking of things I ought to follow up – one being a search through the records of Companies House. I consider this agency one of the glories of the British Civil Service, and its website exemplary: a few swift keystrokes – 'farson holdings' – and I learn the company was recently dissolved, and the names of its now-disqualified directors, one of which catches my eye. After that I try 'christian wagner west london gangs' in various combinations in Google, but it's hopeless: best leave that one to the police.

In the end I give up on sleep completely. It's not my style to creep around at night, but I can't just lie here.

I feel my way down the stairs – gripping the makeshift handrail tight – and listen at the bedroom doors. From Harriet's comes a gentle snuffling sound. Her ladyship next door is snoring loudly, with irregular snorts and whistling sounds: obstructive sleep apnoea – she should get that checked out.

It seems Melanie prefers to sleep with the door ajar. I can tell from her soft, regular breathing that she's out for the count.

I stop for a moment and peer in. On the table I espy the shape of a handbag. I know it's a risk – I know it's wrong – but I tiptoe in and take it.

Back in my room, I suffer a convulsion of guilt. Have I

stooped so low that I'm rifling through ladies' handbags? What would Marcus say?

I know what he'd say, and so would Julie: your situation is desperate, there's a killer in the house, do what you have to.

It's many, many years since I've looked inside one of these – not since my mother caught me playing with hers, and putting on her make-up.

I unzip it. Wow! What a lot of stuff. Who knew handbags were so – capacious?

The interior is divided into two sections, with a side pocket kept shut by means of a magnetic catch. I check this first – it's just the place to keep love letters. Instead I find receipts. Lots and lots and lots of receipts, dating back months. Does she have a reason for keeping them? Is it a woman thing?

The rest is a jumble: a leather purse containing about a hundred pounds in cash, a bunch of keys, hand sanitizer, dozens of pens, a hairbrush. A torch, batteries – always good to be ready for emergencies. And right at the bottom of the bag – I could smell them before I opened it – two tonka beans. Well, now we know.

Mixed in with all this, apparently at random, is a jumble of cosmetics, including the lipstick donated by Rose and a refillable perfume atomizer containing, if I'm not mistaken, Shalimar. You can't go wrong with Guerlain. And a powder compact.

This particular compact has been converted to hold photographs. The top one is of a pretty young woman with a wide smile and red hair, I'm guessing Melanie's daughter. The bottom one shows a proud-looking man, every inch the soldier, with sandy hair and square chin: Ben.

The photographs have evidently been trimmed into circles to fit the compact, and one edge of the bottom picture is sticking out, forming a sort of tab. I give it a gentle tug, and out it pops. Behind it is another picture. Such handsome men: this one bears a striking resemblance to Jude Law.

I'm restoring the powder compact to order when my eyes fall again on her phone. I know it's illegal to break into people's phones, but I doubt very much I'll succeed anyway. I try entering *123456* as the passcode, then *111111*. What was the daughter's name? Jessica? Jemima – that's it. Just for the hell of it, I tap the tiny letters underneath the numerals to spell it out. This gives me *536462* – the phone leaps open.

I must find a way to warn Melanie her passcode is too obvious – it's the least I can do. I'm also aware that the clock is ticking. What if she wakes up and notices her bag is missing?

I start scrolling.

I'm not sure what I'm hoping to find, but I start with her emails. Nothing of interest. Next, I try text messages. I tap 'christian' into the search bar.

Yes! But only one message, which in itself is odd; the rest of the trail must have been deleted. It was sent last Friday.

> Hey, mel, try and come next week if u can get away I managed to fix it so there's 1 space left on the course. Long time no see lets get some QT together. C:

Is it so much more trouble to write proper words and sentences? I'm momentarily puzzled by the colon after the C, till I notice that if you turn it anti-clockwise it's a text emoticon of a grinning face. I must tell Julie.

Melanie pretended she hardly knew Christian, and Rose told me otherwise. Now I know Mel and Christian were intimate; so much so that she let him call her Mel.

I return the bag where it belongs then make my noiseless way down to the first floor.

Rose's private rooms occupy the whole of the back part of the house. The only way in is through a hobnail door in ancient oak – an architectural anomaly, probably reclaimed from a castle. A pair of Beefeaters standing guard each side of it wouldn't look amiss. Cut into it is a small hatch – known nowadays as a 'speakeasy grille' – through which visitors can be vetted. I can imagine it opening a crack and a ghostly voice announcing she's not at home.

In the centre of the door is a colossal ring handle. I'm dying to give it a waggle on the off-chance she has forgotten to lock up. I expect, however, boiling oil would be poured over me through some concealed slit, so I decide not to risk it.

I wonder how she passes the lonely hours, when she's not clicking away at her abacus. Playing solitaire? Cataloguing the celery jugs? Voodoo?

I listen next at Vicky's door. A shallow, irregular breathing pattern tells me she's in the REM phase of sleep. She's an odd one; is she dreaming of fluffy animals – or cleavers?

This floor is also where the men have been billeted. Not a whisper from either of them. Stephen's door is locked – a sensible precaution, given recent events. When I peek into Gregory's room – he's not there!

Sleepwalking? A tryst with Mrs Hoyt? Popped out to meander under the moonlight?

With cat-like tread, I proceed down the Grand Staircase.

The Pink Room is empty and there's a dim light emanating from behind the green baize door. From Suzie's Magic Kingdom waft faint sounds – tinny music, snatches of words. Her laptop must be back.

I pad my way back through the hall and am halfway up the Grand Staircase when the locks of the front door snap back. I freeze as a dark figure enters, looks about as if lost, then launches itself unsteadily across the hall. Whoever it may be is inebriated, dripping wet and humming something.

It's Gregory! I nip upstairs, unsure if I've been spotted. Now what might he be doing out late on his own? As I ascend an aromatic blend of whisky, cigarettes and sex drifts up the stairwell and I recognize that old music hall number, 'One Of The Ruins That Cromwell Knocked About'.

Not just a chequered business history, but someone who prowls about local fleshpots at night and comes back singing snatches of Marie Lloyd. Very Jack the Ripper. If he slipped out tonight, it was probably him last night, too. And if last night, why not murder-night itself, when Stephen heard the front door opening?

Crawling back into bed, I spot the corner of Christian's notebook peeping out of my jacket pocket. Maybe it will unlock a few more secrets. I flick through the pages and notice the last one appears to have been torn out; then fall into a deathly sleep.

CHAPTER 39

Thursday

At 4 a.m. I sit bolt upright, wondering where I am. Now wide awake, I plug in my earbuds and check out the rolling news.

Christian's murder is no longer headlining, but the producers have spliced together some clips of number forty-one's front door, crowds of people standing in the rain and close-ups of teddy bears and balloons attached to the railings.

'One of the tutors at the prestigious Chester Square Cookery School is chef Paul Delamere –' I turn up the volume – don't want to miss a word of this – 'who was standing in for murder victim Christian Wagner at short notice, after he broke his arm in circumstances that the police now regard as suspicious. Delamere was taken in by the police for questioning on Wednesday evening but later released pending further investigation.

'Delamere, who is in his mid-forties and unmarried, is an old associate of Mr Wagner, and himself a Belgravia resident. He is the grandson of one-time Poet Laureate Walter Delamere. He was not available for comment.'

What? How dare they?

I attack Google to find the number for Metro24, then hit CALL so hard I'm surprised my phone doesn't shatter. I am offered option after option. No, I don't want to upgrade my Metro24 package (I don't have one!). No, I don't want Metro24 broadband. No, I don't want to speak to some infernal Happiness Champion about Metro24.

I jab the red button and try the website instead. There's no email address for customer service, just one of those annoying forms with lots of dropdown menus. My thumbs fly across the keys.

Dear Metro24 newsdesk,

At 4.13 this morning your news team broadcast a segment about the murder of Christian Wagner.

I am the 'Paul Delamere' mentioned during your report, which contained numerous presumptions and falsehoods.

1) I was assured by the police that they had no plans to make my name public with regard to their inquiries, information which is – obviously – highly damaging to my reputation. Please tell me how you found out about this confidential matter. (I am not a person of 'public interest' and it is an extreme breach of privacy.)

2) My surname is not 'Delamere' but 'Delamare'. The writer you mentioned was not Delamere either, but De La Mare (three words). I am not related to him – not even distantly – and nor was he ever Poet Laureate.

3) I was 'not available for comment' because you didn't ask me. But in case you want one, here you go: No Comment.

4) Who told you I'm in my 'mid-forties'? Not true, not even near.

I am sure you are planning to repeat this news report ad infinitum, but please remove it at once, because it is highly inaccurate, not to mention slanderous.

In disgust,

Paul Delamare

I slam the send button.

It's a miracle: an email pings in from Metro24. Alas, one of those annoying auto responses, assuring me that 'all messages are carefully read by the team'. Maybe if they spent a bit time more reading Wikipedia they'd know how to spell Walter De La Mare.

All of this is bad enough, but there's something else upsetting me too – the sad realization that in the course of twenty-four hours, Christian has been demoted from national treasure and superstar chef to a filler on the rolling news.

Oh, that's a surprise, another email from Metro24 – an intern, probably. Would I like to be interviewed for the eight o'clock news, to put forward my version of events?

It's probably not the best choice in the circumstances but I settle for something brisk and businesslike: *Drop dead.*

* * *

Three hours later I wake again to a text from Julie.

> 🚀. So 🤩about the 📸🙏4 all your help. May I bring the 🖼 round 2 your 🏠 2 show you 2night? 🪐 entering ♊ 🌧 ahead, 🆘

This I interpret as meaning: We have lift-off. So excited about the shoot – thank you for all your help. May I bring the pictures round to your place to show you tonight?

Followed, inevitably, by my horoscope for the day: Saturn entering Gemini. Storm ahead – DANGER.

Gemini is one of the more colourful star signs. The celestial twins have a reputation for being smart but treacherous; not the kind of people I need around me in the current emergency, but thanks anyway, Julie.

I'll reply later – but first I need to arrange the locksmith.

I'm not sure what time class will finish this afternoon, so we agree an evening slot – six forty-five.

Then, eight minutes later, while I'm drying my face with a rather scratchy towel (at Rose's prices, guests deserve something fluffier), my phone starts jumping up and down in my pocket. Whoop whoop whoop – it's a police siren.

> 🚨🚨🚨 OMG!!! Saw on 📺 something about 👮! What's happening? RU OK?? 🚨🚨🚨

How did she do that? Talking emojis? This is a terrible new development.

Only Julie could worry about someone else when she's just about to embark on the most ambitious photoshoot in the history of magazine journalism, but that's why I love her. I text her straight back.

> TV people got it all wrong. Best of luck for today – can't wait to see the pictures. Minor hiccough at Jubilee Cottage but I'll expect you there at 7 p.m.

I don't like keeping things from Julie, but there's no point in worrying her.

I look out of the window to see it's raining yet again. After the deluge of yesterday, the day looks petulant and menacing. Sweet wrappers and circulars have been picked up by squalls of wind and are fluttering along the pavement, flapping into the faces of pedestrians and onto car windscreens.

With the weekend in sight, traffic is heavy. Steaming cars with their headlamps ablaze run the lights, and taxis and Ubers carve each other up.

The only people left outside are a policeman collecting up crowd barriers and ripping the police tape off them in an irritated fashion, and another hurrying the traffic on. Despite what I told them, the police have evidently decided to treat Lilith's fall as an accident.

I'm first to arrive for breakfast, joined shortly by Vicky and Melanie. There's a chill in the air today and Vicky looks more presentable than usual, in black jeans and a cardigan.

'You didn't knit that yourself, did you?' asks Melanie, stroking it admiringly. I notice for the first time her nails – they're sharpened into points. Vicky smiles brightly and nods.

'Gosh! It's as fine as lace – how clever of you,' Melanie adds.

'I've always got something on the go. Mainly things for family and friends.'

'I bet you're popular,' says Melanie. I watch Vicky carefully: she seems about to say something, but instead rattles cereal into a bowl.

As the others file in, I take Melanie aside and ask her if she remembered to ask Ben about Christian. She claps a hand to her head: 'Silly me. Don't worry – I'll do it later.'

Everyone demands to know how Lilith is, and every time I reply I've no idea. When asked for the sixth time, I suggest Suzie go upstairs to request an update from Mrs Hoyt and she leaves the room.

'The lights on the stairs weren't working,' announces Lady B.

'The bulbs had been twisted out, that's why,' says Vicky, observant as ever. A ripple of alarm runs round the room. 'Of course I'm sure – I screwed them back in.'

'Did you tell that to the police?' I ask.

'I didn't discover it till this morning when I went up for my bath.'

Suzie brings back news that Lilith remains in a coma at Chelsea and Westminster Hospital, and her next-of-kin have been informed. Has she broken anything? the students ask. Everything, replies Suzie tonelessly. Doctors are usually a bit more specific, or they were in my father's day.

I can't help thinking of the poor archdeacon, picking up the phone in the middle of the night in her storm-lashed

North Wales vicarage, to be told her beloved is lying in a hospital bed on life support. I hope Rose will have the grace to put the poor woman up when she arrives in London – assuming she wants to stay in Belgravia's equivalent of the Bates Motel.

The mood remains downcast as we drift along to the Old Ballroom, and I can sense unrest in the air as my students don their aprons for our last day together. This morning we will be covering *Syrups, Spun Sugar and Sugarcraft*, another creaking relic from the days of home economics and Fanny Cradock.

De'Lyse has a thunderous look about her. 'Paul,' she announces, 'can we get real here? No one wants to learn about syrup and fondant and making sugar pansies for wedding cakes. I'm sure it's all very interesting for posh ladies with too much time on their hands –' glancing round meaningfully – 'but a bit, well, out of date.'

'Hmm,' I say – she's right, of course. 'But the point of being here is that you receive a good general grounding across the whole range of kitchen techniques.' I sound like Rose Hoyt.

She rolls her eyes. 'Come off it! Puff pastry was bad enough! I don't want to know how to make toffee. And if I fancy fruit jellies – which is never – I'll buy a bag at the shop.' She has a point.

'Wait here for a minute and I'll go and have a word with Rose. She wasn't very pleased that *Spectacular Seafood* was called off, so I'd better check. While I'm out, think what you might like to learn instead – we've got *Vital Vegetables* this afternoon, so that's something to look forward to.'

Ignoring the pained expressions on my students' faces, I plod off to the Shelley Room to tell the boss we have a rebellion on our hands.

CHAPTER 40

On my way through the front hall, I check no one's looking and dive into the library.

The call jumps to voicemail: '*If you're phoning about a beauty treatment, you can reach me on this number . . .*' One never has a pen in such situations, so I use my finger to inscribe it on the misted-up window then tap it in. Isla answers immediately in a sing-song voice. Quite a difference from yesterday.

'Serendipity Spa – Isla speaking, how may I help you?'

'Isla, please don't ring off. It's Paul again – we spoke yesterday.' I can almost feel her finger hovering over the button and wild ideas flash through my mind. I could make something up about how Isla's been left a hundred grand in his will. Anything to keep her on the line.

'I told you not to phone,' she growls. I hear a door click – she's gone into a cupboard or something, which is a good sign. 'Look, I'm in the middle of a Powerpeel, you couldn't have called at a worse time.'

'I'm so sorry. I know you take great pride in your work – it's really worthwhile, helping people realize their full aesthetic potential. But please think of this as a favour to poor Uncle Chris.'

'You've got two minutes. If I leave that serum on too long, my client won't have any face left.' I hear her open the door and call out, 'Won't be a moment, love!' Then she switches back to her hostile voice. 'What do you want this time?'

'Something you mentioned yesterday. About your brother.'

There's a pause. 'You mean Darren? He's not really my brother, he was fostered.'

'Er, yes. I was hoping I might be able to speak to him. In case he's, well, bumped into Uncle Chris over the years.'

'Look,' she replies, 'I don't know half of what Darren got up to when he went off to London but you're not going to be able to speak to him.'

Surely not someone else dead before his time . . . 'Why not?'

'I haven't spoken to him since High Down. I don't know where he is.'

'Is that another part of Swindon?'

'You pulling my leg? It's a prison. Now, if you're finished . . .'

'I'm sorry about Darren – honestly, that must be tough for you, for the whole family.'

'Tough on Uncle Chris, too. They were close – like father and son.'

I pause to take this in. 'But one last thing. You mentioned Chris's kids.'

'I told you all I know.'

'I wondered if, er, your uncle might have kept in touch with them?'

'No way! He didn't want to know. Mum said he didn't deserve to be a dad.'

What a mess families get themselves into; sometimes I feel glad I haven't got one, though of course I don't mean it.

'Isla,' I add in my most captivating tone, the one I use when trying for a bank loan or a reservation for Sunday lunch at the Hand and Flowers. 'How would I go about contacting the children? I think someone should speak to them.'

'Swindon Borough Council? I'm joking, by the way – good luck!'

'Just a little detail,' I say. 'What were the children's names?'

'Like I told you . . .' Then I hear a squeal of horror. 'The serum! Someone get me some water!' There's a bang as Isla's phone hits the floor, and the line goes dead.

CHAPTER 41

In the plush serenity of the Shelley Room, Rose is deep in contemplation of her laptop. Her rich perfume tickles my nostrils.

'Oh, it's you!' she says, looking up at me with one eyebrow raised. 'I thought class had begun.'

'That's what I'm here about. There's discord among the students.' Mutiny, more like.

'If this is about Lilith, it's very unfortunate, but if people insist on walking about at night without turning the lights on, accidents will happen.' So much for the milk of human kindness.

'Since you mention it, the lights weren't working,' I reply. 'Someone unscrewed the bulbs.'

She looks genuinely surprised. 'They were working when I checked this morning.'

'Anyway,' I continue, 'that's not what I'm here for. De'Lyse is unhappy with this morning's class and doesn't want to learn about sugar boiling. I think she has a point – it's a bit, shall we say, theoretical?' Rose's hackles start to rise. 'The other students seem to agree.'

She takes up her habitual stance at the window. This is evidently where she does her thinking. After a minute, she says, 'Follow the students' wishes. It's disappointing, because we aim to cover the whole culinary spectrum, but what with the, er, disruptions . . . and of course a stand-in tutor—'

'That's hardly—'

'I merely mean that your predecessor taught this course many, many times without dissent. Please bear in mind, however, De'Lyse is here on a complimentary basis, in return for publicizing the course. I have been assured she is an influenza.'

'Don't you mean "influencer"?' I say.

Rose ignores me. 'I'm talking about the trend for young people to be *infected* by the enthusiasms of their peer group. Regardless of which, we expect and deserve a glowing review. So we'd better keep her happy.'

I wonder what De'Lyse's followers would think if they knew that courses at Chester Square involve fatal accidents with cleavers and that if you go to the bathroom at night, you could end up with a fractured skull.

'Any preferences for what I should teach instead?' I say.

Rose gives me a sour look. 'I'm sure with your rich experience you'll manage to think of something.'

Patronizing as ever, but I let it pass . . . because I need a favour.

'Rose, there's something I need to know about one of the other students, and I'm hoping you can help.' She mutters something about confidentiality. 'Gregory Greenleaf. Do you recognize the surname?'

She plays with an earring, then looks at me straight. 'Patricia Highsmith – Mr Ripley's, erm, friend. And what of it?'

'I don't think it's Gregory's real name.'

She cocks her head playfully; this is a new side to her. 'Give me one moment,' she says, putting on glasses and opening her laptop. She taps away for a minute and then her eyes light up. 'His fee was paid by bank transfer from the account of a *G. Farson*. Wonder as one might, it would not be the first time a student has chosen to study at Chester Square incognito; indeed, I can recall—'

'Thank you, that's all I need to know. But while you've got your accounts open, may I mention something else? We never did discuss my fee. I've taken the liberty of calculating it for you, and bearing in mind the hours and the short notice, the figure I would suggest is—'

'Oh, no!' She throws up her hands. 'Quite the misunderstanding. Upon my honour, Christian assured me you were doing it as a personal favour to him, for friendship's sake. I've nothing whatever left in the budget, and what with cancellations pouring in, it's out of the question.'

Unbelievable! A whole week of torment in this hellscape and not a penny to show for it.

'But you have reminded me of a grave omission,' she concludes, sitting down at her desk again, to indicate my time is up. 'On behalf of us all, I would like to thank you for last night's delectable gravadlax. Too, too lavish of you.'

* * *

What would Julie say? Pack up and go home. Instead, conscientious to a fault, I plod back to the Old Ballroom where my surviving students are waiting expectantly. Even if not treated as such, I'm a professional, and I won't let them down.

I'm just at the doors when my phone rings. About time too – it's Detective Sergeant Blondie. 'Apparently you were concerned about a woman who collapsed last night,' he says. 'Note on file to give you a courtesy call.'

'How good of you,' I say, sarcastically. 'But Lilith didn't collapse – she fell down a flight of stairs.'

'The lady with the hair,' he says.

I cup my hands to my phone. 'Before she passed out, she told me she'd been pushed.'

'Let me see what it says here.' Pages rustle. 'Have you

always had a penchant for falling over dead bodies, or is this a new thing?'

'She isn't dead, or at least not yet.'

'So what's your point?'

'It was attempted murder. She spoke with extreme difficulty, but she knew what she was saying.'

'In a coma now, I believe.'

'All the more reason to find who tried to kill her,' I counter.

There's a long pause, during which he's probably checking his nails, wondering if it's time to book a manicure.

'And another thing,' I say. 'Someone removed the lightbulbs, so the staircase was dark.'

'Well, that explains it,' he replies. 'She missed her footing.'

'It was done deliberately! So they could jump out at her in the dark.'

He thinks about this for a minute. 'Right, here's the plan. I'll ask the hospital to inform us as soon as she comes round, and we'll take a statement from her. Till then, best sit tight. Have a good day.'

CHAPTER 42

'OK, everyone,' I announce to my class. 'Snap decision. No more formal teaching – we'll make one glorious final meal together: a feast in honour of Christian, based around his signature dishes.' Upon hearing this, a cheer goes up so loud that Suzie hears it in the Old Scullery, and comes in to find out what all the fuss is about.

There's an art to menu planning; you're looking for an overall framework, which you then populate with contrasting flavours and textures. I produce Christian's notebook and scribble out a selection of recipes which I hope will do him justice.

I put Stephen, with his feather touch, in charge of our amuse-gueule, which will be the cheese biscuit recipe. De'Lyse, pleased at having got her way, will make our hors d'oeuvre (pretty unchallenging): devilled eggs. Lady B can poach the poularde demi-deuil, Melanie make the accompanying sauces and the Hon. the side dish; for this I propose Christian's American potato dish.

Melanie takes me aside. 'Why do I end up with all the boring jobs? De'Lyse's recipe looks much more interesting.' I'm beginning to realize that Melanie is green-eyed in more ways than one, and always seems to want what someone else has got.

'Sauces are the highest form of culinary art,' I assure her.

In a leap of faith, I ask Vicky to take charge of dessert.

Thunder and Lightning Cake requires care and precision, so it should suit someone who spends her life dispensing life-or-death medicaments.

This leaves Gregory. To use an expression of my mother's, he looks like a peeled onion.

'Sleep well?' I ask.

'Did you?' he fires back. So he spotted me on the stairs.

'The menu's pretty much taken care of,' I continue smoothly. 'Is there something you've always wanted to cook, or would like me to show you?'

He snorts and snuffles, wishing I'd leave him alone.

'For instance, some people have problems with meringues – usually it's an egg whipping problem. Or they want to know how to cook rice so it's fluffy, which is really just a question of careful measuring and adjusting the heat correctly.' I fix on a smile: he's not wriggling off the hook.

'Actually, there is,' he says. 'Pasta. I bought a machine, but have never used it.'

'Let's make some tortellini and a batch of linguine – you can take them home and enjoy them for your supper. Ask Vicky – you can probably freeze them.

'Proportions are a cinch: six hundred grams of flour to six large eggs. Let's go and find the tipo 00 flour – I know I saw it somewhere.'

I lead him into a small storeroom where dry goods are kept. 'Gregory, I don't mind if you pop out at night. Mum's the word.' He looks relieved. 'May I ask you a couple of questions, though?'

'If you must,' he says.

'You're Gregory Farson, if I'm not mistaken.' He blinks then nods slowly. 'Did you hold Christian responsible for Farson Holdings going bust?'

This surprises him. 'How do you know about all this?' he whispers.

'Companies House.'

Gregory fiddles with a hearing aid. 'Christian let his investors down – took his eye off the ball.'

'And you came here to confront him about it?' I continue.

'For months and months he refused to see me,' says Gregory with a downward glance.

'And on Monday night you cornered him?'

'We had a very civilized conversation – laid matters to rest.' He sighs, then shuts his eyes. 'I didn't murder him.'

'I'm inclined to believe that,' I say, 'but you had reason to. I also think you're the right type: impatient and somewhat heavy-handed, and capable of planning ahead . . . for instance, it was a nice touch to turn up with a bottle of excellent Bordeaux, which you had thought ahead to *chambrer*.'

'How on earth—?'

'There was no sign of a cork or corkscrew, and the capsule had been neatly trimmed with a foil cutter. I expect you prepared it in your room before dinner.

'The reason I think you're innocent, however, is that a murderer would not be careless enough to leave a folder with his name on it lying around in Christian's sitting room, or fingerprints all over a wine glass. Nor, after committing the deed, would he be likely to go wandering around the seedier parts of Victoria, thus arousing further suspicion.'

'Christian was kind enough to tip me off about, well, useful addresses in the area.'

'I did wonder. My other question: when you arrived at Christian's flat on Monday night, did you notice anything in the hall?'

'Nothing out of the ordinary.'

'Did you hear anything while you and Christian were talking?'

'He had music on – a radio station.'

'And what kind of mood was he in when you left him?'

'He said he was totally bushed and going straight to bed. He may have regretted the wine – he said he was on co-codamol.'

'That's all very helpful,' I say. 'Anything else you can remember about the night?'

'There was one thing. On the way out we found a small gift-wrapped parcel on the doorstep. I've no idea what it was.'

CHAPTER 43

I'm glad to have had it out with Gregory, and interesting that the gift must have been delivered while he was inside with Christian. I'll give that some thought later, but while the students have their heads down, I seize the moment and head to the library.

I've begun to think of this as my private sanctum, but someone's been in recently: the misted-up window has been wiped and dried. I google 'swindon borough council', then try 'swindon adoption services', which brings up the tautological 'Adopt Thames Valley Regional Adoption Agency'. To the best of my knowledge Swindon isn't on the Thames, nor in a valley, but never mind.

I find myself scrolling through swathes of material about the different sorts of adoption, fostering and associated legal rights. I discover I'm eligible to adopt a child myself – I had no idea – though I don't think it's for me.

Contacting someone who's been adopted seems an unbelievably laborious, complicated process, but I guess that's understandable. Screwing my courage to the sticking place, I dial the helpline.

After a few minutes of pan pipes, a snarky voice with better things to do asks me to explain myself.

'Two young children were adopted in Swindon in about 2000,' I begin. 'Their guardian was a Barbara Wagner Edwards and they—'

'If I may interrupt,' says the voice, 'I'm afraid I can't help you unless you're a family member.' You'd think they'd give these people some elementary empathy training.

'I am, in a sense,' I reply, feeling myself overcome by a crimson tide of shame and guilt; although in a Jesuitical sense it's true – I do come from a family, just not the Wagners or Edwardses.

'Then you'll need to apply to join our Letterbox Scheme.' I've just read about this – you register a message saying that you'd like to be contacted, then hope one day the adopted person will pick it up. Not dissimilar from putting a message in a bottle and throwing it into the ocean.

'It's a bit more urgent than that,' I reply.

Ignoring this, the voice continues: 'Obviously we'll need all the details, Mr . . . Waggoner, did you say?' They start reading out a list in a bored monotone: 'Date of birth, place of birth, birth name, date . . .'

It's enough to discourage the most hard-boiled private investigator, and I give up.

On the way out, my eye is drawn to a weighty tome sitting on the table – the *Larousse Encyclopedia of La Cucina Italiana*. I hesitate for a moment, wondering whether the pictures and descriptions of the different pasta shapes would amuse Gregory (there are over 600), but I think probably not.

As I walk back to the Old Ballroom I glance out at the dark little courtyard where Christian met his grisly fate, and notice for the first time a rose twining up a trellis, reaching for the light. This gives me an idea.

Everyone in class is working and chatting away with the exception of the Hon., who is studying her recipe in silent puzzlement. Bless her, she's never heard of hash browns.

'We're going to use frozen,' I tell her. Chefs often keep a stash of tasty standbys in the freezer – not the sort of thing you need to make from scratch.

'It says I have to start by frying an onion. Would you mind?' she asks. 'I'm sorry, it's the smell.'

'It's not much fun being around food when you're not up to par,' I reply as I splash olive oil into a frying pan. 'Still feeling under the weather?'

She doesn't answer. After checking no one is listening, I ask confidentially. 'Harriet, is everything OK?'

She continues studying the floor, then looks up, eyes swimming. 'I only found out for sure on Monday, you see. I'd have cancelled if I'd known.'

Oh, my goodness! She's telling me she's pregnant! I know some people can spot it at a hundred paces, but like most men, I suspect, I'm clueless.

'I honestly had no idea!' I whisper, a sob rising in my throat. Silly, I know, but I always get this way. A new baby in the world – the miracle of human life. 'Congratulations!' I want to give her a huge hug but daren't draw attention. 'Have you told the others?'

'You know Mummy – she's taken charge of the situation. Plus there's a minor complication,' she adds, looking round. 'It's not Jason's.'

So that's why Lady B's had smoke coming out of her ears for the past three days.

I suddenly remember something else. Does this (finally) explain Harriet's mysterious tête-à-tête with Christian on Monday, when I saw him reacting so oddly? Is he the father? And if so, is it too farfetched to imagine an outraged Lady Brash doing away with the charmer who's about to throw her daughter's advantageous marriage under the bus?

Before I can probe her further, I hear a voice call out for me. I give Harriet an apologetic smile and turn away.

It's Vicky, asking how she should decorate her cake (which she insists on calling a gâteau; everything sounds better in

French). I've been hoping to ask her some questions, to follow up on a hunch I've had, and now's my chance.

'You know what would look lovely,' I say. 'Crystallized rose petals.'

She puts her hand to her temple. 'Christian!' she declares. '*Pass the Gravy!* Series Three. Always fancied having a go – but where do you find roses in the middle of London?'

I assure her that the capital is a botanical wonderland if only you know where to look, and lead her out into the courtyard, putting out my hand to check for rain.

I haven't been here since Tuesday lunchtime. The shattered glass has been cleared away, the forensics team and all its paraphernalia come and gone. The only evidence of the murder is the door into Christian's flat, the glass of which has been boarded up with cheap plywood, swinging open. An invitation to the gory-minded to pop in and take a selfie, or a perpetrator still among us to revisit the scene of their crime.

I show Vicky the rose. It staggers me how anything can flower in such Stygian gloom but here it is. Deep pink – sweet-pea scent – no thorns; 'Zéphirine Drouhin', if I'm not mistaken.

I feel my phone buzz in my pocket.

'Excuse me,' I say, 'I need to take this. Pick some extra ones for the table while you're at it. And don't go away – I'll be right back.' I step under the cast-iron stairs, press the phone to my ear and hear the surge of an operatic chorus.

CHAPTER 44

'Hello?' cries a familiar voice. 'Hang on, let me turn that down . . . That's better, who's calling, please?'

'Jerome, you're calling me. It's Paul.'

'Oh, my dear! What a treat. I'm listening to Verdi – nothing like it for a Friday morning. Did you know Verdi means Friday in Italian?'

'It doesn't. Nor is it Friday.'

'Just poured myself a snifter – sun over the yardarm and all that.' My watch says ten to eleven. He continues: 'There's something I omitted to mention the other day . . . and it's been on my – ah – *conscience*.' The Archbishop of Canterbury couldn't sound more penitent. 'Christian begged me to keep it to myself, but I feel that, as events have turned out, one might consider my pledge, well, invalidated.

'Two years ago, he visited me at that little croft I had for a while in Scotland, the one that belonged to the people who made their fortune in raincoats. He delivered a sort of confession. I don't think you ever visited me there, but it was early April—'

'Is the date of relevance?' I snap.

'Well, actually, it is,' he replies in a hurt voice, which makes me feel a total rat. 'I'm only trying to help.'

'I'm sorry. Tell me everything, and take as long as you like.'

'He said it was his children's birthday. It was the first I'd heard of children – I don't think any of us knew – and he was in a blue funk. They were born before he came to London, it seems, and were left in Swindon in the care of his sister. I remember in particular because I asked him if they were left in *a handbag*. By the way, did I ever tell you about the time I set fire to Edith Evans in the dress circle at the Theatre Royal Newcastle?' I hear a cork pop and the glug of sherry.

'Anyway, the idea was that Christian would send a regular sum for their upkeep. To his eternal sorrow, he didn't keep his side of the bargain, and lost touch with them. It was the bitterest regret of his life. To have thrown it all away, his shot at being a parent. Poor Christian . . . he wept in my arms, lamenting his beautiful children.'

To think of my dear friend Christian, suffering such paternal remorse behind that playboy persona. And I'd had no idea.

'Thank you, Jerome, I'm so grateful you called.' If my hunch is correct – that Harriet is carrying Christian's child, and he knew it – how doubly poignant this is. 'I only wish there was some way of tracking them down.'

'Christian told me he tried every which way – but you're a clever boy, maybe you'll have more luck.'

'I mustn't keep you any longer,' I say.

'Delighted to help, I enjoy our little chats.'

'Just one final thing. It's a very long shot, but did he ever mention anyone called Darren?'

There's a pause and slurp. 'I once met a Shaun. And we have a Kyle in the village. Then there's Wayne Sleep, of course . . .'

It's like that scene in *Lawrence of Arabia*, waiting for a pinprick to turn into Omar Sharif.

'Do you know, there *was* a Darren at one point. That louche young man who used to drive Christian about – the one we thought might be mute, or pretending to be, like Harpo Marx?'

I hear the crescendo of a hundred male voices in the background, and Jerome joining in an octave below.

'Thank you,' I say. 'If you think of anything else, let me know.'

I am pondering how Christian's jailbird nephew Darren might fit into the jigsaw when I become aware of Vicky looming over me, secateurs in hand.

'Everything OK?' she asks.

Jerome belts everything out so loudly I'm sure she heard every word. Before I can quiz her, which is why I've dragged her out here, she leaps in.

'I'm glad to catch you,' she continues, moving in on me. 'Have a quiet moment.'

'Oh,' I say, recoiling. Despite myself, I'm reminded of a toy spider I once had, with wibble-wobble eyes. 'How can I help?'

'It might be relevant – to the investigation, I mean. And I haven't anyone else to tell.'

'How about the police?'

She purses her lips. 'It's a bit too . . . *personal* for that.'

Steeling myself for the worst, I ask her to proceed.

'Well, it's my feet, you see. Hubby says I've got wandering feet, but it's not true. Magnetic, more like,' she adds, with a titter.

What the dickens is she on about?

'Our first evening at dinner, the night poor Christian . . . had his accident. Well, I'm not the only one, I know for a fact lots of ladies do it, but I like to slip my shoes off of an evening and give my toes a bit of a wiggle. Under the table.' She points to one foot, then the other. 'It's not medical, but I find it relaxing.

'I've run into problems before – people getting naughty, touching my toes with theirs. *Nudging.* You'd be surprised what goes on under some tables.'

'So . . . you're telling me you were playing footsie on Monday night,' I say, with a wink.

'If you're going to be mischievous, I won't tell you. But there was more than one of them.'

'Two legs, you mean? But they could have belonged to the same person.'

She tuts, then adds, icily: 'They were coming at me from different directions.'

'Go on, then,' I say, enjoying this. 'Who did the legs belong to? Do I get to guess? Give me a clue!'

She sniffs. 'Some people have extraordinarily long legs, which is why you can never be one hundred per cent sure. But one was – I thought so at the time, but now we know – Lilith.' She blushes. 'Then another came along, very insistent. Tap tap tap, like Morse code.'

'Did it spell something out?'

She purses her lips. 'It was a gentleman's shoe – no doubt about it – so that will have been Gregory. Then another one arrives.'

'Goodness – like a game of Twister.'

'This time it's a lady's foot, soft and dainty – not like Lilith's – and it's stroking and rubbing. But not for long because it goes off with Gregory.'

'And who are you guessing this one might have belonged to?'

'I don't need to guess – it had a bunion, so that's Melanie.'

'Well, I never! And what's that got to do with . . . what happened?'

'Since then I've been keeping an eye on the two of them. That Melanie, she wriggles and flutters her eyelashes whenever a man walks into the room. And she watches Rose when she's not looking.'

'I've noticed that too. And Gregory?'

'Call it a woman's intuition, but there's something going on.'

Melanie and Gregory? No shortage of intrigues at number forty-one, but that's a new one. 'Thank you for confiding in me – I'll give it some thought. And before we go back to class, may I ask you something?'

'And what would that be?'

'That was a lovely scarf you knitted for Christian.'

She stops dead in her tracks and stares at me. 'What are you talking about?'

'The stripy one you knitted for him. You wrapped it up and left it on his doorstep.'

She turns red, then I see giant tears welling up in her eyes.

'I never got to give it to him,' she says in a trembling voice. 'I went over after dinner on Monday but he had some *woman* in there.'

'Didn't you knock?' I say.

This question embarrasses her further. 'Well, I admit I may have tried the handle. I almost went in, but I didn't want to disturb him. *Them.*'

'Did you tell the police?' I say.

'Of course not! They'd think I was mad – an ordinary middle-aged woman throwing herself at someone . . . someone like him.'

'You say a woman's voice . . . Could it have been on the radio?'

With this, her face convulses in a mixture of conflicting emotions. She begins to sob and throws herself into my arms.

CHAPTER 45

When the crisis has subsided, Vicky goes off for a quiet moment and I slide back into class unnoticed. 'Your shirt's all wet,' trumpets Lady Brash.

'It's raining again,' I counter.

When you're teaching you tend to do all the talking: this morning I'm going to listen. I will visit each bench in turn, ostensibly to check progress and have a friendly one-to-one. I'm horribly aware that this afternoon they'll all go home and the next couple of hours are my last chance to glean what I can.

'Looking great, Stephen, Christian would have been proud of you.' He stares at me.

'Any questions come up during the week? Culinary ones, I mean.' He's slicing discs of Parmesan biscuit dough, and very neatly, too.

He studies me thoughtfully, then says in his usual affectless way: 'My favourite class was the one on knives. You were saying that chefs are expected to provide their own, but how can you afford to buy them if you haven't got a job?'

I've got a few spare knives at home – ones that have seen better days; I might give him a couple, if it turns out he's serious. 'Do I take it we've won you over to the idea of becoming a chef?'

'I'm keeping my options open,' is all he says.

'When you bake them, take them to nut-brown – darker

than pastry. It was one of Christian's secrets,' I say and leave him to it.

Next I come to Lady B, who is in the process of woman-handling a chicken out of its saucepan, and not making a very good job of it.

'You'll find it easier if you put a wooden spoon into the cavity and lift it that way,' I suggest. Her ladyship hates some-one knowing better than her, but tough.

'It's too hot for me to strip off the flesh,' she says. 'I'll leave it to cool.'

'You know you can do it wearing rubber gloves?' I suggest. 'Keeps it out of your fingernails, too.'

She gives me a withering look. 'I don't want it tasting of washing-up liquid, thank you.'

'Any questions come up during the week?' I ask her, expect-ing something recherché along the lines of how to press a duck or preserve larks' tongues in aspic.

'Yes, there is. Your stepson's mother – Olinda, you said?'

Oh, no! If they're friends, Olinda will find out about the murder and my arrest; probably turn up to give evidence against me.

'I met an Olinda on a cruise last year. If you must know, it was for solo travellers. Can't say I warmed to her. I have noth-ing against women showing off their finer features, but not at the expense of decency. The men were clustering about her, of course, like wasps round a jam jar.'

That's Olinda, beyond a shadow of a doubt. After the split from Marcus, the slatternliness of her dress sense was revealed to the world, in the form of plunging tops and snatch-a-peep hemlines. 'Did you catch her surname?'

'If I did, I put it out of my mind,' replies her ladyship. 'But there can't be too many Olindas out there.'

'Lots and lots. More than you'd think,' I say. I'm turning to go when I decide to risk one more question. 'Wonderful about Harriet,' I say under my breath. Her eyes widen – if she were a dragon she'd emit a puff of smoke.

'I admit to having been taken by surprise,' she says cautiously.

'When did you hear the news?' I've found that if you ask a question head on – even one you have no right to ask – you often get a straight answer; except with politicians, that is.

'Late on Monday night. Just the time when . . . you know, poor Christian . . .' I feel her eyes drilling into me. 'You must forgive me if I've appeared . . . stressed.' She picks up her chef's knife. Once again I find myself wondering if Christian's murder might have been a mother-of-the-bride's desperate attempt to rescue her daughter's honour.

Melanie has prepped and lined up her ingredients in sequence, but seems reluctant to start cooking. Maybe her mind's elsewhere.

'Um,' I say, all casual, 'did you manage to speak to Ben yet?'

'I did but he was in a rush,' she replies. 'I promise I'll ask him when we speak later.'

'Please do,' I say. 'For Christian's sake if nothing else.'

Vicky has made a brave return and set herself up a production line of egg white, rose petals, sugar and a wire rack.

'How's the cake coming along?' I ask. No point in sugared rose petals if there's nothing for them to beautify.

'In the oven,' she says.

'That was quick.'

'I don't know what all the fuss is about, I just did what the recipe said.' She places the first petal on the rack with a surprisingly delicate touch. 'Breaks my heart to think Lilith won't get to enjoy a slice.'

'Although it's hardly gluten-free,' I add.

'I was unkind to her and nothing will ever change that.'

'Did the course in general live up to expectations, apart from the awful bits?'

She takes her time thinking about this. 'I'll be honest with you: I wouldn't have dreamt of coming along if it hadn't been for Christian. Plus I don't expect I'll see anyone from here again—'

I protest, but she continues.

'No, I don't make friends easily at the best of times, and you know as well as I do that these aren't my kind of people. But we've been through a lot together this week, and we've stuck it out—' (She's welling up again.) 'And I'm not going to keep going on about my freezer, and if and when hubby does come home, he can sort out dinner for himself in future, because I've got my own life to lead, and I'm not going to waste any more of it.' She concludes with the words, 'What I meant to say was: thank you.' Before rushing out of the room.

'Nothing to worry about,' I tell the others. 'It's been an emotional few days.'

Next, De'Lyse summons me over. 'Don't think much of your recipe,' she declares. 'How long do you hardboil eggs for?'

I explain that seven or eight minutes is the usual advice, but you can achieve a less rubbery effect and prevent the yolk blackening at the edge by starting the eggs in cold water, bringing them to a rolling boil, clapping on the lid, turning off the heat – and leaving them for exactly ten minutes.

'That's the way I'll do it from now on,' she says. If I get time I'll show her that trick where you roll a hardboiled egg under the blade of your knife so it pops perfectly in two: just the thing for TikTok.

'And in general, has it been a useful week for you?' I ask.

'Apart from the obvious, it's been great. I wasn't sure it would be my thing beforehand, and I'm sorry about making you change today's lessons, but I'm glad I came. I've learnt a lot from you. Or to put it another way: I've learnt that there's a lot more for me to learn.

'By the way,' she concludes, now addressing the class in general, 'did anyone else see Paul on the news this morning? He never told us he was related to some famous poet!'

CHAPTER 46

I wish Melanie would get on with it and speak to her husband. Finally she leaves the classroom, phone in hand, and I'm left to pace about for another quarter of an hour. When I can bear it no longer, I go to see what's happening and find her striding about the front hall as if she owns the place, yelling into her phone. 'Quite so, darling . . . Yes, I'll do just as you say . . . Me too . . . Kiss kiss!' She smiles brightly at me, showing her teeth.

I usher her into the library. The rain is starting to plash down heavily again.

'That was Ben! He's made it to work – sounds just fine. Taking me out to dinner tomorrow night.'

'Well, that's terrific!' I say. The world has fallen to pieces, but at least marital harmony has been restored.

'Maybe we should fix up a blind date for Cressida and Jonny!' she says gaily. 'Kill two birds with one stone.'

Good grief! The very thought. 'Erm . . . Absolutely never going to happen! Jonny's nearly my age. Plus he's already got a girlfriend.' We've never met and my impression of her oscillates; sometimes I imagine her as a Goth she-devil dominatrix, tying Jonny to the bed and whipping him till he bleeds; sometimes as a crushed, powerless victim. I hope for her sake it's the former. 'So what did he say?'

She pretends to look at a book and puts it back down. 'It turns out Ben *did* know Christian.'

'Why didn't you say before?' I protest.

She pauses. 'Ben asked me not to.'

'Why?' I ask.

'I told you the other day. He didn't approve of Rose having an affair – thought she was being taken advantage of: you know, a vulnerable widow. He was reluctant to be drawn in. He still is.'

'And was Ben happy about your friendship with Christian?'

This catches her by surprise. 'How do you—?' She looks me in the eye, which makes a change. 'I don't know who you've been gossiping with, but OK, I was close to Christian, and he may have been something of a sore point between me and Ben. The two of them knew each other from way back – twenty-five years at least.'

'So why are you telling me all this now? Is it Ben's idea or is it just to get me off your back?'

'Ben has nothing to hide – nor do I,' she says defiantly. 'But as you seem set on stirring things up, he thought it better for you to hear the full story.'

'Fine,' I say, praying that this time she's going to speak the truth. 'Fire away.'

She takes a deep breath. 'We have to go right back to the late nineties. I don't know if you're aware, but Chris – as he was then known – was married.'

I nod, and look at my watch, which has the desired effect of speeding her on.

'He and his wife lived in a particularly depressing little MOD flat at Tidworth. Army housing of the period was abysmal – row upon row of pre-fabs disappearing into the distance, with weedy gardens and the odd spindly tree.

'Anyway, one January he went off with his colleagues for a stag weekend and came back on the Sunday evening to find his poor wife slumped across the kitchen table, dead.

'What made it even more dreadful was the babies. They

were found shut in a bedroom, safe and sound. After that there was endless speculation, and various investigations and inquests, though the only really certain thing was that their mother died of carbon monoxide poisoning. Chris blamed himself, as any husband would, because a few weeks earlier he'd installed a wardrobe partially blocking the flue; you know how deadly these things can be. But the boiler itself was prehistoric, and no one could remember when it was last serviced.

'In court he claimed the accommodation provided by the army was substandard and it all got very nasty. He left the service in the worst possible circumstances, though it has to be said the regiment gave him a generous settlement. Ben knows because he signed it off.

'One more thing. Chris was extremely popular with his fellow soldiers, and one of the younger men set up a sort of fund for everyone to pay into, to make sure the twins were provided for.'

'Did you say twins?'

'Twin girls, I believe.' For some reason, this seems to make the story even more poignant. 'It was another large sum. Comforting to think that those poor motherless babes would want for nothing. Once he left the army, though, no one heard from Chris again. It was as if he disappeared.'

Large sums of money vanishing without trace . . . family left behind for someone else to bankroll . . . unexplained bad debts . . . beating by thugs . . . a racing calendar hanging on the wall. Why did I never think of it before?

It had occasionally crossed my mind how strange it was that over two decades he accumulated fame and success but nothing else. The occasional fast car, a couple of Rolexes – which came and went – but never a house or flat. If you'd asked him, he'd have told you he blew his money on holidays, fine living and 'ladies'; but he wouldn't have been telling the truth. Christian was a gambler.

'I still don't understand why you kept this quiet,' I say. 'Did you tell the police when they were interviewing you?'

She thinks about this a moment. 'I can't believe they'd be remotely interested. Speaking of which, please keep this to yourself. It's old history.'

'Just one final thing,' I say. 'Was someone called Darren ever mentioned, in connection with Christian?'

'Of course. They were very close, although Christian was much older. Darren set up the fund for Christian's babies. Another sad story – he was injured in Basra and invalided out of the service. His full name was Darren Edwards.'

* * *

Musing on all this, I turn my attention back to Gregory, who has enlisted the help of Suzie and pulled out a huge chrome food mixer.

'You'll need iced water,' I say. Suzie fetches a tray of ice cubes and a jug of water.

We tip the flour and eggs into the bowl and insert the dough hook attachment. 'Ready?' I ask Gregory, and he nods, jug in hand.

From behind me I hear a crunching sound. *Aargh!* I turn to see that Suzie has slipped a couple of ice cubes into her mouth. Of all the noises in all the world, the one I most hate is the sound of ice being crunched in a human jaw.

I am still flinching when I turn on the mixer and – *BAM!*

The mixer leaps from beneath my fingertips and there's a blinding flash. My body goes numb and I'm aware of being hurled backwards like a rag doll, landing sprawled across the cooker. I hear a scream from De'Lyse and a vicious hiss as her pan of eggs goes over, narrowly missing both of us. A plasticky burning smell fills the air and a veil of soot descends around the burnt-out mixer.

'What the . . .?' I gasp. 'That could have killed me!'

The students help me to a chair. To do them justice, they're as stunned and appalled as I am.

'Short circuit,' declares Gregory, rubbing his chin.

'Lucky you're wearing rubber soles or you'd've burnt to a crisp,' declares Vicky, her pupils huge.

'Did you see that?' says De'Lyse, wishing she'd captured it for her fans.

'Keep your distance, Harriet. It might still be live,' commands Lady B, waving her daughter back.

Suzie capably takes charge. She turns the electricity off at the isolation switch, removes the débris and wipes everything down. After this, she and Gregory test to make sure the socket hasn't been damaged – it hasn't – and she disappears briefly to fetch the Chester Square Accident Book. Producing a felt-tip from her pocket, she fills in three boxes, signs with a large squiggled *S* and we're back in business.

Apparently I've smuts on my face, so I disappear briefly to wash. By the time I get back, everything has changed.

CHAPTER 47

The students have lined up across the room and are glowering at me with accusing eyes. In the centre stand Starsky and Hutch.

'You're back,' I say, trying to sound upbeat. 'How's tricks?'

'It's too late for jokes, Paul,' says the DCI, with a reproachful shake of the head.

Because of its clerestory windows, the Old Ballroom is flooded with natural light. Even though it's rained all week, I've enjoyed the way it dances about, adding unexpected highlights and sparkles to objects and surfaces. A ray of sunshine has chosen this very moment to beam its way down through the clouds. It hovers over number forty-one, shafts through the glass and alights upon Blondie's golden curls, bestowing its beatific radiance on them. If he were holding a harp, you would honestly mistake him for an angel.

I look at the spectacle with astonishment – the students turn in wonder, too. How many hours does that take in front of the mirror each morning? What expert application of conditioners and oils and unguents and pomades and clays and waxes and mousses and spritzes? Or is it possible that someone can just wake up looking so naturally – bouffant?

He gives a modest cough to recall us from our reverie and moistens his sculpted lips. We're all hoping for something from Handel's *Messiah*, or at the very least a psalm, but instead he intones: 'Paul Delamare, you will accompany us to

Belgravia Police Station on suspicion of the murder of Christian Wagner. I remind you that you do not have to say anything but it may harm your defence if you do not mention, when questioned, something that you later rely on in court.'

I look round my students imploringly. All I can see are expressions of scorn and pity. Vicky is shaking her head slowly and wringing her hands. De'Lyse stares at me like a Gorgon. Lady B has curled her lip, as if I'm a dead vole the cat dragged in. The Hon. Harriet and Melanie are dabbing their eyes, and Gregory's jaw is working away noiselessly, as if he's munching seed. Stephen looks on expressionless.

The drama of the moment is broken by a frantic buzzing sound. All eyes jerk around the room. The DCI and Blondie clutch their walkie-talkies, De'Lyse fumbles for her phone and it drops with a crash.

One person alone remains unperturbed – although he does look slightly puzzled. 'Is that me?' says Gregory, poking his ear. The noise stops. 'Battery needs changing – carry on.'

The officers shift from foot to foot, impatient to usher me out, but I realize this is the last time I'll see my students. 'I suppose that's goodbye then,' I say. 'Thank you, everyone, for being such a pleasure to teach and I hope we'll meet again one day, in happier circumstances.'

Stony silence.

'And I almost forgot – enjoy your lunch! Quick reminder about the chicken – don't overheat it when you add it back to the cream sauce.'

Vicky puts up her hand. At least someone has a kind word to say, maybe good luck or thank you.

'Quick question,' she pipes up. 'Do we get to keep our aprons?'

* * *

This time I decide to take up the duty solicitor option, and am duly informed that a certain Krisha Basu is on the way. I'd hate being on call, having to drop whatever I was doing and traipse off to sit in a little room listening to people arguing.

I'm allowed to make one phone call, so I leave an upbeat voicemail for Julie. There's no one like her at times of need – she was in Perth, Australia when Marcus died and at my side twenty-three hours later – but I'm determined not to mess up today for her; it's too important. 'Just checking in,' I say. 'I'll be, er, offline for the next couple of hours, but don't worry, everything's fine. Hope it's going well – see you tonight.'

They say that time passes faster the older you get, but let me assure you, not if you're at a police station waiting to be interviewed on a murder charge. I'm aware that on the floors above and below me, dozens of officers and detectives are toiling away to prove my guilt, poking about in my past and raking up evidence of wrongdoing. I feel the forces of justice gathering against me.

Eventually I ask a passing constable if I'm allowed pencil and paper. Writing things down uses a different part of the brain and may shed some light; perhaps I can even offer to share my conclusions with the detectives, help get them off my back.

SUSPECT	*ALIBI*	*MOTIVE*	*NOTES*
Gang	*N/A*	*Money*	*No evidence of robbery. Darren?*
Terrorists	*N/A*	*Jihad*	*Decapitation. But why Christian?*
Melanie H-P	*Asleep*	*Jilted (or unrequited) lover*	*Unreliable witness. Lipstick at scene. Previous love interest (Alan Hoyt) died in suspicious circumstances. Difficult marriage – drunk/jealous husband?*
Rose	*Doing accounts*	*Jilted lover*	*Perfume at scene. Husband number 1 died in suspicious circumstances.*

Vicky	*Delivers scarf, then bed*	*Crime of passion*	*Stalker. Went to C's flat on murder night. Also: jealous husband?*
Milla	*Unknown*	*Ambition*	*To get her hands on the cookery school.*
De'Lyse	*Online*	*Ambition*	*Accomplice to Milla?*
Stephen	*Gaming online*	*Revenge*	*Insulted/belittled by C. in front of everyone.*
Lady B	*Arguing*	*Punishment*	*For impregnating her daughter.*
Harriet	"	"	*Also: so wedding to Jason can go ahead.*
Suzie	*Watching film online*	*Revenge*	*Sexually harrassed by C.*
Gregory	*Visits C. then prostitute*	*Money*	*Blamed C. for his bankruptcy.*
Lilith	*Asleep*	*Unknown*	*Someone needed to silence her. For what?*

I'm an ardent believer in the power of the unconscious. Scientists may have solved the mysteries of the universe, but they haven't even begun to explain the workings of the human brain. I feel my own churning and chugging now, like my computer when its hard drive spins into action. The answer is staring me in the face, I feel it.

But now my solicitor has arrived.

CHAPTER 48

Krisha is five foot two, very pretty with tawny-coloured doe eyes and a sweet smile. She's wearing a crease-free black skirt suit, and a pair of new-looking white trainers so she can scoot extra-fast from the Tube to the police station. In view of what I'm accused of, I think they could have sent someone with more experience, rather than this clearly very recent graduate.

We sit side by side in the same interview room as last time, under the same harsh lighting. She tells me to listen carefully to everything I'm asked and not to answer anything I'm unsure of . . . not to withhold information nor try to outwit the officers . . . that she's here to support me and we can take a break at any time.

I show her the chart I've drawn up. 'We could pool resources,' I say hopefully. She closes her hand gently around mine, scrunching up the paper.

'I wouldn't,' she says.

'I'm sure I know some stuff they don't, simply from being around the students the whole time. Such as Darren, a nephew of Christian's who's been—'

'Concentrate on answering their questions. It will alienate them if you tell them how to do their job.'

When the DCI and DS stride in, looking like the Big Bad Bear and Goldilocks, they have a gleeful look about them. They're going to make mincemeat out of Krisha – and me.

Blondie announces the recording equipment is on and goes straight in, unable to restrain his excitement. Krisha raises an eyebrow and shoots me a smile of encouragement.

The DS is reading from his notes, rather fast. He asks if I'm sure the glass door to Christian's flat was broken when I arrived on the scene.

'Yes. It was only because I saw the broken glass all over the courtyard that I went across to it in the first place,' I reply, confidently.

'There's a theory—'

'Stop right there, Detective Sergeant,' says Krisha, holding up her hand. 'This is going to take all night if you go off at unattributed tangents. Please stick to the point so as not to inconvenience my client any longer than is strictly necessary.'

'Erm, OK,' says Blondie, looking slightly abashed. 'It's just that there seems to have been a clumsy attempt to make it look like the flat was broken into.'

'Because the murder happened at midnight and the glass was broken in the morning,' says Krisha, with a winning smile. 'It's OK, we get it.' Then she turns to me: 'Paul, they're asking if you broke the glass when you arrived in the morning?'

'Why would I do that?' I ask.

'Yes or no?' she says, sharply.

'No.'

The DCI doesn't look particularly impressed with the way that went, so he takes over, low and slow. 'Tell us about your relationship with Mr Wagner, Paul.'

'As I said last time, we've been friends for twenty-odd years and worked together on many, many occasions. I always thought we were quite close, but since he died I'm not so sure.'

'What do you mean by that?'

'Only that I found out that he'd been married, which I didn't know before. And served in the army.'

'How did you find that out?'

'It was online.'

'And you were surprised?'

'That he'd been married, yes, because he always seemed to enjoy playing the field. Ever since I've known him, he's had a spectacular woman on his arm. Numerous girlfriends. Innumerable, if I'm honest. But no one permanent. I didn't think it was in his nature.'

'And the army?'

'We never spoke much about what he'd done before we met, but military service . . . you'd think he'd have mentioned it.'

'How did you feel about these various relationships?'

'They were of no concern or interest to me. Until Chester Square, I hadn't seen Christian for a couple of years. In case it's relevant, I believe he had an affair with Rose Hoyt, though you'd need to confirm that with her.' Krisha nods approvingly.

'Yes, we're aware of that. What other affairs do you know of?'

After a quick whisper with Krisha, I say: 'Harriet told me she's pregnant, and I think Christian might have been, well, responsible.'

'Lady Brash's daughter. Yes, he was quite the Casanova.'

It crosses my mind that this might be the moment to share some of the other secrets I've unearthed, except that Krisha told me not to. And I have to admit, it sounds as if the police have been doing their homework.

'Incidentally,' I add, while I seem to be on the front foot, 'I was *extremely* disappointed that my name was leaked to Metro24 this morning. You promised me faithfully last time that there was no reason my involvement – in your investigation, I mean – should be made public.'

The DCI shrugs. 'Didn't come from us. There were quite a

few people in the dining room when you were arrested – how about one of them tipping off the news? Mr, er, Greenleaf, for instance. Not the most reliable of characters.'

'You mean Mr Farson?'

He raises an eyebrow. 'I take it that Mr *Farson* has confided in you.'

'You could put it that way,' I reply.

Now the DCI gives a curt nod to Blondie. With a becoming shake of his mane, the DS commences: 'At dinner on Monday evening, you were reported to have said the following, I'll read it out. "It's not the sort of thing you say to people nowadays. There's no place for attitudes like that." Did you say those words, Paul?'

Where on earth did they dig that up from? 'Erm . . . Sounds like the sort of thing I *would* say. Was that when Christian was being such a pillock towards the young student, Stephen Cartwright?'

'That's what we're asking *you*, Paul.'

'Oh, come on,' declares Krisha. 'No need for these theatrics!'

Blondie stiffens.

'Ms Basu,' says the DCI, 'please let's try and keep the tone polite and professional. My colleague would like to know if Paul's criticism was directed at Mr Wagner.'

'Yes. Although it was intended only for Stephen's ears, because he's very young and seemed upset by Christian's behaviour. I felt bad for him.'

'Thank you,' Blondie says, in a crowing tone: he's back in his stride. 'Now, multiple witnesses report the following acrimonious exchange between you and Mr Wagner three hours before his murder: "You said we were in this together, but it's the same old, same old. Just occasionally, you need to think about someone other than yourself."'

Once again, I'm staggered by how they've got hold of this, word for word. Was someone taping me?

'Well, yes,' I reply. 'But what I meant was that Christian had let me down by not phoning me back, and not turning up for classes as promised. Not in the existential sense.'

'Meaning what?' asks Blondie.

'Don't you have dictionaries round here?' I snap back.

Krisha gives me a fierce look and takes over. 'Paul was annoyed Christian didn't return his phone call or behave in a businesslike way – it wasn't a death threat.'

'Your attitude towards Mr Wagner has been described as *jealous*,' Blondie continues. '"Jealous of his glamour and success" is how someone put it. Do you envy his job?'

'I've never heard anything so ridiculous in my life,' I say. 'Who told you that? Have you been conjuring up witnesses from nowhere? People you met down the pub? I said nothing of the kind.'

'It's not what you said, it's how you came across, Paul.'

'Look – I didn't envy his job, I didn't envy his TV career. And most of all, I didn't envy him the glamour models slash actresses slash reality TV stars.'

'Wrong end of the ballroom,' mutters Blondie under his breath, but soon wishes he hadn't.

'What did you say?' cries Krisha, launching herself out of her chair, doe eyes turned cold and fierce.

Blondie looks at the floor.

'That's it! Interview terminated! I am not having you intimidate my client by making homophobic slurs. We will be filing an official complaint.' Krisha throws open the door and ushers me out.

CHAPTER 49

I don't know where this legal firebrand came from, but I'm relieved she's on my side. At the officers' earnest beseeching, she's gone back in with them, leaving me sitting on my own in another small featureless room.

I really must learn not to go by first impressions. Krisha is just the latest example. What about Lilith, who only three days ago I was laughing at? It must take courage to live the life she does in the Bible Belt of North Wales. Or Vicky – trivial, vacuous even, on the surface, but riven by passion and unfulfilled desires. Even colourless Suzie probably has a story to tell, though I can't imagine it being a *Sunday Times* bestseller.

Maybe the trick is to imagine myself stepping into their shoes. For a grim moment I try and picture myself as Rose, endlessly pacing up and down the draughty corridors of number forty-one, catching glimpses of myself in the countless mirrors. Or Lady B discovering my daughter is pregnant by the wrong man, and that I neglected to take out wedding insurance.

My thoughts are interrupted by the return of Krisha. I don't know what they've been discussing out there, but she seems to have lost some of her bounce. 'Paul, you do realize how serious this is?' she says. 'You sound a bit, well, flippant.'

'*Flippant?*' I can hardly get the word out. 'Krisha, if I'm coming across badly, I can't help it, it's who I am. I'm fighting for my life here.'

Nor, when I return to face my interrogators, do they look as castigated as I might have wished. I get the sense that was just the overture.

They offer me water, and I notice Blondie has provided himself with some already. You can tell from his flawless complexion that he takes hydration seriously: a large tumbler (real glass), bobbing with ice cubes. I sincerely hope he doesn't start crunching them.

The DCI goes first. His voice has got gruffer.

'I'm glad we sorted that out. A couple more things that have come up, Paul. When we interviewed you the day before yesterday, this was found in your jacket.'

'How dare you?' I declare. 'Someone offers to hang up your coat and then goes snooping through the pockets? Is that even allowed?' Krisha shrugs; obviously it is.

The officer produces a plastic bag containing some pieces of dried pasta. He tips them out onto the table. 'Do you recognize these?'

Good God! I did pick up some bits of pasta from Christian's floor. I'd totally forgotten.

I've always been good at pasta shapes – identifying them is another of my party pieces. This is that twisted one from southern Italy, usual accompanying sauce is tomatoes and anchovies, but what's happening to my brain? I know the name but can't think of it. Not fusilli, not casarecce, not strozzapreti, not trofie . . . I feel myself getting all hot and panicky, like a tongue-tied student on *University Challenge*.

'The name's completely gone out of my head,' I say. 'If you'll give me a second—'

'We're not interested in what it's called, Paul. Where did it come from?'

'Well, that I can remember: Puglia,' I reply. They look blank.

'The heel of Italy,' says Krisha.

Blondie cuts in, 'We know that, but the DCI is asking how it got in your pocket.'

'Oh, I see – a jar must have got knocked over in Christian's kitchen. The pasta was on the floor. Some kind of fight . . .'

Krisha jumps straight in. 'But you don't *know* that, do you, Paul?'

'Of course not, I wasn't there.'

Krisha leans forward, clears her throat and says in a loud, clear voice: 'I'm confirming for the benefit of Metropolitan Police cameras and recording devices, and any other Orwellian spyware that you guys may have stashed away under the floorboards, that my client is not suggesting there *was* a fight . . . or that he *saw* a fight . . . let alone that he was *in* a fight . . . Have I made that clear?' The DCI nods, but he's still looking pleased as Punch.

I continue: 'There was some pasta on the floor when I went into the flat and, I can't explain why, I just picked some up and put it in my pocket.'

'Were you trying to clear it up?'

'It was all over the place – I'd never have been able to get it all into my pockets. Besides, why would I want to?'

'Leave the questions to us, please.'

'Oh, for Pete's sake,' cries Krisha. 'Can you two stop trying to score points the whole time?'

The DCI gives a patronizing smile and passes the baton to his colleague. It's the moment Blondie's been waiting for – there's a gleam in his eye almost as bright as his shimmering locks.

'Last but not least,' he says, his voice rising. He produces what looks like a cheap photo album, the sort of thing Woolworth's used to sell before its sad and untimely demise. 'We'd like to talk to you about some evidence we've had in from forensics. It appears that Mr Wagner died of a lethal drug injection before the decapitation occurred—'

'Oh! I had no idea . . .' I say. A wave of sickness passes over me. 'Are you sure?'

'Since then, we've received anonymous information—'

'You mean a tip-off?' interrupts Krisha. 'I'd look very carefully where that came from if I were you.'

'If I may finish, we received information that an article belonging to you contained items of interest.' He holds up a photo of a small brown vial, with a ruler beside it to show scale. Then one of a syringe sticking into a cork. 'These were concealed in a leather bag of yours.'

'Whoa!' I say. 'Hold it right there. A syringe? You're out of your minds.'

Blondie shrugs and slides back in his chair, then produces another photo.

'They were hidden inside this.'

'That's my dad's old medical bag!' I cry. 'How dare you interfere with my things without my permission?' Krisha motions with her hand for me to calm down.

'A Gladstone bag, I believe it's called,' says Blondie, pleased with himself, though I bet he had to google it. 'We'll take you through the formal identification process later, but it was dropped off to us anonymously. Said syringe was found in a concealed compartment in the base of this Gladstone bag.'

'Concealed compartment?' I declare. 'What are you talking about? I don't believe such a thing exists.'

He flicks over another page and dangles an incriminating image carelessly before me. Damn, I always knew I should have inspected that bag more carefully.

'Well, someone hid it there.'

'We have your fingerprints on the cork, Paul. Perfect fingerprints – textbook, according to forensics. And I expect you remember the cork itself?' He holds up another picture.

'Of course not. Anyway, all corks look alike.'

'Anything in particular printed on this one?'

'Oh, come on!' says Krisha. 'My client can read, probably a whole lot better than you two.'

I continue, sounding defensive: 'So what? A third of all French wines come from Languedoc. I opened the wine the other night at dinner, for instance – I'm sure everyone there must have seen me doing it.'

'Which evening?'

'Tuesday. The night after Christian's . . . death.'

Blondie slides even further back in his chair, in what I believe is called a man-splay, and pushes back a stray curl. I'm surprised Krisha doesn't throw a glass of water in his crotch, but she is frowning, worried by the way this is going.

'Hmm . . .' he says, his pitch rising further as he moves in for the kill. 'Something not quite right there, Paul. The hypodermic was used on Monday night, so you must have handled the cork *before* that.'

I can't think of anything to say, except I never had anything to do with any syringe stuck in a cork and someone please wake me from this nightmare.

'Another thing came up,' he says, mock-casually. 'We got the guys browsing through old police records . . .' I know what's coming '. . . and we gather you are – how shall I put this? – not unfamiliar with illegal substances, stimulants, narcotics, hallucinogenics, et cetera.' His lusciously quilted lips linger over the last word as if savouring a caramel and sea salt truffle. 'Which bring us to the vial. The vial containing Gamma-Hydroxybutyrate.'

I look at Krisha imploringly and she raises an eyebrow. I can see written across her forehead: *Oh, great, now I find out I'm defending a crackhead*. I start to sweat.

Unable to resist turning the thumbscrew, the DCI leans in. 'You may know it by its common name, GHB.'

The last time I heard a voice that low was the Commendatore's ghost in *Don Giovanni*. I whisper in Krisha's ear that I need a break. This is catastrophic.

The officers consent to half an hour, in a cell this time, but they'd like me to sign something before I go. I know it's vital that everything should be done in the right and proper way, but is it really necessary?

What they hand me on this occasion, however, is a blank piece of paper.

'What's he signing?' asks Krisha, sharply.

'His name,' says Blondie. I'm really not happy – they could type a full confession above my signature and say I'd signed it! I look at Krisha, but she shrugs.

'Well, I'll need a pen,' I say.

The officers place a ballpoint on the desk in front of me. They're watching me with such obviously intent expressions that I'm tempted to sign 'Mickey Mouse' or 'Judy Garland', but there's been enough aggro for one day so I settle for my own name.

As I hand it over to them, I observe a quick exchange of glances, as if they're somehow . . . disappointed.

* * *

An hour and a half later, Krisha steps into the cell and tells me I'm being released on conditional bail. I have to ask what this means, but I want to hug her, spin her round in the air. It's all I can do not to burst into tears.

How did she manage it? It's a miracle.

'I wasn't going to tell you, but it's the first time I've done one of these on my own. I only qualified last week,' she informs me with the widest smile. I haven't the heart to admit I guessed as much. 'I was able to do some bargaining – there were some sloppy bits of procedure.'

'They're making total fools of themselves,' I say slowly. 'They haven't the first idea what happened, so they're trying to pin it on me. They don't even *mention* Lilith being pushed down the stairs – what kind of investigation is this?'

'Look, they've got some serious stuff on you already, and when the rest of the forensic findings come in, it'll likely make things even worse.'

'By the time that happens, the bird will have flown. In fact – it's too late already. They'll all have gone home by now.'

She ignores this. 'You're my client – you're the one I'm worried about. I think you should expect to be brought back into custody tomorrow, so tonight is your last chance to get your story straight. And if you seriously believe someone is setting you up, who and why?'

After that, she takes me to the custody suite and I receive back my wallet and keys. I'm not just hot and sweaty but trembling all over. 'You've forgotten my phone,' I say. My voice has gone wobbly, too.

The constable explains my phone can be returned for one quick call, but otherwise it will be impounded while the tech guys examine it. I know about this from Julie: it's not just a question of who I've been ringing, or who's been ringing me – they can usually track exactly where you've been while you've had your phone about your person. I must remember to use a burner next time.

Five minutes later, to my surprise, Blondie arrives, bearing my phone on a little tray.

'Oh, it's you,' I say.

I refuse to meet his eye but can't help noticing him glance over his shoulder to check we're alone. 'I'm genuinely sorry about all this,' he says. 'I'm only doing my job.'

What the bejesus is he talking about?

'The PC will be back in a minute to collect the phone,' he adds, 'but I wanted to say . . . Well, I hope . . .' He smiles straight at me. 'You seem like a nice guy, that's all.' And walks out.

Did that just happen?

I shake my head in disbelief and pick up my phone. I want to speak to Julie, but my battery is showing red, so I decide to text instead. Three words in, it starts flashing that it's about to die, so with trembling finger I hit an emoji and press send.

DESSERT

Friday 2nd April 2021

I don't mind admitting it's been a tough old time since the brasserie biz went down the tube. My agent has been knocking on the doors of Food Network – zilch. When pushed, my book publisher asked if I fancied doing an air-fryer book. No way.

I've moved in with Rose – a flat at the cookery school. It's tiny – hardly any light – and strings attached: I have to do ALL the teaching. She thinks she's doing me a favour, I reckon the opposite.

Milla's up to something . . . she brought her boss round the other day when Rose was out and I caught her giving him the grand tour and snapping photos. The atmosphere's pretty toxic.

While clearing out I came across a recipe I brought back from when I was posted in Düsseldorf. Blitzkuchen. Happy days.

This is their birthday, so it seems right to be making a cake.

THUNDER AND LIGHTNING CAKE

My version is called Thunder and Lightning to celebrate the Cornish teatime treat – a Cornish split spread with clotted cream and drizzled with golden syrup.

For the cake, cream 120g softened butter with 100g caster sugar and 4 egg yolks, then beat in 1 teaspoon vanilla, 3 tablespoons milk and 120g self-raising flour till just mixed. Divide between two buttered and base-lined 20cm tins and spread thinly and evenly.

Whisk 4 egg whites till frothy, then continue whipping, gradually adding 150g sugar, until thick and meringue-like. Spread evenly on top of cake batter and sprinkle each layer with 3 tablespoons toasted flaked almonds and ½ tablespoon demerara sugar. (This will give the layers a nougatine topping.) Bake at 160°C fan for about 30 minutes, till puffed and nuts are browned; the meringue will sink (it's meant to).

To assemble, put one cake layer meringue-side up on your serving plate. Spread delicately with home-made or bought salted caramel icing (about 250g) and the same of clotted cream (don't beat the cream or it'll go runny). Top with remaining layer. Finish with a sprinkling of chocolate curls and for a bit of bling, edible gold leaf. Serves 8–10.

CHAPTER 50

The one time I'd actually appreciate a lift in a police car, there isn't one available. I step out into lashing rain and the occasional flash of lightning: the full power of the storm is upon us.

My plan is to get home and wait outside till the locksmith arrives. So what if I'm soaked to the bone? At least I'm out of that place.

It's hard to run in wet clothes – they catch and chafe in all the wrong places – but it feels good. I want to put as much distance between me and Buckingham Palace Road as I can. This area is so ugly. What can the developers have been thinking?

They say that running is good for the brain, and I feel it now. When this is all over, I vow to take more exercise.

I jog through Ebury Square and cross the road into Eaton Terrace, splashing water about like Gene Kelly in *Singin' in the Rain*.

Just as I turn into South Eaton Place, a brilliant flash of lightning illuminates a row of shops and I stop dead. A signwriter has been at work above the door of a new childrenswear shop called 'Princess'; the *S*s have been painted as squiggle shapes, like snakes.

I stop and stare. Rain trickles down my collar as my mind races. What is it about that sign? By the time the thunder rumbles, I'm running again.

* * *

I must phone the police without delay – I can't wait to see their smug faces when they find out how wrong they were. But first, there's something I need to check at the school: I must be rock-solid certain and I need proof.

I pick up my pace, trying to keep my distance from trees and lamp posts: now wouldn't be the time to be struck by lightning.

Through Chester Square – more dark and glowering than ever – and round to the door of number forty-one. I punch *1904* into the keypad, glad I'll never have to do it again.

The locks spring back and I step inside. It's deathly quiet. No coats on the rack, no umbrellas in the stand, no lights on – they've all gone. I've never been on my own in this great big house before, and it's not a friendly feeling.

'Anybody there?' I cry.

The disinfectant smell has returned, along with the moribund chrysanthemums. They look ragged and are dropping petals, but even so it's not natural for flowers to last so long: Rose must put something in the water.

First I make my way to the library. This is a minor detail, hardly germane to the case, but it's been nagging at me – like a song you can't get out of your head. It'll take twenty seconds to sort out, but someone has tidied away the *Larousse* I saw earlier. I'll look it up later.

This time of evening, when twilight is so thick you can almost touch it with your fingers, and cats wake to go out hunting, is what my mother used to call *dimpsy*. 'It's coming in dimpsy,' she would say. It's a West Country expression – her family came from the cold, high plateau of mid-Devon, land of bright-pink soil and twisting, high-hedged lanes. Another was, 'I've let my cup of tea go zimzaw,' meaning cold. I wish people would revive the old words rather than keep inventing new ones.

For some reason she's been on my mind during the last few days. Julie's always trying to get me to go and 'talk to someone' about what happened, but I've resisted. Sometimes I try to imagine Mum aged seventy, which is what she would have turned this year.

Among the many puzzles of this case, one of the most frustrating has been how someone pushed Lilith down the stairs then vanished without trace. I think I know how it was done, and that's what I'm here to check.

I pad my way up the Grand Staircase, across the first floor landing and— What's that? I freeze. But it's nothing – probably a pipe gurgling; I wonder when Rose last had her radiators bled.

Up and up I go, right to the top of the house. Here's the box room from which Alan plunged, and the bathroom where Lilith enjoyed possibly her final soak. I stand for a moment on the landing, studying the *Vertigo* poster, then lift it off the wall.

Behind it, just as I suspected, is a familiar pair of sliding doors in burnished mahogany and a button marked Down. So handy if a guest fancies breakfast in bed, or if someone wants to nip up unnoticed in order to shove a Welshwoman down the stairs.

A vicious flick of lightning illuminates the scene in brilliant blue, then five seconds later there's a wallop of thunder. Everyone thinks that five seconds means the storm is five miles away, but that's not true: it's five seconds per mile. By my calculation, as it's coming from the north, that means it's currently over Hyde Park.

I reach into my pocket – time to phone the police. I'm looking forward to an apology from the DCI and his poncy sidekick. Maybe even an MBE.

But of course there's no phone there – the police took it.

I pad my way down to the first floor, pick my way through the obstacle course on the landing and step into the Shelley Room. A gust of Rose's cloying scent greets me at the door: the lingering sort that sinks into carpets and curtains. Everything is in its place, except that the ornate cast-iron safe yawns wide. I peer inside – just dust.

I don't know how much she found in there, but enough to vanish on. Good riddance, though I'd much prefer her to have been brought to justice.

What patience it must have taken, waiting till a vacancy came up at the school. What sangfroid, to talk her way into a job for which she wasn't qualified (though the fact she'd work for a pittance must have sweetened her way). She must have been planning it for years. Because, of course, the person who murdered Christian was one of the daughters he abandoned as babies.

Suzie.

In time I'll be able to puzzle out every detail of her plan – the misleading clues she planted, her attempts to pin the crime on me. That business with poor Lilith.

There's one small, circumstantial detail that plants her centre-stage on the fatal evening, however. Someone visited Christian in his flat and felt-tipped a distinctive *S* onto his plaster cast.

Seeing the Princess shop sign jogged my memory. There's only one person at number forty-one who writes her *S*s like snakes. The murderer literally left her signature at the scene.

I shake my head ruefully, wishing I'd been quicker on the uptake, and decide it's time to take off.

I pick up the landline – not often you get to dial 999 – and it's dead.

A cold chill settles over me. Did I just hear a noise on the landing outside, the creak of a board?

I put the phone down as quietly as I can, despite my violently shaking hand.

There's something – or someone – at the door.

My hair stands on end, a shiver runs up my spine. She should have made her getaway hours ago. What's she doing here?

The door flies open and there she is, eyes dilated. We eye each other for a split second then she jumps at me, brandishing a marble rolling pin – one of those monstrous French affairs they use for making croissants. I dodge but it's already blurring through the air.

So this is it. Thank you for a wonderful life, I say to anyone listening, as the marble lands with a sickening thud on the top of my skull and the world turns black.

CHAPTER 51

My eyes open and and I realize I'm in the Old Scullery. My hands are tied behind my back and I can't move. Suzie must have dragged me down with her bare hands, breaking my neck in the process.

From my peripheral vision I'm aware of a pair of devils capering about, sprinkling liquid around the place from two jerry cans, then I realize I'm seeing double. For some reason I can't smell anything, though I'm guessing it's petrol or paraffin, which means she's going to try and make it look like an accident. *Whoomph!* Paul flambé.

I manage to lift my head a fraction and look about. There are the remains of dessert on the kitchen table, sagging in the warmth, plus a dish of chicken, both of which should rightfully have been put in the fridge hours ago. Piles of dirty plates are jumbled together with smeary glasses; I strive to be open-minded about such things, but on no account was this a menu with which red wine should have been served.

On a side table I spot the *Larousse* I was looking for earlier, though I won't be needing it now.

I try to roll over, wriggle my hands free, but it's hopeless. I feel as if my body is made of lead and I'm sinking, sinking. I close my eyes and prepare to meet my end.

I've said my final goodbyes and am halfway through the Lord's Prayer when, above the *glug glug glug* of sloshing petrol, I make out the sound of footsteps. Footsteps growing louder.

I open my eyes with a start. My line of vision includes the stairs, and I see a pair of ankle boots come into view, followed by a paisley skirt and a black woollen cape. I could swear that's the outfit someone I know bought two weeks ago in that designer sale in South Molton Street. From the bottom step I hear a much-loved voice sing out: 'Paul? Are you down here? You weren't at home, so I—'

Can it be? Has someone sent my guardian angel to rescue me?

My elation turns to freezing horror as I realize the deadly trap into which I've drawn her. Then another pair of feet appears, and I see Julie's not alone: it's the young student, Stephen.

I try to shout a warning to them, but nothing comes out – not even a gurgle. Instead I stare paralysed as they look about them in astonishment.

I kick out with my feet, then manage to stagger onto my knees. 'Stop her!' I croak, trying desperately to draw their attention to Suzie, now crouched behind the table. Seeing me covered in blood, Julie jumps in horror.

'She killed Christian,' I splutter, though it doesn't sound like my voice.

Julie is lightning quick on the uptake, and in the same way as a cat fluffs up its tail fur to make it look bigger for combat, she visibly expands before me. In one hand she raises a large, dripping umbrella, in the other a hefty messenger bag containing her laptop. If you're ever intending to use a computer as a slingshot, you won't do better than a sixteen-inch MacBook Pro, with forty gigabytes of memory and eight terabytes of solid-state storage.

'Let's do this,' bellows Julie to the weedy figure beside her, who reaches into his backpack and pulls out his glasses.

'Ready when you are,' he replies, softly. *Rready when you arrr.* Another rhotic speaker – I never noticed.

The newcomers edge towards Suzie in a pincer movement. I try to stand up but lose balance and fall back down again.

No matter, because it's over in a matter of moments. Suzie's hands go up in surrender. I'm genuinely surprised – I'd have expected her to put up more of a fight. While Stephen holds her, Julie helps me onto a stool and unties my hands. I realize now that I was secured with butcher's twine, which is great for joints of meat but doesn't half cut into your wrists.

My next ordeal is to watch my rescuers make a hopeless mess of tying Suzie up with more of the twine. Knots being one of my things, I'm able to take them step by step through a Spanish bowline and thus ensure she's firmly attached to the table leg.

By this time I've recovered enough to get back on my feet.

'We'll keep her tied up – you get help,' Stephen tells me, taking command of the situation.

In the struggle, Suzie's sweatshirt has ripped at the shoulder, revealing a mark on her neck. It's a tattoo, of a curvy little cherub blowing a horn. Something starts to tug away at the back of my my mind.

'We'll be OK,' says Julie, seeing my hesitation. 'She's not going anywhere.'

CHAPTER 52

Maybe it's the petrol fumes, maybe it's being coshed with the rolling pin, but I'm not thinking clearly: at the top of the stairs I remember the landline is dead.

What I'll do instead is dash out into Chester Square and scream for help.

Halfway across the hall I stop in my tracks. I feel the cogs of my brain whirring, shunting into gear.

Clunk. What was Julie's astro-prediction for the day? Something about Gemini.

Clunk. Suzie's tattoo . . . I'm no particular fan of the things; a Celtic band over buff, toned triceps can be striking, but once that skin starts to wrinkle and sag? Jonny's smothered in them, as you could probably guess. Why would Suzie and Stephen have matching cherubs inked onto their clavicles – hers playing a horn, his a harp?

And then the final *clunk.* Those intertwined pasta twists – the forgotten name that kept bugging me . . . *gemelli.* Twins!

As in a film, when the cameraman pulls focus and a blurred picture gradually becomes pin-sharp, the mist lifts from my mind. Christian was murdered not by one person, but two acting in concert. The pair who did it were twins. Not just any old twins – but Christian's.

Perhaps because I'm an only child, I've always found twins fascinating. The Kray twins, Maurice and Robin from the Bee Gees. Those Swedish girls who went crazy on the M6.

That peculiar French pair who overdid the plastic surgery. Jedward!

The only thing that doesn't add up is that Christian had twin *girls*. But what did I overhear Suzie call Stephen the other day? *Stevie.*

What if . . . what if . . . Stephen's not a man at all?

Suzie and Stevie. Christian's long-lost *twin daughters*.

'*Ye Gods!*' I gasp.

So that's it. Stevie deceived us all into thinking she was a man, and the pasta was a clue, left by Christian in his final drugged moments. A clue meant for the one person he thought might work it out. Me.

In the blink of an eye, the world has changed . . . The sisters from hell are waiting at the bottom of the stairs to ambush me – with Julie at their mercy.

It's too late to get help – too late for the police. My friend's life is on the line and I'm the only one who can save her.

Through the swirling horror a plan begins to form. I approach the dumb waiter, perch on the edge of the compartment and reverse in. I feel my joints click and I suck in my breath.

Once I'm in, I somehow reach out a hand and whack the down button, then start my slow descent to the underworld. As luck would have it – someone must be looking out for me – there's a long, low growl of thunder overhead, which covers the noise of the winch.

CHAPTER 53

I erupt from the dumb waiter like a popped champagne cork and let out a colossal roar.

The twins shriek and spring back from their hiding places at the bottom of the stairs.

The stench of petrol rushes to my head, but what have they done with Julie? I spot the handle of Suzie's bedroom door waggling frantically up and down and hear furious pounding and muffled cries from within.

'Stand back, Julie,' I scream, then shoulder-charge it with all my might. Fortunately it's made of deal (no French-polished mahogany for kitchen maids) and splinters on impact: out leaps my friend.

I turn to see Suzie creeping along the wall with chef's knife in hand – a thirty-centimetre Wüsthof with olive-wood handle. Meanwhile Stephen – or rather, Stevie – has armed herself with an electric carving knife. She tosses away her glasses and moves in on me, swishing it in figures-of-eight.

Electric carving knives are something of a joke nowadays – certainly at Sunday lunch – but as every food stylist knows, nothing can touch them for slicing delicate cakes or pavlovas oozing with whipped cream. The serrated blades are designed to cut fast and clean, with tips sharpened to needles.

'I'm going to cut your balls off!' she growls.

'Yourr balls': there's that *rrrr* sound again. Maybe if she'd said more than half a dozen words during the week, I'd have put two and two together.

I kick out at her and a sickening line appears on my calf, as if drawn in by a pen, before the blood starts to fountain. On the plus side, I feel nothing.

From the corner of my eye I spot my sharpening steel on the kitchen table. Well, that's a relief – it wasn't put out with the recycling, or hung on the wall so Rose could claim it once belonged to Henry VIII. I snatch it up.

By alternately goading and luring, I succeed in manoeuvring a panting Stevie in front of the colossal wooden dresser; as I do so I notice her painted beard is beginning to run from the exertion.

Julie is far fitter than the rest of us – all that swimming and Pilates. Using a toasting fork she's grabbed off the wall and shielding herself with a roasting tin, she also succeeds in backing Suzie towards the dresser.

Seeing our opponents side by side, it's suddenly so *obvious*. They're certainly not identical – and their hair gives each a totally different look – but I'm gazing at the same oval faces, the same milky skin, the same shadowed, impenetrable eyes. Even the same ring of chocolate round the mouth, because they've both been eating mousse that *I* paid for.

Suzie now comes at me with her Wüsthof and the clashing of metal rings in the air. I'm horribly aware that with each stroke and counter-stroke her blade is being honed to more lethal sharpness by my steel. *Zing zing sing* – just the way I taught the students.

I'm beginning to lose hope when I get an idea. I leap to the back of the dresser and wedge my steel behind it, to use as a lever. You can't beat a good old-fashioned steel – it's a solid piece of kit, no bending or buckling. The top-heavy piece of furniture creaks under the strain and its dismal display of sauceboats, figurines, jugs, and ramekins tinkles on woodworm-infested shelves.

I scream at Julie, 'Now!' and she hops backwards in a jeté of which Nureyev would have been proud.

I yank the steel with all my might. There's a judder, and a splintering sound, and over the dresser goes. It may be because of the low ceiling and stone floor, but the crash is *tremendous*. Teapots spin through the air, egg coddlers bounce off the walls, figurines careen across the floor and cruet sets explode in mid-air.

Through the mushroom cloud of dust and débris can be heard the wheezing of Stevie, trapped underneath and gasping for breath. Suzie, who managed to leap clear, looks like a volcano that's about to erupt, ferocious eyes tinged with red.

CHAPTER 54

Suzie moves in front of the staircase to close off our means of escape. From the rubble she has dug something of a kitchen rarity – a tomahawk knife.

'Suzie,' I say, in a beseeching tone, lowering my steel. 'I want to be a friend to you, and to your sister.' I've caught her attention. 'I know life hasn't treated you kindly and this isn't your fault.' She fixes me with her cold fish eyes but I see the muscles in her wrist and arm relax a little.

'There are people who can help, who want to make up for what happened.' She blinks, and for a millisecond I actually feel sorry for her. Then I take a deep breath and scream as loud as I can: '*BEHIND YOU!!*'

Autonomic reflex: works every time. As she turns, I leap forward and deliver a brutal blow to the knife-bearing hand.

God alone knows how she holds on to her weapon, but she does. With a banshee howl, she falls back into the corner, rubbing her wrist. Her face, normally so pale and expressionless, is suffused with fury and her eyes narrowed to slits. My stomach gives a lurch as I realize this hideous transformation was probably the last thing Christian saw before he died. His child, his killer.

There's nothing more dangerous than a cornered beast. She crouches down, coils herself into a ball, twirls the tomahawk in the air above her and spins it towards me with all her might. As if in slow motion, the weapon hisses through the air and my hands shoot up to protect my head.

The weapon hits me blade first and I sink to the ground. I grovel on the floor, my left arm totally numb. My hand has been chopped off. Then I glance down to see a mangled steel watch strap, adorned with the shattered glass of a dial – and my hand still attached to my arm. Thank you, Marcus.

I stagger to my feet in time to see Suzie head for the staircase. It's never happened before, but a lesson from the rugby field comes to my assistance. I floor her with a flying tackle. She collapses, winded.

Julie has also been busy. My resourceful friend has managed to drag the kitchen table on top of the dresser and has found from nowhere half a dozen huge water cooler bottles to weigh it down. Stevie isn't going anywhere.

Then I get an idea. Why bother with hand-to-hand when you can send in missiles? I grab a water jug and lob it at Suzie. She ducks in time, it smashes on the wall behind, but there's plenty more where that came from.

Soon the air is filled with crashing and smashing, breakages piling up like snowdrifts. Chester Square has never seen anything like it. And everywhere, there seems to be food. Cake is stuck to the ceiling, biscuits are shattered like confetti and gobbets of chicken squelch underfoot. I see Suzie slip on a devilled egg – wipe a crystallized rose petal out of her eye – but it's not over yet.

Stevie has got an arm out from under the dresser, and is shouting and gesticulating to her sister . . . something about a lighter. *Lighterrr.*

An eerie smile creeps across Suzie's face. With the speed of Lucifer, she flies across the kitchen and snatches up a gas lighter lying on the stove. She punches the air, lets out a blood-chilling cackle and laces her finger into the trigger.

Julie and I are one click from going up in smoke.

No time to think: instinct takes over. I seize the only thing within reach – the sumo-weight tome on the cooking of Italy. I take a deep breath, swing and release the *Larousse*.

It whooshes through the air like a discus, in an elegant curve, pages lightly a-flutter. I'm no expert in aerodynamics, but along its trajectory it makes three perfect rotations on the horizontal axis. I know even less about cricket than I do about rugby, but I believe this delivery would technically be described as a 'beamer'. Our umpire at school would have called it as a no ball – unsportsmanlike, even – but in the words of our school motto, *quidquid requiritur, fiat*.

The ribbed leather spine of the book smacks into Suzie's forehead, accompanied by the dead weight of 786 pages, 130 colour plates and heavy-duty 'library' hardcovers.

For the first, only and most important time in my life, I've thrown straight.

* * *

I pinion Suzie's arms behind her and drag her semi-conscious to the dumb waiter. She starts to come back to life – kicking, biting, hissing – but not before I've got her head into the hatch. Holding her in a vice-like grip, I balance on one foot and reach out with the other towards the control button. With a delicate toe action, I hit 'up'. A shriek of pain pulses from my bloodied leg.

The mahogany doors glide slowly to, and I finally realize what they remind me of – the sliding doors at a crematorium, closing while the coffin is borne away.

Suzie croaks as the doors judder and bounce against her throat. There's a grinding sound as camshafts and tension belts and gears crank into action. 'Let me go!' she gurgles, but there's no way this mechanism is giving up its grip on her. Quality Victorian workmanship, not like today.

I keep the button jammed down and shout to Julie to run for help.

'First things first,' she cries back. That's Julie all over – thinks things through. She pulls a fire extinguisher off the wall and shoots foam everywhere, adding extra squirts into the dumb waiter and under the table for good measure. A sprinkling of flaked almonds and glacé cherries and the room would look like a giant trifle.

'Shall I set off the smoke alarms? Trip the sprinkler system?' she asks, eyes sparkling; no, I say, we're good. After which my dear girl adjusts her cape and shoots up the stairs to summon help, while I make a mental note to retrieve my steel, so I haven't had a completely wasted evening.

EPILOGUE

Eight Weeks Later

'I should have known all along,' I say, shaking my head, which is a bad idea if you're recovering from a cracked skull and delayed concussion. We're sitting in front of the fire at Jubilee Cottage sipping a sumptuous Californian Chardonnay with a Mozart piano concerto – K467, with its sublime Andante – playing softly in the background. It's a live recording from 1950, Dinu Lipatti is the soloist.

'The very first words Stevie said to me were obvious lies,' I continue. 'Why would the Royal Parks send an apprentice on an upmarket cookery course to see if they wanted to change career? Just shows what people will believe if you're in a circle introducing yourselves.' (The Royal Parks wasn't a total lie, by the way: Stevie did once pick litter in Kensington Gardens while on community service.) 'Besides, have you ever seen a gardener that pale?'

Tonight was Julie's concert, and she, by contrast, is aglow with success. She looked sensational in a flamboyant silk top and flares à la Mama Cass, and the way she tooted her clarinet in the air during 'When I'm Sixty-Four' earned a standing ovation.

I'm flattered she's chosen to spend the evening with me, when she could have gone after-partying with her orchestral friends. Apparently the McDreamy new double-bass player has asked for her phone number – twice.

The sixties are on the tip of every tongue just now, because the early copies of *Escape*'s Christmas issue have hit the newsstands and it's breaking every record. *PSYCHEDELIC CHRISTMAS!* screams the cover; no one has ever seen anything like it.

It's not just that every page pops with kaleidoscopic colour, not just the jazzy party clothes and the way-out decorating ideas. It's full of verve and panache and *fun*. Needless to say, Julie's pages steal the show. Never has a turkey been roasted to such permatan succulence, potatoes to such crunchy Day-glo glory, amid a rainbow of trimmings and sauces. Mince pies, tricky to sex up at the best of times, literally sparkle under a crust of crushed rock sugar, and the multi-coloured flames on her Christmas pud would do Cirque du Soleil proud. Everything is photographed against a palette that pops and fizzes – and where the heck did she find those dip-dyed wolfhounds?

Yesterday, Richard Buzz dropped in on the *Escape*'s editorial team to tell them the good news (en route to *Lovely*, to tell Tammy the opposite). He said *Escape*'s Christmas number had not only bust all records, but would go down in magazine history. To which Dena added as an aside to Julie, rewriting the truth in her usual way, 'I *knew* you had it in you, love. I said all along *Nutcracker* was done to death.'

To her credit, she did have the grace to publicly thank her heroes of the hour: instead of the usual boring staff and contributor list on page three, she had it redesigned in homage to Peter Blake's *Sgt Pepper* cover, with Julie, Spencer, Lucinda and herself in the middle dressed as the Fab Four. She's reneged on our lunch invitation, but hinted to Julie that she might ask her to step up to deputy editor when Celia goes on maternity leave. Win-win.

'What gave you the sixties idea?' says Julie, curiously.

'Oh, just came to me,' I say, lightly. Disingenuousness not really being my thing, I add: 'If you must know, Lilith used to dress up in these bizarre multicoloured outfits, and she happened to walk past at the right moment. And then, of course, there was your concert. But you take the credit – it was your shoot.'

'Oh, get on with you!' Julie protests. 'But we're not here to talk about me. I want to hear the full story.' What with rushing *Escape*'s Christmas issue to the printer, Julie's rehearsals and my spell in hospital, tonight is the first time we've been able to sit down and have a proper chinwag since that epic night. 'All the details, please.'

I top up our wine; there's much to tell. But first: 'Can you just explain how you happened to waltz into the basement in my hour of need? Love that cape by the way – it has a fabulous swing to it.'

'Well, when I saw your terrified-face emoji I knew things must be desperate. I rang you and there was a sort of muttering sound, then whoever it was hung up—'

'The police helpfully took my phone.'

'So the second we wrapped up the shoot I raced to Jubilee Cottage and arrived fifteen minutes early. Finding no one there, I ran all the way to Chester Square. I'm surprised I didn't mow anyone down – I was like a runaway express train.

'Luckily I still had your text from the other night, so I tapped in the code and went in.

'I called out for you and no one answered. There was just one light on, over a little staircase. I was making my way over to it, in case you were down there, when this young guy with a shaved head appeared from nowhere and asked what I was doing. I sensed there was something wrong and carried on down. I hardly expected to find myself on the set of *A Nightmare on Elm Street*.'

'OK, there was something very weird about them both, but extenuating circumstances too, now we have the full story.'

Julie rolls her eyes. 'Please don't tell me you're going to come over all compassionate?' I have this habit of feeling sorry for people when I shouldn't, and she's always ticking me off for it. 'So now, over to you.'

'I told you I'd received a letter. It's a personal, off-the-record account sent to me by someone formerly high up in Gloucestershire Social Services, who has been haunted ever since by what the Wagner twins were subjected to while they were meant to be "in care". Her feeling is that however dreadful the things that happened to me, what happened to them was far worse.'

I hand her the paper.

In 2015, I was a Young Person Liaison Officer working with Gloucestershire Social Services, which is when I met the Wagner twins.

Susan and Stephanie lost their mother in an accident in the early 2000s. At first they went to live with their aunt but were given up for adoption and went to live with a couple in Trowbridge. It was an unfortunate match: the girls described their adoptive parents as 'religious nutcases' who were determined they should become missionaries. By the age of ten, the girls had gained a reputation as troublemakers, bullying and stealing, and were taken into care.

They were sent to a home specializing in children with behavioural issues. One evening, a group of youngsters escaped onto the roof and threw down tiles. A supervisor was hit in the face and blinded, and Susan named as the ringleader. There was an official inquiry, revealing that staff members had sexually as well as physically abused those in their care.

The twins were moved to another home, which was shortly afterwards closed down in similar circumstances. They appear to have been victims of a flawed system.

The twins are dyzygotic (non-identical). Of the two, Suzie (as she called herself by this time) was the more presentable and manageable. She could have been placed in better circumstances, with a family, but refused to leave her twin. Stevie (Stephanie) was dexterous and had technical ability – she completed courses in both woodwork and IT skills – but too aggressive and unpredictable to be employable. On several occasions Stevie went on sprees of theft and vandalism disguised as a boy. She was interviewed about this, on the grounds that she might want to talk to someone about her gender, but she refused vehemently.

The last time I encountered them the Wagner girls were unemployed and living in Gloucester. According to a fellow social worker, they had begun to develop an unhealthy fixation on their birth father, whom they had never met.

I am shocked, saddened but not entirely surprised to hear of their recent, tragic misadventure. It is my opinion that the girls never recovered from the trauma of losing all family contact suddenly and at a highly impressionable age; and that this trauma mutated into anger and ultimately Paranoid Personality Disorder (PPD).

With regard to the crime itself, there are examples in medical literature of <u>Shared Delusional Disorder</u>, in which a dominant partner with severe mental illness (for instance, paranoid schizophrenia) incites and coerces the other into acts of extreme violence. Suzie was diagnosed as being the dominant twin.

I do not believe there is any particular significance in their choice of method (decapitation) beyond, perhaps, the obvious symbolism: to annihilate the cerebral as well as biological existence of their father.

On an entirely personal note, in my opinion the Wagner twins are victims of society – they have been let down not just by their family and 'the system' but by all of us. No one is born bad.

Julie pauses to let this sink in. 'So they were stalking Christian for years.'

'He lived a very public life. They saw their dad parading his fame, glamour and wealth and compared it with the upbringing they'd received – the squalor and the misery.

'They dug out an old newspaper report and discovered a fund had been collected on their behalf by their dad's colleagues; then spun themselves a story that he'd run off with a fortune that should have been theirs. In fact, it was a decent amount for a voluntary collection by his soldier mates, no more than that.

'It's easy to hate someone in the abstract. The tragedy is that if Christian had had the chance, he would have tried to make amends; he makes that perfectly clear in his diary.'

I *almost* wish I'd never read it – Christian laying bare his soul on those closely scribbled pages; something I can never un-see.

'The worst thing from the twins' point of view is that they've been split up while they're on remand, and when they're sentenced could end up at different ends of the country. That will double the punishment for them both.'

Julie frowns. 'Don't forget you're talking about a couple of homicidal maniacs who almost killed us both!'

'And that brings us to the night of the murder.'

We fortify ourselves with another glass of wine and I continue. 'Stevie booked herself onto a course at the cookery school into which her sister had inveigled herself, posing as a young man called Stephen. Suzie *Wheeler* and the disguised Stephen *Cartwright* were finally in close proximity to the father they despised. Wheelers and cartwrights are traditionally the same trade as waggoners, of course – or, in this case, *Wagner*. They must have given that some thought, it's a nice touch.' I'm doing it again, and Julie tuts.

'But the police must surely have checked their IDs? It's pretty basic stuff,' she says.

'The twins had been living under their assumed names for some time, and organized themselves a trail of addresses and work history.

'They deliberately chose a busy week, so there were plenty of potential suspects at the school to confuse the police. The weekend before Stevie was due to arrive, however, they hit a problem: Christian broke his arm.

'At first it seemed to throw their plans into disarray, but in the end it worked in their favour because it sent the police off in the wrong direction, chasing money-lenders.

'The first time Stevie saw her father in the flesh was when he walked into the classroom and she fainted from shock. Suzie jumped to her twin's assistance – a bit too fast.

'I kick myself for not seeing the similarity between them, either then or later. If Stevie had disguised herself using a false moustache or a fat suit it maybe would have rung alarm bells, but there's nothing stand-out about a young man wearing teashade glasses and a radical haircut.

'There were other clues I missed, too. Suzie somehow seemed to know how Stephen liked his tea, and once let slip the name "Stevie" – though she managed to distract my attention by dropping something. They were both left handers, too – as was Christian.'

'But that doesn't have any bearing on what happened, does it?'

'Only that Christian was injected by someone using their left hand and the cleaver was struck from the left. Which is why Blondie's face fell at the police station when I signed my autograph with my right.'

'Aha! That would be your gorgeous and very talkative detective friend!' says Julie.

I don't blush often, but I feel myself go crimson to the roots. 'Don't be ridiculous . . . although he did text again. I said it's still too soon for me. He's going to keep in touch.'

Julie takes my hand. 'One day, perhaps.'

After a short pause, I resume. 'Now for the night of the murder. After dinner, Gregory turned up at Christian's flat. While they were talking, Vicky arrived to give Christian his scarf. She overheard Gloria Hunniford on Sentimental FM – her Monday evening late show – and assumed he had a floozy in there, and left it at the door. When Christian let Gregory out, he found the parcel, tore off the giftwrap and left it on the windowsill.

'Suzie hung about till the coast was clear and knocked at her father's door. It was late, but she made up some excuse or sob story; he felt sorry for her and let her in.

'When he wasn't looking, she spiked his drink with GHB. While waiting for it to take effect, she asked if she could sign his plaster cast, and when he was past putting up a fight, let Stephen in. They locked the door and one of them jabbed him with the fatal syringe. By the way, it'll be interesting to see how that plays out in court, because each of them can say the other administered the injection.'

'Barristers call it a cut-throat defence,' says Julie.

'After that there was a scuffle, during which Christian was able to overturn the jar of gemelli pasta. He died from an opioid overdose shortly after midnight.'

Julie sighs, then asks: 'This cleaver business. Wouldn't it have made more sense to make it look like a botched burglary?'

'I'm afraid our twins were rather into beheading; forensics found some horrific downloads on Suzie's laptop. That's the way they wanted to do it, so they created a narrative to fit.

'They went online and found that if you decapitate someone the blood spray is phenomenal. Therefore they needed to kill him first to allow his blood pressure to drop.'

'So cruel and calculating,' says Julie.

'Meanwhile they tidied up, wiped their fingerprints off everything and went about scattering misleading clues. Why bother? Partly as an insurance policy; partly to confuse the police; partly out of simple malice. Melanie's lipstick under the sofa . . . A spritz of that heavy perfume Rose wears . . . A couple of Lilith's hairs dotted about. I'm surprised they didn't chuck in a false eyelash from De'Lyse and a couple of Vicky's footprints for good measure.

'The following morning, possibly as an afterthought, Suzie returned to break the glass door and make it look like jihadists had smashed their way in. She told the police some cockadoodie story about Middle Eastern-looking people watching the house and sitting in a parked car in the square. The anti-terrorism squad were having none of it, but they did wonder why she was lying to them. Now we know.'

'Why hang about? Why not just scarper straight after the murder?'

'If they'd fled on murder night, the police would have launched a manhunt and they'd never have got away.'

'But surely Rose would have raised the alarm when she found Suzie had taken off?'

'There was no reason to. As far as Rose was concerned, Stephen left after lunch with the other students. And Suzie left a note saying there was a family emergency and she'd been called away. They bought themselves plenty of time.'

'Shame they couldn't put their talents to better use,' says Julie, shaking her head. 'How did they fix their alibis?'

'Stevie installed a simulation app on each of their laptops which made it look as if they'd been pressing buttons and sending messages into the early hours. Afterwards, she deleted the app but left the history for the police to find.'

'And how did Lilith get mixed up in all this?' asks Julie. 'And more important – how is she?'

'Still in hospital,' I reply. Bangor Ysbyty Gwynedd Hospital to be precise, but try saying that after two large glasses of Au Bon Climat. 'She's a little better every day. The archdeacon and I speak once a week and she's invited me to visit in spring for the wild daffodils.

'Lilith was smarter than I gave her credit for. She spotted that Suzie and Stevie had the same tattoo.'

'Does she have X-ray vision?' asks Julie.

'She noticed Stevie's tattoo when she fainted in class, and Suzie's when she dropped the baking sheet. This led her to the conclusion they were lovers, and she couldn't resist letting them know. After that she announced to all and sundry that Christian was "a man of secrets". What she *meant* was that she'd worked out that Harriet was pregnant by him, but the twins thought she was hinting she knew they were his kids.'

Julie lets out a sigh.

'At this point they freaked out and decided they needed to silence her by pushing her down the stairs.'

'And they really believed they could get away with all this?'

'They very nearly did. They knew the murder scene in Christian's flat must have been covered with DNA and fibre evidence, but those tests always take weeks to come in: by which time they'd be in Casablanca drinking champagne.'

'It takes money to go into hiding. Did they have any?'

'On Thursday afternoon, as luck would have it, Rose went to Harley Street for some medical tests. This gave the twins the run of the place for four hours. First job was to ransack the Shelley Room safe. The girls wasted half an hour trying to find the key.'

'Let me guess. Rose keeps it in the urn containing her grandmother's ashes.'

'It's not been locked since the First World War – you simply turn the knob. And it was empty. They had enough money to get away, however, because Suzie had been fiddling the petty cash. So Stevie went off to Victoria to buy Eurostar tickets then came back to find you'd arrived.'

'Not before disconnecting the phone,' says Julie.

'That wasn't them – it was Jonny's fault, surprise surprise. Before Rose left, she received another of his hoax calls and she was so angry she yanked the wire out of the wall.

'Now, of course, DNA evidence has come in and the twins are all over it. And once forensics knew where to look, there was more. For instance, they checked the washing machines in the basement and someone ran fourteen deep-clean cycles at ninety degrees centigrade between twelve thirty-seven a.m. on Monday night and midnight on Wednesday.'

'Suzie could get a job at *Which?* magazine,' chuckles Julie.

'Maybe she will, in thirty years' time,' I reply.

'On the subject of household appliances – what about the exploding food mixer?'

'Incorrect overload thermal relay – I reckon it should have been twelve to eighteen amp rating. Just one of those things. But if it hadn't been for that – and the accident book – I'd never have seen Suzie's snakey signature, and linked her to Christian's plaster cast.'

I shrug and decide it's more than time to crack open the second bottle. The hard part is coming.

'Blondie found a piece of paper in Suzie's rucksack and passed it on to me. It was scrunched-up into a ball – almost got thrown away.' Part of me wishes it had, but too late now. 'It was the last page of his recipe diary, which she'd torn out.'

I place the crumpled page on the table and push it towards Julie.

<u>*Sunday 21st August 2022*</u>
Hard times. More disasters on the betting front but I feel in my bones it'll come right soon. To add insult to injury, poor Rose – her palsy seems to be getting worse. Milla blames it on me as usual – says I bring bad luck.

We've got a new general assistant, Suzie. Strange girl, wary of me for some reason. Yesterday she was polishing a mirror in the hall. I caught her reflection and for a fraction of a second she reminded me of my wife. Weird but also very frightening.

It started me off on one and I had a bit of a crisis. When I think of my poor kids and the way I abandoned them . . . I'll regret it till the day I die. It's years since I registered with the agencies that are supposed to link you up with your adopted kids – but still nothing. Is it that the girls don't care? Or do they hate me? Maybe I'll find them one day. Mustn't lose hope.

They're young women by now, of course. I keep thinking: where are you? Were you brought up in a good home, by kind, loving people? Do you have boyfriends, girlfriends, who look out for you? I hope you're still close and take care of each other. I hope you're happy.

Maybe you're even thinking of starting families of your own, in which case – your dad would say wait till you're a bit older. I can talk – your mum and I were only 19. But that was true love, the sort that only strikes once in a lifetime.

If I had the chance, Susan and Stephanie, I'd tell you this: 'Your dad loves you and would give his life to make amends.'

May God give me the chance.

There's only one thing that makes me feel better at times like this: I'm going into the kitchen. I'll make something for Suzie. (She loves chocolate.) Here it is, my killer version of Rocky Road.

DEATH BY ROCKY ROAD

Gently melt together 130g butter, 200g best dark chocolate and 50g golden syrup. Stir in 100g broken biscuits – something plain like rich tea – and 6 tablespoons broken crunchy honeycomb pieces, then 50g mini-marshmallows. Turn into an 18cm square shallow tin lined with baking paper. Chill for 2 hours or longer. Cut into squares or rectangles – depending on size, anything from 12–20.

Specially for Suzie, I'm pushing the boat out with a coating of dark chocolate ganache, more marshmallows, swirls of white chocolate, a dusting of grated tonka and crushed crystallized violets. She's all on her own and deserves a treat.

Julie wipes away a tear and we sit in silence for a minute. Then I put the piece of paper away and pour more wine.

Finally, she gets up and crosses to the mantelpiece. 'I've never seen so many cards,' she says. It's true – who knew I was so popular? Maybe time to stop being a hermit.

I don't suppose she ever will, but I'd like her to have met my students. I feel tender towards them.

Vicky sent hers to the Chelsea and Westminster while I was in for observation. A bandaged flamingo on the front, and a message saying she's had a heart-to-heart with hubby and they've booked a holiday to Madeira – together.

Harriet tucked a note in with hers. She and Jason have brought forward their wedding and will have a small family ceremony. He's 'totally cool' about fathering Christian's child. How very modern.

Lady Brash sent flowers! Not just an ordinary Interflora job, but a huge and lovely box of country flowers, 'grown not flown', including my favourite – fragrant stocks. Scrawled on the accompanying card:

Wishing you well and hope we cross swords again. Harriet says I talked too much – forgive me if I ruined the course! Warmest love, Serena B.
P.S. Always a bed if you come to Bath.

I've had no sense of smell since being whacked on the head – though my consultant tells me if I'm lucky it should slowly come back. Stocks I can survive without, but there are other scents I miss more.

'Aha, you know about this one,' I say. A couple of weeks ago I tipped De'Lyse off about a vacancy at Buzz for a 'freelance social media ambassador-at-large / food', then a mystery parcel arrived, containing a climbing plant with thick glossy leaves, labelled *Hoya carnosa*. It was a thank-you gift – she got the job. I've never tried my hand at houseplants, and this could be the start of something new.

'Tell me about Melanie,' says Julie. 'She sounds, well, weird.'

'She dropped me off an ancient press cutting, from which I learnt Christian's middle name – Stephen – and that his wife was called Susan. Also, two tonka beans.'

'No! At least she gave them back.'

'We decided Stevie must have put them in her bag to make trouble. We're having coffee next week to chat about Ben.' You'd be surprised how often gay men are called in as unofficial marriage guidance counsellors.

'And did you seriously think she might have been the murderer?'

'At one point, yes – I had it all worked out. She latched onto Rose's handsome Alan, and then her dishy lover Christian. If she couldn't have them for herself, the next best thing would be to bump them off; possibly with the help of Ben. Only of course it wasn't true.'

'She still sounds a bit of a nightmare.'

'It's Ben I feel sorry for . . . many a bored and neglected husband has turned to booze.'

'So were they real love affairs? Or all in her mind?'

'That's the very question I asked Rose when I met up with her.'

I hold up a stiff cream card with From the Desk of Rose Hoyt engraved in navy blue along the top and Chester Square Cookery School across the bottom.

Ten days ago, Rose invited me over for a drink, 'for old times' sake'. Not wishing to offend, I asked if we could meet somewhere other than the school, and so, when the time came, I found myself heading for the bar in Sloane Square where this whole adventure started.

When I arrived, I had misgivings – all those mirrors – but she strode in wearing a sheer black dress complete with veil; the latter studded with tiny hearts, clubs, diamonds and spades. Everyone looked round – you don't see veils much nowadays, except at funerals.

I stood to greet her – the room had fallen silent – and she raised her hand and drew it slowly back. It was done with such elegance and panache that – I jest not – there was a ripple of applause.

What was under the veil? Had her affliction healed – or taken a lurch for the worse?

In the event it was neither – she looked the same as before – but I realized something in *me* has changed. I wouldn't wish pain or discomfort on anyone, but Rose is beautiful the way she is. Her asymmetry no longer makes me feel uncomfortable and I'm ashamed it ever did.

'Once we were settled down with our champagne, she apologized for being late. Thanks to the publicity, she's been overrun with bookings, though I can't believe they're coming along to learn how to de-vein prawns.'

'Then she broke her big news: she's selling number forty-one and moving to Somerset, where her Hoyt relatives live.'

'So they forgave her for pushing Mr Hoyt out of the window?' asks Julie, who has a fine memory for detail.

'She called it a *rapprochement*. Obviously, I had to ask more.'

'Do tell.' Julie also likes a juicy bit of gossip.

'I said I was sorry to hear about what happened to Alan, and she gave me an odd look, as if to say, "Who've you been talking to?" Then she pondered for a moment and asked if she could tell me something in strictest confidence.'

'I don't count,' says Julie quickly.

'Ha! I said I would share it with you. Alan wasn't born to money but he had a real talent for making it. He did extremely well playing the markets until Milla was ten, when things went wrong for him and he lost the lot. Normally when that happens, financiers simply start again and build up a new fortune, but Alan was hit by depression. He refused help and ended up throwing himself out of the attic window.'

'What a ghastly story. I hope it doesn't stir up—'

'It doesn't get any easier, if you're referring to my mother. But it kind of explains why Rose is the way she is. You don't recover from someone close to you committing suicide, you learn to live with it.' We sit in silence for a minute.

'Alan left a suicide note,' I continue, 'asking Rose to destroy it after reading because it would void his life insurance. She used the money from that to set up the cookery school, hoping it would provide for her future. It was fraud, I'm afraid, and she's had it on her conscience all these years.'

'She could give the money back when she sells the place,' suggests Julie. 'Or donate it to the Labour Party.'

'I took advantage of her being in a confidential mood to ask about Melanie,' I continue. 'As you can imagine, I had to tread carefully.'

'Rose explained that she was aware of Melanie's "pashes" on Alan and Christian – there were others over the years – but felt sorry for her old friend; protective even. You won't believe it, but the old skinflint let Melanie come on the course free, because she sounded as if she needed a break.'

'And as far as Christian was concerned – Melanie was just a casual flirtation?'

'Nothing more, I'm certain of it. His diary is full of dalliances – like lots of guys, he was proud of his prowess at seduction – but there's not a single mention of her.'

'How will Rose amuse herself in Somerset?' asks Julie.

'She's going to open a museum of culinary history and put all her junk on display. I can just see her rattling round with a bunch of keys, terrifying tourists.'

Someone else read the story with especial interest, of course, and bestirred himself enough to craft me a bespoke *Don't Get Well* card. Coffin-shaped, it has a caricature of me sitting in my favourite chair holding my severed head. Inside is a thoughtful message, of which this is the profanity-filtered version: *As you must be finding all the stairs in Jubilee Cottage too much for an invalid, perhaps it's time to seek an alternative address.* We laugh and chuck it in the bin.

At this point there's a long pause. I look down at my watch, which isn't there because the lovely Audemars Piguet people are repairing it, free of charge.

Julie says, 'Look, Paul, you must learn not to let people take advantage of you. Christian, then Rose. And Jonny – first and foremost Jonny.'

'I know exactly what you're going to say next, Julie. I've given it a lot of thought, but I can't just cut him off.'

'Surely—'

'He's Marcus's son,' I say.

A long pause.

'Look, can we talk about him some other time?' I ask.

'Of course,' says Julie. Then: 'I keep meaning to ask: what are all those cardboard boxes by the front door?'

'Nothing really – having a bit of a clear-out.'

'Looked to me like books.' You can't hide anything from Julie.

'I'm donating them to the Law Society.'

'My goodness. Are you sure?'

I let out a deep breath. 'I'm sure. Know anyone who'd like a Toby jug?'

She laughs and touches my hand again. 'Great to hear. Any more thoughts on a cat or dog?'

'How about we call in at the animal rescue place at the weekend – see if anyone's wagging his tail at us?'

With that, we clink glasses and raise our usual toast.

'To new adventures!'

END OF BOOK ONE

AUTHOR'S NOTE

Although this is a work of fiction, the recipes from Christian's notebook are working recipes; photographs of the finished dishes, for those who find them helpful, can be found on the author's website.

If this story has whetted your interest in knives, I would recommend a visit to the Japanese Knife Company, with branches in London, Paris and Stockholm. Despite the name, it offers knives (and everything knife-related) from all over the world, as well as an inexpensive sharpening service for personal callers or by post.

Should you need to divest yourself of old, worn-out knives, some police stations have an amnesty bin, recycling centres sometimes accept them (carefully wrapped) or they can be donated or sold on to those over eighteen. Chefs speak mistily of a 'knife graveyard' in Germany where you can post beloved knives once their day is done, to be melted down with their colleagues and turned into new. Alas, it's a myth.

Tonka beans are available from Steenbergs in Yorkshire and Sous Chef; use sparingly. Those wishing to track down Marcus Berens' signature cologne, 'Après un Rêve', will be disappointed, but Les Senteurs in Elizabeth Street, London SW1 offers a selection of heady tonka-based fragrances, as does Parfums de Nicolaï.

ACKNOWLEDGEMENTS

This is my first work of fiction and it's involved a surprising amount of teamwork. At home, I have a living reference library and sounding board in the form of my husband Robert. Good fortune steered me into the hands of an exceptional mentor in the form of Lynn Curtis; starting out in fiction is daunting and I was lucky indeed to find an editor as encouraging, patient and insightful.

Thank you Oli Munson at A M Heath, for your confidence in the project and talking me down from the ceiling when I was panicking over rewrites and line edits; also at A M Heath, the inestimable Harmony Leung. My editor at Transworld, Finn Cotton, has frankly astounded me with his eye for detail and all-round creativity – thank you for the untold time and effort put in on my behalf.

For the cover and artwork, a warm hand to Irene Martinez, and for so adroitly publicizing and marketing the book, Tom Hill and Louis Patel. I am grateful to my copy-editor, Fraser Crichton, for fine-tuning the manuscript with flair and insight. To the sales team, Emily Harvey, Tom Chicken and Laura Ricchetti, a huge thank you. I feel very at home in the Transworld 'family', so thank you Larry and team for making me so welcome.

Christian's recipes are for real, and have been tested and

finessed by the best in the business, Angela Nilsen. Poularde demi-deuil is based, with permission, on a Jane Grigson recipe passed down through her daughter Sophie, and Death by Rocky Road inspired by a confection made by Cocorico of Exeter. Paul learnt the finer details of filter coffee brewing from Maxwell Colonna-Dashwood.

Every crime writer needs a policeman in his pocket, and mine is Ian Pike, retired of the Metropolitan Police; not only did he lift the veil on the mysteries of forensic procedure but dramatically heightened Paul's discomfort at Belgravia Police Station. My friend Titania Hardie, expert on folklore, magic, symbols and divination, added her unique sparkle to Julie's astrological predictions and helped transform them into emojis.

Before becoming a food writer, I had the privilege of working for several outstanding magazine editors, including (at *Living* in the late 1980s) Dena Vane. The character of Dena in this book is a tribute to – emphatically *not* a portrait of – a very remarkable woman, and I'd like to thank Karol-An Kirkman and family for allowing me to borrow her name. My depiction of Jerome Marnier is fondly dedicated to that prince among chef-restaurateurs, Robert Carrier.

Three years ago, Olwen Rice – another great editor – invited me to write a regular column for *Waitrose Weekend*. I would like her to know – as also Alison Oakervee – that this favour opened up to me a whole new way of writing, and helped me 'find my voice': thank you for believing in me and giving me the chance.

My friend Stephen Mudge resides in the 'land of bright-pink soil and twisting, high-hedged lanes' and I am grateful to him and his late mother Susannah for keeping alive such Devon idioms as dimpsy and zimzaw. For their help on other details of the text, my thanks to Samuel Goldsmith and Rory Manchee. For technical advice on dealing with objectionable cookery students, I am indebted to Ken Hom CBE.

Warm thanks to my beta readers – Ruth Watson of Watson and Walpole and, of course, Robert; Joanna Toye – for her warm encouragement during the submission process; and Barbara Baker and Mary and Nick Forde for their eternal support and encouragement (and for finding me my policeman). I am proud to be a member of The Seven – a group of writers who met a dozen years ago at the Arvon Foundation: Pauline Beaumont, Kristen Frederickson, Samuel Goldsmith (him again), Foxie Jones, Katie Socker, Susan Willis. Long may we continue to gather, like nuts, each May. You are such a talented bunch.

It has taken several million keystrokes (yes) to write this story, and my ultra-efficient and ergonomic set-up was masterminded for me by John Sage of The Keyboard Co; for her good-humoured patience in printing out the many drafts, I commend Julie Greenaway of Quickprint, Exeter.

All the best stories return to their beginning, so I would once again like to thank those who make my domestic life – literally – blissful: the aforementioned Robert, Benjamin and Maxim. To new adventures, indeed.

ABOUT THE AUTHOR

After being flung into the culinary limelight as a semi-finalist on *Masterchef*, Orlando Murrin edited *Woman and Home*, *BBC Good Food* and founded *Olive* magazine; then he switched track to become a chef-hotelier in South West France and Somerset.

He has written six cookbooks and is President of the Guild of Food Writers. An ever-popular guest on TV and radio, he presents the *BBC Good Food* podcast with Tom Kerridge.

From his grandfather, a Met detective who rose to become a crack MI5 interrogator, he inherited a fascination with crime and mystery. He lives in domestic bliss in Exeter, Devon, and *Knife Skills for Beginners* is his debut novel.

You can find Orlando at

@orlandomurrin

@Orlando Murrin

@orlandomurrinauthor

or via his website: www.orlandomurrin.com